PARADISE COURT

PARADISE COURT

A Mark Yeager Sports Mystery

MIKE BEFELER

Encircle Publications, LLC
Farmington, Maine U.S.A.

Dedication

To my wife, kids, and grandkids, and to all those who enjoy the sport of pickleball.

Acknowledgments

Many thanks to Wendy, Eddie Vincent, Cynthia Brackett-Vincent and, in particular, Greg Johnson who originally pointed out the location of a paradise court.

Chapter 1

The flight from Denver to Maui did not go well for Mark Yeager. First, the airline mixed up the seat reservations for Mark and his wife, Sophie. Rather than sitting together, they ended up in different rows, and with the flight already overbooked and as much as Mark argued, he had no success at finding a way to convince the powers-that-be to reassign their seats together.

Once on the plane, neither of Mark's seatmates expressed any interest in changing seats. The two large men on either side of him only glared at him when he made the suggestion, as if he were trying to steal their firstborn child.

Then the snack pack meal ended up being stale crackers and some mystery salami that had indigestion, at the best, and ptomaine, at the worst, written all over it. The final indignity—being stuck in the middle section between those two beefy men who kept taking over the armrests—added nothing to his flight enjoyment. He only hoped the plane didn't have a problem, forcing the oxygen masks to descend from the ceiling. He could picture his two seat companions fighting to grab his mask as a backup while they elbowed him in the ribs and stuffed him down in his seat.

He watched the flight attendants scurry around to attend to a woman struggling to retrieve her carryon from the overhead compartment, almost dropping it on an unsuspecting older traveler. A man needed a blanket even though the cabin temperature must have been in the eighties, and a runaway child raced down the aisle as if the school bully was after him. In the row ahead a crying baby punctuated the cabin vibration, and

1

behind him he received periodic kicks from an overactive child who was probably on a sugar high from too many Gummy Bears, one of which had flown over the seat and landed in Mark's cup of Cranapple juice. The bulk to the right sneezed every ten minutes, never once covering his face, and the hulk to the left coughed continually, also not covering his mouth. Mark pictured a hoard of germs fighting to determine which would be the first to infect him. Finally tiring of this form of entertainment, Mark only wished he had a magical shot to give to his seat companions to reduce them to normal size.

Two hours into the flight after having finished reading the airline magazine that had an article describing the multitude of Hawaiian celebrations planned for the upcoming holiday season of 2003, he squeezed out of his seat and moseyed back to find Sophie peacefully asleep. He decided not to bother her. She had a skinny older man and equally skinny young woman on either side of her. He shook his head at the inequity of their respective seating arrangements.

He visited the restroom, needing to do this much more often after his prostate cancer surgery a year and a half earlier. He thought back over all he had been through the last two years. Retiring from the company he had started, making enough money from the sale of that company when it was acquired that he wouldn't have to work again, settling into an uneasy retirement, only to be slammed by prostate cancer. He clenched his fists. But he had survived and now had a clean bill of health. He unclenched his fists, recognizing the gratitude at being alive. The last year had been a whirlwind. He and Sophie had considered taking this vacation a year ago, but Mark had fallen into a consulting gig helping a startup company in Boulder, Colorado. During the last year, he also had to take a hiatus from playing platform tennis during the reconstruction of the North Boulder Recreation Center and relocation of the platform tennis courts. Fortunately, he and his buddies had discovered pickleball during this period and took up this new sport, which he became hooked on quickly. He now played pickleball at least twice a week, the benefit of being sort of retired. On this vacation, he and Sophie had an opportunity to relax in a beautiful place for the first time since the fear of cancer spreading had been eliminated.

Shortly after Mark returned to his seat, a member of the flight crew announced that the scheduled movie, one that Mark had not seen and was looking forward to, would not be shown because of equipment failure. Equipment failure. If they had trouble with a simple movie system what did that say about keeping the engines running and the wings attached?

The announcement continued to say that there would be a contest to pick the time of the halfway point of the flight to Maui. After a few minutes, flight attendants headed down the aisle handing out forms for the contest. Mark took out a pen and prepared to make his best estimate. Another announcement came over the intercom giving the departure time, expected arrival time, distance of the flight, anticipated average speed for the first and second halves of the flight as well as head wind estimates.

Mark listened carefully and made notes on the cocktail napkin left over from his Gummy-Bear-infested Cranapple juice. After much thought and recalculation, he came up with his answer, convinced he would be in the running for the prize of a bottle of champagne. At least that might make up for the other inconveniences of the flight so far.

He noticed the brute to his left had slept through the whole project, while the equally large man to his right had quickly jotted down an answer without any of the elaborate calculations Mark had made.

Mark asked the man, "Came up with your answer quickly, didn't you?"

"Yeah, I've been on this flight before. Doesn't pay to over-think it." The man shut his eyes and turned away from Mark.

So much for friendly conversation.

Mark's thoughts turned to the time he and Sophie had vacationed in Acapulco. They had spent a wonderful week lying in the sun, parasailing behind a boat, and watching the cliff divers. He smiled to himself at the memory of the luxurious meals, punctuated by some world-class love making. Ah, the good old days. Now they could have a similar experience in Hawaii.

Struggling through a few pages of a thriller, he eventually nodded off only to find himself in a strange dream: he hit the water feet first, the force of the fifty-foot fall momentarily stunning him. An explosion of automatic rifle fire burst around him. He yanked his arms in a strong underwater stroke to gain depth and felt bullets striking his head and back, spent by the mass of the ocean water, but still stinging like angry bees. He continued to swim underwater until he reached a rock outcrop before bursting to the surface to gasp for air. He was out of range of his pursuers, but he sensed they would be after him again. He was gasping for air when a tree branch struck him in the ribs.

Mark let out a loud, "Oof," and awoke to an elbow intruding in his personal space, well over the armrest and planted directly in his ribcage. Readjusting his position, he sighed loudly and shivered, even though the airplane cabin remained toasty warm. The dream seemed so real. He rubbed his eyes at the realization that his recent thoughts of Acapulco cliff divers had led to this strange dream of jumping off a high precipice into the ocean. But where had the image of being shot at come from? That had never happened to him. There's no way a fifty-seven-year-old retired entrepreneur should be in this situation—both the dream and the actuality of this gruesome flight. He hoped this was not a portent of things to come on this long overdue vacation.

Chapter 2

Unfortunately, things didn't improve. When the announcement came for the winner of the half-way time to Maui contest, Mark's companion to his right won. The guy raised his left fist in the air, missing Mark's chin by inches, accepted the bottle of champagne, stuffed it in the pocket in front of him and adjusted his posture to lean even farther across Mark's armrest. Mark resisted the urge to tear the flight magazine in half.

After another hour of discomfort, the intercom crackled with the announcement to secure trays and return seats to their upright position. Mark obliged but then tried to spot the island destination. Unfortunately, in his middle seat, no matter how he contorted himself, he was unable to see anything distinct through the windows on either side. He could only spot a faint image of pale blue sky and white clouds. He unclipped his seatbelt and tried to raise himself to see past his large companions, only to be admonished by the flight attendant to sit down and attach his seatbelt. Back in jail.

The bumpy landing jarred Mark's teeth. He wondered if the pilot had left a dent in the runway. The plane continued forward without any further lurching, so, apparently, no tires had been ruptured.

Once off the plane, Mark's suitcase was nowhere in sight. After inquiring and completing the requisite paperwork, he received the news that the suitcase would be tracked, redirected to Maui when located and delivered to his hotel room. No estimate whether this is would be hours, days or weeks in the future. Mark had visions of wearing the same clothes for the whole vacation.

The one consolation—being in Hawaii he could buy new swim trunks and get by most of the time in those. Fortunately, he had kept all his valuables in his carryon.

His frustration increased when the car rental agency had lost his reservation, and he and Sophie had to wait half an hour because the attendant indicated there were no cars available. After some more shuffling of paperwork and peering at the computer screen, the attendant announced that someone had turned in a dented dark blue subcompact.

Mark decided to cut his losses and take it. The attendant said he could have it cleaned within an hour, but Mark wanted to get going and as far away from this suitcase-eating flight as possible, so he said he would take the car in its current condition.

At that point, the car rental's computer reservation system went down, so he had to give his credit card and wait while the attendant used a paper form for the credit card. The man happily ran the card by hand, giving Mark a periodic smile as he wrote something on the carbon paper form. Obviously, this guy was in no hurry.

Sophie grabbed Mark's arm and whispered in his ear, "It's the island way. No rush. Don't let your blood pressure build up."

Right. After everything that had happened on this flight, Mark pictured his head being a pressure cooker and steam shooting out his ears.

After the attendant double-checked and triple-checked the paperwork, Mark grabbed the proffered keys and dragged Sophie and her suitcase to their not-so-magic carpet.

The car started on the second try, backfired, but after disgorging a black stream of soot settled in to hum like a dissonant preteen garage band. Mark happened to look in the back seat and spied empty chip bags littering the floor and some green goo that reminded him of melted Gummy Bears. The back seat had obviously been the residence of a kid like the one behind him on the plane. He wondered if that would be the theme for his vacation—the attack of the Gummy Bears. Maybe he should have waited an hour to have the car cleaned. Welcome to paradise.

Sophie stretched. "I had a good long sleep on the flight. And you?"

"Not so hot. I dozed briefly but most of the time tried to keep out of the way of overactive elbows on each side of me. I think my seatmates were either retired professional wrestlers or participants in an upcoming Maui sumo wrestling tournament."

She gave him a wifely pat on the arm. "It couldn't have been that bad. But in any case, we can turn our attention to relaxing on the beach."

"Except that my swim trunks are in the errant suitcase."

"I'll help you buy new ones at the hotel. I know you hate to shop, but I'll select something appropriate for you. By the way, the man I sat next to, Dexter Kwan, lives on Maui, is a real estate developer and said he would call the hotel to invite us to his house sometime this week."

Mark arched an eyebrow. "Some guy hitting on you?"

"No. Dexter said he and his wife like to entertain mainland visitors. That's all. My attention on this trip will be focused entirely on you. After the *chaos* of last year, it will be nice to concentrate on us in a beautiful location."

Chaos. That said it exactly. Mark thought back to what had transpired with his attempts to be an amateur sleuth after a murder on the platform tennis courts in Boulder. He had survived several attempts on his life, but his escapades had not been well-received by Sophie. That was one of the reasons for this vacation. He had promised her a trip, but then the consulting job came up and Sophie became consumed in her volunteer work. Finally, both agreed the time had come, and Mark had made the reservations. Here they were, the two of them without any distractions. Relaxation and sightseeing together. He owed that to her.

"Look out!" Sophie shouted.

An oncoming old truck veered into his lane, and Mark's eyesight became tunnel vision. He jammed the steering wheel to the right, missing the intruder by inches.

Mark took a deep breath to calm himself and slow his heart beat. "That was close."

"I guess you have to watch for erratic drivers here. Dexter also taught me some of the important words we should be familiar with while on Maui. Caucasians are referred to as *haoles*, and local residents are called *kama'ainas*. A woman is known as a *wahine* and a man a *kane*."

"You're a wealth of information. I'm now armed and dangerous with my Hawaiian vocabulary. What do you call the guy who swerved into our lane a moment ago?"

"I can think of some inappropriate four letter words, but Dexter gave me one other word. *Pilikia*. It means trouble. Enough of that. I'm so looking forward to swimming and lying on the sand. No worries, no schedule, no *pilikia*."

"I'm for that."

He was pleased that she had taken an interest in their destination. Of course, she had been the one wanting a vacation, and Mark had broken down, taken out his credit card and made the necessary reservations. He looked out the corner of his eye to see Sophie smiling.

"Did your new Maui friend have any suggestions on places for us to visit?"

"That he did. He said to be sure to see Iao Valley. It's very lush and scenic. He mentioned some beaches—Kaanapali and Flemings Beach on the west side of the island. He also recommended walking around Lahaina with its yacht harbor and shops." Sophie rubbed her hands together. "I won't mind doing a little shopping on this trip."

"As long as it's a little."

"Oh, don't be such a tightwad. I'm going to spend a lot of your money. We're on vacation."

"How about some less expensive sights?"

"I don't know what it costs, but Dexter said many tourists enjoy biking down Haleakala at sunrise. Imagine being on the top of a volcano that hasn't erupted since 1790."

"As long as it stays dormant during our stay. You received a history lesson as well as instructions on sights to see."

"Dexter is quite knowledgeable about Maui. But in regards

8

to riding down Haleakala at sunrise, I'll leave that to you since I plan to sleep in every day."

"I don't want to do that by myself, and I don't plan to pick up any local *wahines* to join me."

"You better not. And one thing he said we shouldn't miss. He recommended taking the road to Hana. It's a long and twisty drive, but past Hana is a spot called 'Ohe'o Gulch'. It's supposed to be one of the most beautiful places on the island—a cascade of pools."

"We have lots of tourist activities to look forward to. Too bad they don't have platform tennis or pickleball on Maui. I wouldn't mind getting in a game while I'm here."

"I'm sure you could play regular tennis. The brochure I read indicated there are courts right near the hotel where we're staying."

Mark sighed. "Regular tennis doesn't do it for me anymore now that I'm hooked on sports played on smaller courts."

"Oh, look." Sophie pointed. "There are two little dark blue cars ahead that look the same as ours."

Mark rolled his eyes. "We must have the popular local model. I wonder if the others also come with melted Gummy Bears."

"Oh, don't be such a grump. We'll blend right in. But there's another important thing we need to do while we're on Maui."

Mark waggled his eyebrows at Sophie. "I hope you're thinking what I'm thinking."

She batted his arm. "Behave yourself. We need to hunt for seashells."

"What I had in mind is more exciting, but I'm up for looking for shells as well. First, I need to have someone find my suitcase."

★ ★ ★ ★ ★

The good news, they made it to the hotel with no traffic accidents or assaults. When he went to check in and the clerk of the Maui Queen Hotel asked for his credit card, Mark discovered that he had lost his Visa card. Sophie came to the rescue with her

MasterCard, but Mark had to spend an hour calling the car rental at the airport to see if they had found his card, which they hadn't. Then he had to go through the rigmarole of canceling his credit card and ordering a new one.

The only saving grace—they could rely on Sophie's MasterCard for the rest of the trip. That was only appropriate since she was the one who wanted to spend money. Not that it wouldn't eventually come from their joint checking account anyway.

He nudged her. "Looks like you're going to be treating for the rest of the trip."

Sophie playfully swatted at him, and he ducked out of the way.

With only one suitcase to deal with, they went up to their room. Sophie twirled around inside. "I love it. Look at the view."

Mark had to admit it was spectacular. The sliding glass door led to a balcony overlooking coconut trees, cabanas and a brilliant white beach. Sun sparkled off the ocean that separated Maui from the island of Kaho'olawe. He had read an account of this being called the Target Island, since it had been used as a bombing range by United States armed services during World War II. Currently, it was a wildlife preserve.

The room had all the amenities: a king size bed, small bar, desk, table for two on the balcony, and choice of cooling from air conditioning or opening the sliding doors for the trade winds.

"We'll have to order room service and have breakfast on our balcony some time while we're here. Or maybe lunch, since I don't plan to be up before noon."

"Think of the sights you'll miss if you sleep that late."

"I can make up for it in the afternoon and evening."

After purchasing a new pair of bright green and yellow swim trunks in the hotel store, a quick swim with no shark attack, and a pleasant dinner without food poisoning, they called it a day. Mark hoped their vacation was getting back on track.

Chapter 3

Mark awoke early, as usual. He might be on vacation, but his internal clock had now synchronized with sunrise, and at the first sign of light, his eyes shot open. He stretched and watched Sophie as she snuggled under the blanket, still sound asleep.

Getting out of the bed quietly so as not to awaken her, he peeked out the curtain to see the small island of Molokini and a fishing boat bobbing in the gentle swells. On the hotel grounds the coconut trees swayed in the breeze like graceful hula girls, the fronds telling stories of island history and romance.

Sophie stirred. "Why are you up so early?" came the muffled inquiry from beneath the pillow she invariable kept over her head after a night of sleep. She turned over and her short blond hair became momentarily visible between the pillow and the covers that she clutched to stay warm in the air-conditioned comfort of the room.

"After two days of sleeping late, taking naps, swimming and relaxing on the beach, I'm ready to go exploring."

"You go ahead. I'm sleeping in. But remember to wear the swim trunks that don't have a hole in the pocket." She gave a weak smile, blinked her eyes and dived back beneath the pillow.

Mark smiled at the lump in the bed. Since his suitcase had arrived the afternoon before, he now could wear either of his two pairs of swimming trunks. And nothing was missing from his luggage. In spite of the bad start to the trip, this had certainly been a relaxing vacation so far. Since retiring he hadn't often done nothing. It was against his nature. Of course the bout with prostate cancer had sucked away his energy and threatened his life, but according to his doctor the cancer was gone. That had given him a new outlook on life.

Mark continued gazing through the opening in the curtains. A young couple walked down the beach hand-in-hand. He remembered when he and Sophie had been newlyweds. Sure, he had aged, but he kept himself in good shape playing platform tennis and pickleball and jogging back in Boulder. Even did a little weight work in the basement several times a week. He tightened his bicep. A healthy amount of muscle mass for a guy his age. He had all his hair, wasn't overweight for his six-foot height and could keep up with people ten years younger when he ran the Bolder Boulder, the annual 10K race on Memorial Day. He patted his stomach. No flab. Life was good.

In the dim light, he rummaged through the drawer and grabbed his swim trunks. He put these on and added a T-shirt and a Colorado Rockies baseball cap. He searched around in the drawer and found two white socks and donned his tennis shoes. He grasped the shoelace where it had broken and he had tied a knot. If his platform tennis and pickleball friend, Shelby Prescott, were here, he'd make a snide comment such as, "You own a million dollar home, but not a new pair of shoelaces." Mark gave himself a mental pat on the back. Even though he could afford it, he wasn't about to waste money when a simple repair would do.

After kissing the back of Sophie's neck, he thrust the room keycard into his pocket and left Sophie in charge of sleeping.

This place was perfect for relaxation—low key and not crowded as it would be in a few weeks when families took their holiday vacations. After he left the hotel lobby, he whistled what might be recognized as "Here Comes the Sun" and walked across the driveway to a grove of coconut trees. Leaning against one, he stretched his legs to get ready for a run. Got to warm up. He didn't want to cramp or pull a muscle on his jog.

He and Sophie had spent only a short time looking for shells the last two days and hadn't found any whole ones yet. Some pieces of cone shells and cowries, but that didn't count. They would have more time for that in the next few days. He marveled at this unusual situation. Nothing scheduled. He thought back over his work career. Every day planned, often weeks ahead. And now, whatever they chose to do.

As he stood erect with his hands behind his hips to stretch his back, out of the corner of his eye he noticed a young boy approaching.

With a gap-toothed smile the boy, probably eleven or twelve, held up a necklace made of polished black kukui nuts. "Only ten dollar."

Mark's first reaction, given his propensity not to spend money, was to send the kid packing. But after a moment's thought, he reconsidered, recognizing a fellow entrepreneur, and scrutinized the rumpled black hair, bare feet, cutoff jeans, white T-shirt and backpack. "I don't have any money with me, but if you're around later, I'd like to buy a necklace for my wife."

"No problem. I come back."

"What's your name?" Mark asked.

"Kealamauloa but everybody calls me Kea."

At that moment, one of the hotel staff, a man wearing the signature blue and white Hawaiian shirt with a tag indicating assistant manager, came running up, shaking his right index finger at Kea. "Get out of here. I've told you before. No harassing our guests."

Mark held up a hand. "It's okay. He isn't bothering me."

The assistant manager opened his mouth as if to argue but apparently thought better of it.

Kea saw his chance for a graceful exit, waved to Mark and dashed away.

"I have to apologize," the assistant manager said. "We've had problems with that kid selling junk to our guests."

"He wasn't obnoxious, only asked if I wanted a kukui nut necklace."

The man pursed his lips. "He starts that way but doesn't give up. You haven't seen the last of him."

Mark waited until the assistant manager returned to the lobby, and completed his stretches. Then with a slow, loping gait he headed up the hill to the hotel entrance and turned right to jog along the narrow road that ran past the entrance to the tennis courts and golf course. Mark thought of the times he had played tennis when on vacations in his younger years, before he had discovered platform tennis and, more recently, pickleball. Particularly pickleball. He enjoyed the challenge of dinking the ball into the non-volley zone or "kitchen" area seven feet from the net and having long rallies while trying to cause the opponents to make an error or hit a ball too high that could be slammed back. Too bad there wasn't a pickleball court here on Maui. That would be the one remaining item to make this vacation perfect— now that he had recovered from the atrocious flight from Denver.

The morning sun peeked out from behind Haleakala. He turned a bend in the road and jogged along a stretch bordered by kiawe trees. He had already had the unpleasant experience of walking barefoot under one of these trees and stepping on a thorn. From then on, he had worn sandals until he reached the safety of the sparkling sand.

The bumpy highway ran almost directly south and parallel to the ocean. Above him, seagulls circled. Sea birds made him think of fishing. He remembered seeing one dive to tear a piece of flesh off an unattended tuna he had caught in Acapulco.

He should rent a fishing boat and go out for a day while he was here. That is, if Sophie was interested. He intended to spend as much time as possible with his wife on this trip. That was the objective—time together. No distractions.

His thoughts turned to the idea of living permanently in a place like this. Buy a little place, become a *kama'aina*, toughen his feet to walk barefoot like that kid, Kea. He loved the beach but also the mountains of Colorado. No, he probably would continue to do some consulting with startup companies when he returned to Boulder. Even though he had sold his company, he knew he couldn't stay fully retired. There was only so much leisure he could stand before getting antsy. But he didn't need to work full-time either. Some part-time consulting gigs would suffice. And he could play more pickleball as well. Yes, he had many possibilities when he returned from this vacation. But for the time being, he would enjoy a healthy run with the ocean and greenery around him.

Mopping his brow, he realized he had jogged over a mile, and he marveled at how fast he could run with the extra oxygen at sea level versus the thinner air at over a mile high where he usually exercised in Colorado. Much like the day before when he had swum for over an hour in the ocean, he sensed he could keep up this pace forever.

As his gaze returned to the road, he could see a framed fence with two coconut trees behind it. Ten yards farther, he stopped dead in his tracks. He squinted at what looked like a pickleball court. He rubbed his eyes. His recent ruminations on this sport must be leading to a mirage.

Pickleball was a fairly new sport but growing in popularity. His buddies who played platform tennis and he had made the transition to pickleball during the six-month period when their platform tennis courts were out of commission. They had played outdoors on a court outlined on a basketball court and indoors at the gym at the South Boulder Recreation Center. Mark had taken some lessons as well to learn the strategy of the game. Compared to tennis and platform tennis where power was essential, pickleball relied more on touch and placement. Sure, you blasted a ball when it came to you high and you were just behind the non-volley line, but the essence of the game was getting quickly up to the non-volley zone and then dinking into the non-volley zone of your opponents. The same held true with the serve and return of serve. Power wasn't necessary. Having only one serve, you wanted to get it deep into the court, and on a return of serve, a high deep shot was effective since it gave you time to get up to the non-volley zone.

Here in this remote stretch of road on Maui, the last thing he expected to find was a pickleball court. Yet, this certainly was the outline of a pickleball court he could see through a wire fence

15

above a five-foot tall stone wall next to the asphalt road.

His heart beat faster. Maybe he could get a game in while here on Maui. That would really make this a good vacation. He had his regular foursome in Boulder, but it was always fun to find some new players. He wondered if many people used this court here in this remote part of Maui.

The north end of the court faced a vacant lot, and here the top of the wall stood only three feet above a dirt hill.

Mark scrambled up the mound to get a look inside the court. Sure enough, there was the playing surface that appeared to be the size of a badminton court with two rectangular service areas at the back on both sides. The difference from tennis and platform tennis, in pickleball you served to the back of the court. If your one serve ended up outside the diagonally opposed service area, you lost the serve. The net looked new. A few dirt clods cluttered the playing surface, probably thrown over the wall, but those could easily be swept away. This court gave off an implied invitation to have Mark and three others grace its surface with their tennis shoes for a lively game. Wouldn't that be a blast?

Mark's attention refocused on the property beyond the court. A large yard opened up to a red-roofed house and matching cottage. Quite an estate. Right on the ocean, well-maintained grounds, professionally landscaped. This certainly was a pickleball court in paradise with plumerias, palms swaying in the breeze and bright blue water.

From his perch, Mark looked along the road. Not a person in sight. A scraggly mutt sat on the other side of the road, scratching its ear. The morning was quiet, interrupted only by myna birds cawing in a nearby banyan tree. Mark took in a deep breath and could smell the aroma of jasmine. This would be an ideal place to live. He raised his hands and the gentle breeze caressed his arms.

He peered again at the pickleball court, wondering who lived there. Then as he directed his gaze directly downward and to the right, he involuntarily flinched. A man's body was wedged between the dirt mound and the wall.

Chapter 4

Mark put his hand on the fence to lean directly over the contorted figure below. He couldn't believe what he was seeing. The man was obviously dead, his body twisted in an unnatural angle and his head lolling to one side. He wore blue swimming trunks, white tank top and no shoes. A red spot dotted the center of his forehead and dried blood caked the side of his face.

Bile rose in Mark's throat, and he had to force down a gag reflex. This find was definitely not what he was expecting in this remote location. *What to do?* He needed to notify someone but hadn't brought his cell phone with him.

Leaping down the hill, he ran along the wall to find the entrance to the house. Twenty yards along the road, the wall ended and was replaced by a large sliding wooden gate eight feet tall. The wood was weathered with a few patches of remaining rust brown stain. He shook the gate to find it solidly locked. A small speaker box was mounted in the stone wall. Mark pressed the red button and could hear the sound of static. He noticed a microphone imbedded within the box.

"Hello, is anyone there?"

No answer.

He pushed the red button several more times and shouted into the microphone again and again.

Still no answer.

He pounded on the wooden gate, but the house was too far back for anyone to hear him.

There was no way he was going to get in unless he scaled the wall and high fence, and that wasn't a realistic plan.

Still no people out walking and no traffic in sight. Even the dog had disappeared. Only a few unoccupied cars parked along the side of the road. He ran south following the remaining section of wall. The estate extended for a hundred yards, all enclosed. The south end of the property was bounded by more stone wall and wire fence that jutted toward the ocean and equally high shrubs that fronted a small beach and ran along the beachfront. The whole place was sealed in. It reminded him of a protected fortress.

Mark scanned both directions along the road. Still no traffic of the human or automobile variety.

The next house, on the other side and twenty yards down the road, was not as isolated. This green two-story structure with tile roof had a door and doorbell that could be reached from the street. Mark dashed up and rang the doorbell.

A balding, middle-aged man in Bermuda shorts and T-shirt answered, holding a coffee cup.

"I hate to bother you, but I need to have you call 9-1-1. There's a dead body up the road."

The man raised his eyebrows. "Is this some kind of joke?"

"No. There's a dead man lying behind the stone wall at your neighbor's place."

"It doesn't surprise me. What a bunch of racket that group of yahoos made there last night. I almost called the police myself. Wait here."

The man closed the door, but returned moments later with a cell phone.

"Here." The man thrust the phone into Mark's hand. "You make the call."

Mark pushed 9-1-1, identified himself and described his location along the deserted road.

He handed the phone back to the man. "Someone will be here soon."

The man stepped outside and shut the door. "I'll wait with you, but I'm not going to go look at any dead body."

"I don't blame you. I certainly didn't want to find it. Who owns the property with the pickleball court?"

"What's pickleball?"

"It's a sport played with a paddle and a ball similar to a wiffle ball. Your neighbor has a court off the road behind a wall."

"Okay. I've heard thwacking noises that must be balls being hit. The owners are people named Reinholt. They live in California most of the year."

"Are they here now?"

"No. There's someone staying in the guest cottage and watching the house for the Reinholts. Guy's the tennis pro at the Maui Queen Tennis Club."

"I'm staying at the Maui Queen Hotel, and the tennis courts are up the road."

The man nodded vigorously. "That's the place."

"You said there was commotion last night."

"Yeah. Some kind of party. I don't know why the Reinholts let that guy stay there. I had to put up with a bunch of rowdies whooping and hollering. And lights glaring. As I said, I was getting ready to call in a complaint when they finally settled down. Jeez. You move from the big city to get away from all that, and it follows you."

★ ★ ★ ★ ★

After another fifteen minutes, a dark gray Ford Taurus with a blue light on the roof pulled up. A large, part-Hawaiian man extracted himself from the passenger side of the car.

Mark walked toward the car. He saw that a rather skinny man in khaki uniform had also emerged from the driver's side.

The large man stood nearly six-foot-four and must have weighed well over three hundred pounds. He glared at Mark. "You the guy who found a body?"

"I stopped to look at the pickleball court," Mark pointed up the street. "When I climbed up a dirt hill next to the retaining wall by the court, I saw a man wedged between the wall and the dirt mound. I think he was shot."

"Why were you up there?"

"I play pickleball back in Colorado and was excited to find a court in this remote place. My curiosity. I had to get a closer look."

"Akahi, go check the hill," the large man, obviously in charge told his sidekick.

"Okay, Puna." The skinny cop ambled up the street.

Puna took out a notepad. "I'd like to see some identification."

"I don't have any with me. My wallet's back in my hotel room. My name is Mark Yeager."

"Where're you staying, Mr. Yeager?"

"My wife and I are at the Maui Queen. I'd be happy to let you see my driver's license if you give me a ride back to the hotel."

"You're kind of out of the way for a tourist."

"I was taking an early morning jog, enjoying the sunshine and ocean. Until, I stopped here."

Puna eyed him suspiciously. "You happened to be at this place and found a dead body?"

Mark straightened. "That's right. I just happened to be here."

"Let's go take a look. You come with me."

As if Mark intended to argue.

Mark and Puna walked along the road and climbed the hill to the retaining wall. Akahi had jumped down and was examining the body. Mark realized that no one would ever see the body from the road. You would have to be on the top of the dirt mound as he had been to spot the dead man.

"Shot through the forehead, Puna. Looks like he's been dead for several hours. Also found a Maui Queen room card next to the body."

"Maybe that card belongs to you, Mr. Yeager?" Puna sneered.

"I don't think so." Just to be sure, Mark put his hand in his pocket. *Uh-oh.* No card. His fingers poked through a hole. *Crap.* He'd forgotten that these old swim trunks had a hole in the pocket. And Sophie had even warned him to wear the new pair, but in the darkness he had put on the old swim trunks and dropped the room key in the torn pocket. Warmth spread across Mark's cheeks as he turned his pocket inside out. "I seem to have a hole in my swim trunks. It could have fallen out when I was up on the wall and spotted the body."

"Hold the card on the edges, Akahi. We'll want to check for Mr. Yeager's fingerprints."

"Look, my fingerprints will be on that card since it slipped out of my pocket. I was passing by. You don't think I had anything to do with this, do you?"

Puna gave Mark a cold stare. "All we know is that there's a murdered man and probably your room card. We'll see."

Akahi climbed back up the hill to join Puna and Mark. "It's George Tanabe."

"Our favorite suspected drug dealer," Puna said. "You wouldn't happen to be involved in drugs, Mr. Yeager?"

Mark clenched his fists. "Of course not. Any chance this was suicide?"

Akahi wiped dirt off his uniform. "Doesn't look like it. No gun lying near the body. Suicides don't usually get rid of the weapon after committing the act." Akahi grinned.

Mark resisted the urge to roll his eyes. Island humor.

Puna pointed to his cohort. "Akahi, call to get the coroner's assistant out here. I'm going to see who's living in the house."

"Got it, boss." He jogged back to the police car.

"I tried to reach someone from the microphone by the gate," Mark said. "No one answered. I understand people named Reinholt own this property and the tennis pro from the Maui Queen Tennis Club is staying here."

"You seem to know an awful lot for someone who claims to be only passing by." Puna's lips curled.

"The neighbor who loaned me a cell phone shared that information. You now know everything I do."

They walked to the gate, and Puna tried the microphone with the same lack of results that Mark had experienced.

Puna turned on his large heels as his assistant came jogging back. "Akahi, go climb the wall and fence near the victim and get the gate open."

21

"Right, boss." Akahi dashed along the road and disappeared up the dirt hill.

"You wait here with me, Mr. Yeager."

Mark nodded as he watched the antics of this two-man sideshow. "No problem. I wouldn't want to miss anything." He sat down near the gate with his back against the stone wall. No other cars came by. Then after a wait of five minutes, a grinding noise caught his attention, and the gate slowly opened.

Akahi came out. "There you go, boss. All fixed."

"You watch Mr. Yeager." Puna motioned toward Mark. "I'll go look around inside."

After Puna disappeared into the compound, Mark said, "Take charge kind of guy."

"You got that right." Akahi laughed. "You want to stay on his right side. He's one tough cop and a good detective. He played football at Lahainaluna High School and was a starting defensive tackle at the University of Hawaii. No one messes with Puna."

Mark inwardly concurred that he didn't want to rile up someone that size. Except for a darker shade of skin, Puna could have been related to the two men who impinged upon his space on the airplane.

Mark scanned the enclave and tried to imagine what had happened to George Tanabe. Was this a random act or did it have anything to do with the noisy game from the night before? Mark had experienced rowdy players in Boulder, although his foursome consisted of staid middle-aged guys. From the appearance of George, this was a younger crowd.

His thoughts were interrupted by a static blast from the radio in the police car farther along the road.

"Stay here." Akahi pointed to Mark's feet and then hustled to the car to answer the radio. He waved a hand and spoke intently, although too far away for Mark to make out the conversation.

A few minutes later, Puna returned from inside the wall, accompanied by a tall, lean, barefooted man in his early thirties with wild blond hair and wearing white tennis shorts and white T-shirt.

The man rubbed his eyes. "What's this all about?"

"I'll ask the questions," Puna said. "Who are you, and what're you doing here?"

"I'm Ted Franklin, the tennis pro at the Maui Queen Tennis Club. I'm staying here and taking care of the place while the owners, the Reinholts, are on the mainland."

"What went on here last night?"

Ted's stare focused down at Mark sitting beside the wall and back up at Puna. "I had some people over to play pickleball. We do that once or twice a week."

Puna took out a pad, which almost disappeared in his large hand. From his shirt pocket he extracted a pen. "I'd like the names and when they left."

Ted scratched his arm as if ridding himself of sand fleas. "Let's see. One was George Tanabe. Said he was going to take a walk on the beach before driving home."

"What time was that?"

Ted shuffled his bare feet. "Must have been nearly ten o'clock."

"Who else?"

"Lefty Kalama. He lives in Kihei. He packed up shortly after George took off."

Puna wrote on the pad. "And?"

"Keone Ahuna. He has a cabin up in the hills above Waikapu. He was the last to leave."

"What time did Keone go?" Puna asked.

"Probably ten fifteen or so."

"Do you know this guy?" Puna jabbed a thick finger in Mark's upper arm.

Mark flinched and felt a twinge in his muscle. There was power behind that finger.

Ted rubbed the stubble on his chin and looked closely. "No. I don't recognize him."

Just then two cars pulled up. A woman climbed out of the first vehicle, holding a black bag. Puna went up to her. "The body is around the side of the fence. Let me know when you're done so we can look closer."

Two policemen in uniforms got out of the second car.

Puna signaled to one of the police officers. "You start containing the crime scene. As soon as the coroner's assistant is finished with the body, check everything close in." Then he pointed at Mark. "Get up."

Mark slowly raised himself, and Puna gave him a push toward the other policeman. "Manuel, make sure Mr. Yeager here isn't carrying. Then have Akahi take him to get his identification and bring him to the station house. I'll be there in an hour."

"Okay. This way, Mr. Yeager."

Manuel led Mark back to the first police car. "Put your hands on the roof."

"This isn't necessary. I'm only wearing swimming trunks and a T-shirt."

Manuel snorted. "Orders. Hands on the car."

Mark complied, and Manuel patted down his back and sides. Some early morning run this had turned out to be.

"You sit in the back." Manuel opened the door, gave Mark a shove inside and slammed the door.

Mark discovered he was in a locked back seat with a clear panel separating him from the front seat. What a way to spend his morning. He watched the activity going on around him, unable to hear what anyone said.

Manuel and Akahi spoke for a moment, before Akahi climbed into the driver's seat and started the car.

Mark glanced at the beaches and coconut trees on the short drive back to the Maui Queen Hotel. They passed a group of kids happily chasing each other along the side of the road. He'd rather be out swimming, snorkeling or laying in the sun than confined in the backseat of a police car. He remembered being trapped between the two large men on the plane. From one type of confinement to another. He longed for the freedom of an open beach.

Akahi pulled into a parking spot at the hotel, jumped out of the car and opened the back door. "Let's go up to your room to get your identification, Mr. Yeager."

Mark got out of the car, and they proceeded into the lobby. The assistant manager Mark had encountered earlier stared at them but made no comment. The sight of a guest being accompanied by a police officer probably didn't occur every day.

At the room, Mark knocked on the door. Nothing. He knocked again. Footfalls sounded, and Sophie opened the door. She blinked at him. "Don't you have your room key?"

"No, and I need to get my wallet. The police want to talk to me."

Sophie's eyes widened. "What happened?"

"I found a dead body while I was out jogging."

Her eyes narrowed. "You're not getting involved in another murder investigation are you?"

Mark gave a nervous laugh. "I happened to be in the wrong place at the wrong time."

"You have a way of doing that."

"Hurry up," Akahi shouted from the hallway.

Mark grabbed his wallet and cell phone and gave Sophie a kiss. "I hope this won't take long."

"I'll go get some breakfast. If I'm not in the room when you get back, I'll be out on the beach."

* * * * *

As they walked back to the police car, Akahi nudged Mark, "Your wife seemed pretty calm. Before I became a policeman, if I'd been in your spot, my wife would have gone crazy."

"I was involved in a murder investigation back in Boulder, Colorado. I guess she's used to this."

Akahi came to an abrupt stop. "No kidding. What happened?"

"A man was murdered. I helped solve the case."

"So you're one of those guys who attracts dead bodies." Ahaki slapped his thigh and laughed. "Kind of like with flies."

Mark resisted the urge to grab and wring Akahi's neck. "I guess so."

25

Rather than putting Mark in the back, Akahi let him sit in the front seat this time.

"You're not concerned that I'm sitting up here with you?" Mark asked.

"Nah. You're not armed."

"What if I'm a hardened criminal and know some deadly martial art?"

Akahi chuckled. "First, you've been patted down so you're not armed. Second, I have some experience with martial arts, and I can tell from how you handle yourself that you're not familiar with deadly techniques."

This piqued Mark's interest. "How do you know that?"

"Simple. How you walk. How you move your arms. How you position yourself next to other people. How you handle yourself. Someone could easily take you because you're not paying attention. An expert walking with me would have noticed my location at all times."

Mark tried to think how someone could act who knew deadly techniques. Then it struck him. Someone like Akahi who appeared casual but was always watching. Mark decided to see if he could get a little information. "Back at the crime scene, there were several names mentioned—Lefty Kalama and Keone Ahuna. And the guy who lives there is Ted Franklin, the tennis pro at Maui Queen."

"You may not be an expert at martial arts, but you're pretty good with names." Akahi glanced over his right shoulder toward Mark. "Sure you don't know these guys?"

"Never met any of them before. What about you?"

"I never met Lefty. From what I know he grew up on Kauai and only moved to Maui five years ago. Puna suspects him of drug dealing but hasn't been able to pin anything on him. Only heard of Ted Franklin." Then he smiled. "Good old Keone. I used to play tennis with him."

"So you're a tennis player?"

Akahi nodded so vigorously that it reminded Mark of a bobble head doll. "Used to be pretty good. Keone and I played against each other in high school. He won more matches, but I beat him a number of times."

"Do you still play?"

"Not very much. Between my wife and Puna, I'm kept pretty busy."

"Ever play pickleball?"

Akahi swished his right hand from left to right as if hitting a backhand shot. "Actually I did. Spent six months at a police academy on the mainland a few years ago. I met some people who played, and we went to a pickleball court whenever we could escape from the punishing training. Took me a while to get used to dinking the ball into the kitchen. Fun sport. I really enjoyed it and got pretty good."

"Yeah, some friends hooked me on it in Colorado. Easier on my body than tennis. I'm surprised Keone never asked you to play pickleball."

"Nope. Didn't know he played or that there was even a court here. He and I didn't keep in touch after high school."

Mark thought of all he was doing to assist local law enforcement and educate them on the surroundings. Maybe he could become a consultant on Maui. Provide dead body and sports advice for the police force. He considered slapping his cheek to stay focused. "It surprised me to find that court... and the body. You seemed to know the victim."

"He was also suspected of being involved in the local drug scene. We've never been able to nail him. Too late now."

Mark watched a car speed past. "Sounds like you have a big drug problem here."

"Not too much of the hard stuff. But marijuana grows quickly here, and there's lots of forest to hide plants." He shrugged. "Bunch of people make extra money that way. Maui wowee."

Chapter 5

At the police station in Kihei, Mark turned over his driver's license to the desk sergeant and submitted to the fingerprint process. Then after cleaning his fingers with a wet wipe, he was led to an interrogation room to wait.

Mark scanned the room. Besides the hard metal chair he sat in against the bare back wall, the only other furniture was a table and one other chair. Up in the corner of the room appeared a camera. He resisted the urge to stick out his tongue or wave. No one-way mirror. He settled in to wait. What had transpired the night before? Had a pickleball game got out of control? What had happened to George Tanabe after he left the gathering? Did his death have to do with a drug deal gone bad? Did one of the other three pickleball players kill George or had it been someone waiting for him outside?

A drop of sweat trickled down his forehead. No air conditioning in the room. This could be a torture chamber if the heat increased.

Before Mark reached the point of pounding on the walls, Puna showed up and closed the door, filling the small room with his large presence. He went through the Miranda routine and concluded by asking, "Do you understand everything I've told you?"

Mark sighed. "Yes. I don't need a lawyer present." Mark knew his platform tennis and pickleball buddy, Ben Quentin, a Boulder lawyer, wouldn't agree with this decision, but Mark wanted to get this over with and had nothing to hide. "I've been through the Miranda rights before."

"That a fact? You been convicted?"

"I have no criminal record as you know from the checking you've already done."

Puna actually smiled. "That's right. I was interested in what you'd say. But I have a few questions for you. First, what were you doing from ten until midnight last night?"

"I was reading in my hotel room and then sleeping."

"Can your wife verify that?"

Mark's head jerked up. "Actually, she was down watching the late *hula* show at the hotel. I wasn't interested so I went to the room."

"So no one can confirm your whereabouts at that time."

"No. She probably got back around eleven forty-five, but I was asleep by then. You can check with her."

Puna leaned over the table toward Mark. "So you could have driven to the Reinholt property, killed George Tanabe and been back without anyone noticing."

"But I didn't. Besides, I have no motive."

"You involved in buying and selling drugs?"

Mark's eyes flared. "No!"

"What do you do for a living?"

"I'm retired. I ran my own company and sold it last year."

"What kind of company?"

"High tech. It was a network products company. I sold it to Cisco."

"How long you been on Maui?"

"Three days."

"How long you planning to stay?"

Mark felt as if Puna were pointing a machine gun at him, peppering him with questions. "Two weeks altogether. Look, I'm willing to cooperate in any way. As I mentioned, I'm not asking for a lawyer because I have nothing to hide. I don't know any of the people involved, including the victim. You can talk with the hotel staff and find out that I didn't leave the hotel last night."

Puna sat back and folded his large arms. "Nice try, Mr. Yeager, but just because no one remembers seeing you last night doesn't mean you didn't sneak out of the hotel. We'll be doing some more checking on you. I don't want you leaving the island in the next week."

Mark's face grew warm. "I told you I'm not planning to leave. I'm here on vacation."

"I'll be wanting to talk to you some more. Wait in one of the chairs in the lobby."

"I need to get back to join my wife at the hotel."

"Don't be so impatient." He gave Mark a sly grin. "This is Maui. No rush."

Mark groaned. The same warning Sophie had given him when he got impatient with the car rental clerk at the airport. He was on Hawaiian time now. When things were done, they were done.

Puna led Mark out to the lobby, where he sat by himself. His mind swirled with the recent events. He should be concerned about the threat of being arrested, but the circumstances were too farfetched to really scare him. But would he be able to relax with this hanging over his head?

Fifteen minutes later, Puna accompanied Ted Franklin, the Maui Queen Club tennis pro, out to the lobby, and Ted sat next to Mark. Akahi came through the outer door escorting a short man in his thirties with long black hair and goatee. The guy waved to Ted before he disappeared inside.

"Who's that?" Mark asked Ted.

"Keone Ahuna. He was one of the people playing last night. They question you?"

Mark nodded. "And you?"

"Yep. They wanted to know all about last night. We had a good evening of whacking the ball. Too bad something happened to George Tanabe."

"So you have a regular pickleball game?"

"We did. With George dead I don't know if we'll be able to get a foursome. Not many people play the game here."

Mark could recommend Akahi as a replacement, but he had a better idea. "I happened upon the body because I was interested to find a pickleball court in this remote part of Maui. I play back in Colorado."

Ted carefully scrutinized Mark. "What level player are you?"

"I play two or three times a week and would rate myself at the 4.0 level."

"We were supposed to play at seven tonight... but with what happened to George..." Ted paused, then smiled. "Say, you want to join us?"

Mark knew Sophie wouldn't be happy, but he would like to get a game in. Besides, if he were a suspect in the murder, he'd better learn more in order to clear his name.

"Sure, if one of you can lend me a paddle."

Ted slapped Mark on the back. "No problem. I have a whole collection of paddles back at the house."

"So how did a pickleball court get built way out here?"

"Actually it was here when the Reinholts bought the house. Apparently the previous owner was an avid pickleball player from the mainland who had the court installed."

"And the Reinholts play?"

"No. Actually they had a moveable basketball hoop added for their kids and took down the net. When I came to Maui and found the court, I convinced them to set up the pickleball net again. They play it once in a while but are more into regular tennis."

"So where did you find out about the sport?"

"I discovered pickleball in Seattle. I was a teaching tennis pro there after graduating from UCLA. Enjoyed the change from a racquet to a paddle."

"How long have you been the pro at the Maui Queen Tennis Club?"

"Two years. It's a great life, and once I made friends with the Reinholts, I had a place to stay. I give them tennis lessons when they're on Maui, and they let me stay in their guest cottage. They need to have someone watch the property, so it's a win-win."

"And the other guys you played pickleball with last night?" Mark asked.

"Lefty Kalama was one of the better junior tennis players on Kauai a number of years ago before moving to Maui. He owns a sporting goods store at the Kihei Gateway Plaza, and he strings racquets. I went to the store to try to buy a paddle. He had never heard of the sport but ordered some demo models from the mainland. I convinced him to take up the game after that."

"And the guy in there?" Mark pointed toward the door leading into the police station.

"Keone Ahuna. Another good local tennis player. He helps me out at the club from time to time. Doesn't really want to work a whole lot though. Built his own cabin somewhere up in the forest. The only time he's dependable is showing up for our pickleball games."

The door opened and Puna and Keone came out. A policewoman handed Puna a folder. He regarded it for a moment before signaling to Mark. "Mr. Yeager. Come with me."

They went through the inner door, headed down the hallway, entered the interrogation room, and Puna slammed the door.

"Mr. Yeager. The fingerprints on the Maui Queen room card found near the body match your prints."

"Doesn't surprise me. As I told you, I think the card fell through a hole in my pocket when I was leaning over to get a look at the body." Mark pulled the pocket inside out. "See there's a hole here."

"You claim you jogged from the hotel?"

"I don't claim. I did jog from the hotel."

"And the card doesn't fall out of your pocket during all that time, but only when you're leaning against the fence?"

Mark paled. "That's the only explanation I have."

"I'm not going to arrest you yet, but I may reconsider at any time."

"Sounds like I should get a lawyer."

Puna continued to stare at Mark. "Whatever. Remember, I have my eye on you."

* * * * *

After being led back to the lobby again, Mark's heart sank. What kind of vacation mess had he got himself into? He needed some legal advice. He retrieved his cell phone from the pocket without a hole and called Ben Quentin, his pickleball friend and a lawyer back in Boulder. With the three-hour time difference he hoped to catch Ben returning from lunch. Fortunately, he succeeded.

"Ben, I need to tap your legal expertise."

"Mark, you're supposed to be relaxing on the beach and sipping a Mai Tai. What the hell gives?"

"I'm embroiled in a murder investigation."

"Up to your old tricks again."

"Paddle sports seem to cause me problems."

"You mean other than your weak backhand?"

Mark prepared to take exception to that statement but heard a burst of static and thought the connection had been broken. Then Ben's voice continued loud and clear, "Don't tell me they play platform tennis or pickleball on Maui?"

"Actually, I found a pickleball court. I'm in a game tonight, but I'm also a suspect in a murder investigation."

"You don't waste any time getting into trouble."

"No, it seems to seek me out. I need to find a good lawyer on Maui and thought you might have a recommendation for me."

"Hold on a second. Let me check my file."

There was a pause on the line. Mark imagined Ben waving his fingers over a file cabinet and summoning the gods of lawyer networking.

In a minute, Ben returned and cleared his throat. "A law school classmate of mine grew up in the islands and returned to Maui a number of years ago. Homer Nagano practices in Kahului. Here's a phone number."

Mark obtained a pencil and piece of paper from the desk sergeant and wrote it down. He would have one ally.

Chapter 6

Mark punched in Homer's number. A pleasant receptionist informed him that Homer was in court. Mark resisted the urge to say that he'd rather be on a court than in court and instead left his cell phone number with a message that he was a friend of Ben Quentin's and needed Homer's legal assistance.

Mark had done what he could for the moment. He sat back down, and shortly Puna ambled into the hallway and wagged a finger at Mark. "Remember, you stick around."

"So am I free to go?"

"Yeah, but keep in mind we'll be watching you."

"How'd you like to watch me back to the hotel? I'm kind of stuck here."

Puna revealed a hint of white teeth. "It'd be a pretty long walk. Maybe we can work something out for you other than jail." He shouted for Akahi who came running from the other end of the hall.

"Yes, boss."

"Take Mr. Yeager back to his hotel."

"Okay."

Mark expected Akahi to salute, but he only nodded.

Puna handed Mark a card that bore his full name, Puna Pa'a. "Here's my phone number in case you decide you have something to confess to me. And in the meantime, don't do anything I wouldn't do."

★ ★ ★ ★ ★

Akahi allowed Mark sit in the front seat again.

"I feel like I'm getting the royal treatment," Mark said.

"Hey, you're staying at the Maui Queen Hotel, why not?"

Mark looked toward the roof of the car, hoping for deliverance. "Everyone around here wants to be a comedian."

"Why not? It makes the job more fun. You want me to tell you some Portagee jokes?"

"No thanks." Mark stared out the window and spotted a kid eating a mango alongside the road. It reminded him of Kea, barefoot with unruly black hair. He returned his attention to Akahi, who could be what Kea would look like in twenty years. "How long have you worked with Puna?"

"Over a year. He's the best."

"Seems like a tough detective."

Akahi tapped his fingers on the steering wheel. "You have that right. He may be big, but he's fast. And no one's taken him down in a fight."

"Probably not many around bigger than he is."

"Nope, but it's not only his size. Puna is strong. I bet he could out arm wrestle anyone on the island."

"I'll have to remember not to challenge him. He sure likes to order you around all the time."

Akahi raised and lowered his shoulders. "No problem. I'm learning a lot from him. He likes to be the boss. I'm fine with that."

"What do you think of the tennis pro, Ted Franklin?"

"Must be a good tennis teacher, because the tennis club seems happy with him, although we had one complaint that he cheated a woman out of money."

Mark raised his eyebrows. "What kind of complaint?"

"A rich widow staying at the Maui Queen Hotel. Said he took money for an investment that never panned out. It looked like a poor investment, but no one forced her to spend the money. Nothing indicated Ted Franklin did anything illegal."

"What did you think of that charge?"

"I think he was trying to hustle the woman, but a lot of guys try that around here. One of the island occupations. If people want to throw their money away in a poor investment, there's not much we can do. As long as it's not a scam, which this didn't appear to be."

Mark thought of the assistant manager's warning when Kea tried to sell a kukui necklace earlier. Sometimes a fine line between a hustler and an entrepreneur. Mark had dealt with that distinction when he ran his startup company. He had to believe in himself, his company and his product and promote at every possible chance. But he had kept to the truth. The people who made blatant false claims were the ones who got in trouble.

Mark climbed out of the police car in the driveway in front of the hotel. "Thanks for the lift."

"Anytime, Bruddah. We'll be seeing a lot of each other."

"So, you'll be watching me?"

Akahi waggled his eyebrows. "Could be."

"I'll save you some trouble. I'll be at the beach today and tonight playing pickleball on the court near where I found the dead body. I'll be there with Ted, Lefty and Keone. But you don't have to give me a ride. You can come watch on your own. That way you can keep track of all four of us."

Mark shut the door and headed toward the lobby.

Before he reached the door, Kea sprang out of a bush. "You ready to buy the kukui nut necklace?"

"I thought you'd never ask." Mark got out his wallet and took out a ten dollar bill.

The boy took the money and gave Mark the necklace and a business card. "You ever need anything, you ask for Kea. Also, on the back of the card are my cousins. Abe has the best photo gallery on the island in Lahaina, and Nora runs a primo shop for muumuus and Hawaiian shirts in Kaanapoli. You be sure to visit them. Tell them Kea sent you, and you'll get the number one discount available. Uh-oh, here comes that guy who's always bugging me." As the assistant manager hustled out the door, Kea disappeared into the bushes.

"Was that kid bothering you again?" he asked.

"Not a problem."

"You shouldn't buy the kid's cheap merchandise."

Mark regarded the necklace. Each nut gave off a polished sheen, and a sturdy cord held it together. He tugged on it to assure himself. "Looks to be good quality."

The assistant manager sniffed loudly, turned on his heels and stalked back into the lobby.

Mark figured the assistant manager would have preferred Mark spend twenty dollars for a lower quality kukui nut necklace in the hotel store. Nothing like a little friendly competition. He glanced at the business card. It read, "Kea Puahi. Kukui nut necklaces, flower leis, shells, tour guide, fishing expeditions, storyteller, expert on local culture."

Since he and Sophie hadn't yet found any good shells, maybe he could buy something from Kea to give to Sophie. She had her heart set on shells. He turned the card over, and read the printed addresses for Kea's two cousins' shops. The kid was cross promoting.

Mark laughed. Definitely an entrepreneur.

* * * * *

After getting a replacement room key at the front desk, Mark proceeded upstairs. Not finding Sophie in the room, he dropped the kukui nut necklace on the bed. Then he noticed a note on the dresser telling him to join her on the beach. He stashed his wallet before heading downstairs and outside to where he spotted her lying on a towel on the sand. He sat down and looked at the rocky point on the south end of the beach. Kiawe and coconut trees clustered in the grass above the rocks and blocked part of the view of Kahoʻolawe in the distance.

Sophie raised herself on her elbows. "So tell me the details of what you've gotten into this time."

"It was strange. I found this pickleball court while jogging. I couldn't resist looking at it more closely. And then I spotted a dead body."

Sophie eyed him. "Why does there seem to be a connection between paddle sports, murder victims and you?"

"Some guys are chick magnets. I guess I'm a dead body magnet. That's what the police officer who brought me back to the hotel earlier thinks."

"Maybe I should worry about the chicks as well, now that you're functioning again, and I must say, functioning pretty well." She ran her hand along his thigh.

Mark experienced the warm surge that had finally returned. He had wondered after his prostate cancer surgery if that feeling would ever occur again. This trip was like a second honeymoon.

"I've also been invited to play pickleball tonight. If you'll wait for me we can go out for a late dinner afterwards."

Sophie lowered her sunglasses and looked at him above the rims. "Is it playing pickleball or solving the murder that interests you?"

"Actually, it's you that interests me."

She removed her sunglasses completely. "Don't change the subject. Answer my question."

His cheeks grew warm and not from the sun. "You know me so well. I really want to play, but my curiosity is piqued."

"Already trying to solve it? Aren't the police taking care of the investigation?"

"The police detective, Puna Pa'a, seems competent. Plays the bad cop to his sidekick, Akahi, the good cop."

"We've been through this before. Leave it to them."

"That's the problem. I'm a person of interest. Puna thinks I'm involved, so I need to clear myself."

"Don't get too involved. By the way, I bought you a present." She reached in her beach bag and pulled out a kukui nut necklace.

Mark laughed. "How about that? I bought you one, too. It's up on our bed. From a kid named Kea."

"Same one I bought this from. Nice young man—twelve years old with interesting Maui stories. I bartered him down to eight dollars."

Mark winced. "I had to pay ten dollars."

"He said I earned a discount for being a nice *wahine*."

"You are a nice woman, but what have you been doing besides flirting with twelve-year-old kids?"

"I took a swim and tried the snorkel and mask. There are an incredible number of colorful fish in the water. You should give it a try."

Mark decided to follow her suggestion. He adjusted the mask and went in the water. As he stroked away from shore, the warm ocean soothed his body. Back in Colorado, the lakes were freezing over, but here he could swim in this tropical warmth. He swam for half an hour to limber up his muscles and then turned over on his back to float for a few minutes watching swatches of white sail past against the dazzling azure. Ready to enjoy the sights underwater, he adjusted his mask and snorkel and dove. Sure enough, he swam over a section of reef and spotted angelfish, snapper and an eel. No sharks. He'd deal with the human variety later.

★ ★ ★ ★ ★

That evening Mark put on his tennis shoes and tied the laces securely. He gave Sophie a parting kiss.

She put down her novel long enough to give him a withering stare. "Don't stay too long."

"Aye, aye, admiral." He ducked out of the room before he got in any more trouble.

★ ★ ★ ★ ★

He passed a pleasant drive, retracing the route he had jogged in the morning. The sun had set and the tropical darkness descended rapidly. He parked by the hill outside the court and, resisting the urge to check where he had seen the body earlier, walked to the gate, which was partially open. When he reached the court he saw Ted in a blue UCLA baseball cap and another man warming up. They stood behind the non-volley "kitchen" zone and hit short dink shots to each other that landed within the kitchen. Ted had long arms and occasionally reached to cut off a ball before it hit the court. You could lean over as much as you wanted but couldn't step into the kitchen to hit a volley. You could step in if the ball first hit within the kitchen. Then they did a drill where they hit hard shots to each other standing just outside the kitchen line. Mark saw the speed of the ball and gulped. These were young, hard-hitting tennis players who had taken up pickleball. Might be a little different from the old man's game he was used to.

Ted pointed. "There're several paddles on the bench. Pick one and come warm up."

Mark lifted each of the paddles, checked the grips and selected one. He slapped the blue playing surface against his left hand, satisfied that the material was solid—no cracks. He swished it back and forth several times feeling the smooth motion of the light paddle.

Mark joined Ted's side of the net.

"Mark, meet Lefty Kalama." Ted pointed toward his opponent, a thirty-something with a solid build, wavy black hair and wearing a ragged T-shirt.

Lefty waved his paddle.

Mark found that although Lefty pounded the ball, he tended to over hit, and some of the shots would go out. Also, by watching the ball carefully, Mark could handle the pace. He would have to pay attention at all times, particularly at the kitchen line. He tuned the timing of his dink shots and then hit a few serves and shots from behind the baseline.

Keone ambled in and dropped an equipment bag on the grass outside the court, picked up a paddle and entered the court, joining Lefty.

As Mark and Keone hit short shots back and forth from the kitchen line, Mark studied the young man. Slight pock marks on his cheeks, wiry build and a tattoo of an eagle on his right forearm. Keone didn't hit as hard as the other two, but seemed more consistent than Lefty. It would be a good match.

Lefty and Keone won the toss and chose to serve. One of the unique aspects of pickleball was the scoring. Points were only scored when the serving team won a point. Except for the first serve of a game, both players had a chance to serve before the serve reverted to the other team. A server started on the right side of the court serving diagonally to the opponent. If the server's team won the rally, a point was scored and the same person then served from the left side of the court again diagonally to the other opponent. If the serving team lost the rally, then the other person on the serving team served from whichever side he was on. Once a rally was lost by the second server on the team, the serve reverted to the other team. Calling score consisted of giving your team's points, the other team's points and saying one or two for being the first or second server for the team. The only exception was the first rally of the game when the serving team had only one server and called out zero, zero, two. Game was eleven but had to be won by at least two points.

"What side of the court do you want to start on?" Mark asked Ted.

"I'll take the backhand."

"That's fine with me. I play equally on either side."

Lefty served first. He gripped his paddle and before serving the required below the waist underhand serve, called out, "zero, zero, two," and hit a deep shot that clipped the baseline. The left-handed spin was tricky, but Mark blocked the ball back cross court, barely clearing the net, not the deep shot he wanted. Lefty lunged, but was unable to get his paddle fully on the ball so that his shot didn't clear the net.

Ted's eyes widened. "Good return."

"Lucky shot," Mark replied somewhat surprised himself.

Lefty glared and returned to the baseline to receive Mark's serve.

Mark called out, "zero, zero, one." He hit a deep serve, and the return came back to him. One of the rules was a one-bounce rule that no one could hit a volley until the ball had bounced once on that team's side. Mark and Ted therefore waited behind the baseline until Lefty's return struck the court. Mark hit a short shot that landed in the non-volley zone, and he and Ted rushed up to their non-volley line. Lefty hit a short dink back to Mark who fielded it and returned crosscourt to Lefty's backhand. Lefty tried to hit the ball too hard and it went into the net.

"Shit!" Lefty shouted.

Mark gave a sigh of relief. At least they wouldn't be skunked. He changed places with Ted and called the score, "one, zero, one."

As play continued Mark missed a few shots he shouldn't have but got in the rhythm of play. Ted covered the court well, and they made a solid team. During one rally, the four players were all at the kitchen line, dinking back and forth. Mark leaned in expecting another dink, when Keone instead lobbed over his head. Caught by surprise, Mark yelled, "Help!"

Ted, young and agile, responded and Mark switched to the other side as Ted raced back and returned a looping shot into the opponent's kitchen. Mark marveled at his accuracy. Lefty lunged for the ball and popped it up. Ted charged in and hit a crisp volley down the middle between Keone and Lefty.

Lefty slapped his paddle into his right hand. "Damn. You guys are too consistent."

"That's the name of the game." Ted gave Mark a high five.

That's what Mark loved about this sport. The challenge of trying to hit a ball into the opponent's kitchen without hitting too short into the net or too far and high allowing a slam from the opponents. And the long rallies, sometimes going on for ten or fifteen hits. That was fun. Not like tennis, where one hard shot ended the point. Here the strategy was to keep the ball in play in the kitchen until the opponents made an error or popped the ball up so it could be killed.

* * * * *

During the evening, they teamed up twice for each of the three combinations of partners. Mark held his own, and Lefty only drilled him in the stomach once. Ted won all six games, obviously the dominant player.

After they shook hands, Ted said, "Let's go to the patio and have a beer."

They crossed the closely mowed lawn to the guest cottage where Ted lived. This "cottage" occupied a good two thousand square feet, had Persian carpets over a polished wood floor, was decorated with Greek vases and oil paintings of European mountains. Ted brought a cooler outside where they sat under an awning on folding chairs.

Mark whistled. "Not a bad place."

"The Reinholts know how to live," Ted replied. "They only spend two to three months a year on Maui. I'm here to make sure no one breaks in. They have housekeeping and gardening crews that maintain the house and grounds. Most of the year it's like I have my own estate. And I don't have to pay for any of it."

"Yeah, you have a sweet deal," Keone said. "If you ever need someone to take over for you, let me know."

"Hey, you have your own place up in the mountains." Ted held up his beer. "Here's to our accommodations."

After they recounted some of the choice shots and bad misses during the match, the conversation got around to George Tanabe, the murder victim.

"He wasn't as good a player as you, Mark," Lefty said. "He usually lost all six games. Even Ted couldn't often win with George, who was a little too inconsistent."

"Who was the last to see him?" Mark asked.

Lefty gritted his teeth. "He was the first to leave last night. I went out shortly after he did. His car was parked next to mine in the grassy area on the other side of the dirt hill. There's a path to the ocean in the vacant lot. I walked down to the beach. He was sitting on a rock, looking at the surf and tossing pieces of broken coral into the water."

"He say anything?" Mark asked.

"He was pissed that he had lost six games again. Said he should give up the game and stick with regular tennis. I tried to console him, saying his game was improving, but he wasn't buying. I left him there to sulk and went back to my car. Little did I know."

Something had been bothering Mark. "Was he wearing tennis shoes when you saw him by the ocean?"

"No. He had changed into some loafers. George had tender feet and never went barefoot. Not like most island boys."

Mark scratched his chin. "When his body was found, he was wearing blue swim trunks and a white tank top."

"That was his pickleball outfit." Keone crinkled his nose. "Always wore the same things, which should have been washed more often."

Lefty elbowed Keone. "You're one to talk. How often do you change those old grimy, gray shorts?"

Keone took a swig of beer and turned away from Lefty.

Mark scanned the faces of his companions. "But don't you think it's strange that he didn't have any shoes on when his body was discovered?"

They all looked at each other. Then Keone put his beer bottle down. "That wasn't like him. I wonder if the police found his shoes."

Mark made a mental note to pursue that question with Puna or Akahi.

"Did George have any family?" Mark asked. "Anyone who might have missed him last night?"

"I spoke with his wife this afternoon," Ted said. "She was taking it pretty hard. She never saw him after he left to come play here."

"Didn't she get concerned when he didn't return home last night?" Mark asked.

Ted burped loudly. "Nah. She's used to George being out late. He often stays with friends until three or four in the morning. She went to sleep and didn't notice anything until the police woke her up this morning."

"So no one saw him after Lefty did on the beach?" Mark asked.

Ted and Keone shook their heads.

Mark looked at Ted. "Did you hear a gunshot?"

"No. I had music blasting so didn't notice any unusual noises."

Mark tried to picture the scene. "Was there anyone else around last night?"

Ted wrinkled his eyebrows. "No one I saw, but there were several cars parked up the road. When I went to close the gate after everyone left, I got the impression someone was in one of the cars."

"Did you mention that to the police?" Keone asked.

"Yeah, but I couldn't remember any useful details."

Mark wondered if George might have some enemies. "So maybe someone was waiting for him."

Lefty looked at his watch and stood. "It's possible, I suppose. I need to hit the road. I have a full day at the shop tomorrow."

"So it gets down to two things," Mark said. "Who was waiting for him, and where are his shoes?"

Chapter 7

While Mark drove back to the hotel, he reviewed the pickleball game. He had played pretty well and not embarrassed himself. Just before Lefty departed, Mark had told the guys to give him a call when they scheduled another game. He looked forward to playing a few more times while on Maui. He'd have to balance that, though. Sophie wasn't delighted that he had taken off tonight. He'd temper his interest in the game and a chance to query the three who had been there the night George Tanabe died.

His thoughts turned to what had happened earlier that day. He needed to learn more about George. He looked in his rear view mirror and saw a pair of headlights behind him. When he turned into the hotel driveway, the lights followed him. He slowed, and the vehicle behind him slowed as well. Was he getting paranoid? He considered circling back. No, maybe it was only Akahi keeping an eye on him. By the time he reached the parking lot and checked the rearview mirror again, the lights had disappeared. Must have turned off on the service road.

Mark checked carefully before getting out of his car. On his way to the building, he stopped once and did a complete three-sixty to survey his surroundings. Nothing out of the ordinary. A few steps short of the lobby, a hand touched his arm. He spun around and found Kea standing there with a conch shell in one hand.

"I have terrific souvenir here only ten dollar."

"Isn't it kind of late for you to be here?"

Kea gave his gap-toothed smile. "Nothing better to do."

"Don't your parents want you home?"

"Nah. My mom is entertaining her boyfriend. She said not to come back until eleven."

"What about your father?"

Kea scuffed the ground with his bare foot. "He took off three years ago. Went to the mainland and never came back."

Mark looked at his watch and was surprised to see it was ten thirty. "Tell you what. It's almost time for you to be home. Bring the shell back in the morning, and we'll work a deal."

Kea grinned. "You betcha." Then he walked across the parking lot and disappeared into the undergrowth.

Mark rubbed his hands together. Buying a conch shell would be a perfect gift for Sophie. And this would allow them to go back to the mainland with one good seashell. He watched for a moment assuring himself that no one else was around and headed into the hotel.

★ ★ ★ ★ ★

When he stepped into the hotel room, Sophie looked at her watch. "Kind of late, aren't you? I thought we were going to get something to eat."

"We still can. Let's grab some food in the coffee shop."

"You better shower first. I'm not going to want to sit with you as sweaty and smelly as you are."

Mark took a quick shower, changed into walking shorts, T-shirt and sandals, and they went down to the coffee shop to order sandwiches.

The service was quick, and Mark took a bite of his club sandwich. "Not a gourmet meal tonight, but we can go out for a fancy dinner tomorrow."

"I'll hold you to it. I want macadamia nut encrusted mahi-mahi."

★ ★ ★ ★ ★

The next morning at seven Mark planned to take an early morning drive up the coast while Sophie slept in. When he reached his car, he noticed one of the tires was flat. Upon closer inspection he found a huge nail with a note attached driven into the side of the tire. He bent down and read the block letters: "Stay out of what doesn't concern you."

Mark went back up to his room and retrieved his cell phone and the card with Puna's phone number. He returned to his car so as not to disturb Sophie's sleep.

Mark called the number and asked for Puna. The detective was unavailable so Mark left his cell phone number with instructions for Puna to call as soon as possible. Then he opened the trunk, removed the spare tire and began working to replace the damaged tire, being careful not to disturb the attached note.

Mark heard the sound of footsteps and looked up to see Kea. "Someone mess up your car?"

"Yeah, a flat."

"I brought your shell." He set the conch down on the parking lot surface. "Only ten dollar."

"I'll give you nine," Mark said.

"Whoa. You bargain like that nice *wahine* who talked me down for a kukui necklace yesterday."

"Yeah, that nice *wahine* is my wife."

"No kidding. I give you the conch for only eight dollar."

Mark paid the ransom and put the shell in the backseat of the car. Kea looked toward the lobby. "Uh-oh. Time to leave." As the assistant manager strode toward Mark, Kea scampered off into the bushes.

"Is that kid hassling you again?"

"No, but someone put a hole in my tire."

"Probably the darn kid."

"No. I don't think he had anything to do with it."

"Can I call the auto rental agency for you?"

"Thanks, but I can get the tire changed." He set to work.

The assistant manager watched for a moment before returning to the lobby.

Mark wrestled the old tire off the rim, put the new tire on, tightened the nuts and started lowering the jack when his cell phone rang.

Mark answered.

"Is this Mark Yeager?"

It wasn't Puna's voice.

"Yes."

"This is Homer Nagano. You called me yesterday. I'm sorry to be so long in getting back to you, but I was in court the full day yesterday."

"Thanks for calling back. You must be a morning person like me."

Homer chuckled. "I start my day at seven. That way I can enjoy the late afternoon at the beach when work permits."

"My friend, Ben Quentin, gave me your name."

"I haven't seen Ben in years. How's he doing?"

"Has a thriving practice in Boulder, Colorado. That's where I live. I'm visiting Maui and staying at the Maui Queen Hotel. I got in a little jam and may need your assistance."

"Oh?"

Mark described what had happened.

Homer clicked his tongue. "That Puna is quite a pit bull. You and I had better get together today to discuss the situation in more detail. Could you come to my office in Kahului this morning at ten thirty?"

"Assuming no one punctures another tire, yes."

"Tire?"

"Yeah. Someone put a nail in the side of one of the tires on my rental car and left me a threatening note."

"You have some enemies on the island, Mr. Yeager?"

"I didn't think so, but obviously I've riled up someone. I'll explain the whole situation when we meet."

After Mark signed off, he lowered the car and put the jack into the trunk. He heard a car stop and looked up to see Puna lumbering out of a police car.

"You wanted to talk to me?"

49

"Yes. Someone left me a love note." Mark pointed to the tire lying in the parking lot with the note attached.

Puna bent his large body over and inspected the note. "Making some enemies or trying to divert attention away from yourself?"

Mark clenched his fists. "This is a threat to me that I hope you take seriously."

Puna held his hands up in the air. "We'll look into it, Mr. Yeager."

"Detective, there are several things you should know in regards to the George Tanabe murder."

Puna's eyes narrowed. "I'm listening."

"First, last night I was over there playing pickleball with Ted Franklin, Keone Ahuna and Lefty Kalama, and Ted mentioned that someone may have been sitting in a parked car down the block the night of the murder."

"Yeah, he told me that. Didn't have anything specific, though. What else?"

"Second, I might have been followed back to the hotel last night. Maybe it was one of your people or maybe it was someone interested in my movements."

Puna's expression didn't change. "You seem to be right in the middle of trouble."

"I want to clear my name. Also, I'll assist any way I can to find the murderer."

"Quite the good Samaritan, aren't you?"

"Look. You have your job to do, but I don't enjoy being harassed when I'm trying to help. Homer Nagano will be representing me."

"Our own local Perry Mason." Puna gave Mark a steely stare. "You've located a good lawyer."

"There's one other thing I've learned that may be of use to you. George was found barefoot. I was told that was not characteristic of him since he had tender feet. Did you find his shoes?"

Puna looked surprised. "No."

"You may want to go back looking for them. That's one of the pieces that doesn't fit."

Chapter 8

Puna put the threatening note Mark had received in a plastic bag.

"You going to dust the tire for prints?" Mark asked.

"Not worth the effort. I'd find your prints and those of people from the car rental, and it would take all day to verify. If the perpetrator wasn't you, I'm sure he wore gloves or avoided touching the tire."

"And the note?"

"We'll check that out. Did you touch it?"

"No. If you find any prints on it, they won't be mine."

"We'll see."

After Puna departed, Mark threw the damaged tire into the trunk. He'd stop by the car rental agency later to replace it. Then he was finally able to begin his trip up the coast, checking occasionally in his rearview mirror to make sure no one was following him. He needed a break to clear his mind and a chance to take a few photographs. Finding a deserted beach, he strolled along, snapped a few pictures of the waves breaking over the reef and found a few cowry shells. Maybe he should try to sell them to Kea the next time the kid showed up. Nah, he'd add these to the conch shell to give to Sophie. He sat on the sand and contemplated his existence, reaching no new conclusions about the murder and his involvement in it.

On the way back to the hotel, he periodically peered in his rearview mirror but didn't notice anyone suspicious. He'd have to keep up his guard in this dangerous tropical paradise.

Back in their hotel room at nine, he found Sophie on the

balcony reading a book.

"You're up early today," he said.

"I woke up and even took a short walk while you were gone."

Mark suggested they head downstairs and have breakfast at the hotel restaurant.

Once seated next to each other, Sophie shook out her cloth napkin. "Guess what I bought this morning?"

"A conch shell from Kea."

Sophie gave his arm a playful punch. "How'd you know?"

"Because I bought one from him as well. I talked him down to eight dollars." Mark didn't mention that that last dollar of discount was because of her.

Sophie winked at him. "Not bad. Mine was seven dollars."

"That kid has my number."

Sophie patted his hand. "I know it offends your Scottish miserliness to spend money. You just didn't get the full *wahine* discount."

"Ah, the perils of being a man. We now have two conch shells and some cowries I found for you this morning. We can strike finding shells off our to-do list. We don't have to go hunting—we have Kea."

"That's a good start, but I want to find some on my own as well."

They ordered papaya and coffee, with Sophie going for the French toast and Mark the macadamia nut pancakes. Once the food arrived, Sophie pointed her fork at Mark. "Kea is quite a kid."

"Definitely a good salesman. He's talked both of us into buying more than we have anywhere else on this island."

"More than that. He wants to eventually start his own company. He told me he's saving money from his sales to go to the University of Hawaii and get a business degree."

"That so?"

"You should share some of your business experience with him. He's a good listener and eager to learn."

"Speaking of learning, shouldn't he be in school? It's not quite time for a winter break from school and since there's no winter here anyway..."

Sophie dabbed the corner of her mouth with the napkin. "I asked him that same question. He said he's home schooled. His mother bought some books that he studies on his own. He has a good memory and quoted some Shakespeare lines to me. Says that by studying on his own he can learn what he wants fast and still have time to earn money. He has a good head for numbers and definitely knows how to communicate."

"Definitely an entrepreneur. I'll chat with him the next time he accosts me to buy something."

"And some other news. We've been invited to dinner. Dexter Kwan, who I met on the flight to Maui, called to say he and his wife, Harriet, would like us to join them tomorrow night at seven at their house."

"You have all the men on this island wrapped around your little finger."

Sophie waggled her eyebrows at him. "I have eyes only for you."

* * * * *

Sophie decided to get a massage while Mark drove into Kahului to meet with Homer Nagano. He could also stop at the airport to replace the damaged tire. Once again he kept an eye on the road ahead while periodically checking the rearview mirror to make sure no one followed him. Would he be paranoid during this whole vacation?

Homer's office was in a two-story building near the airport, listing various professional people including accountants, attorneys, insurance agents and Realtors.

"Perfect location," the skinny, late forties lawyer in slacks and Hawaiian shirt said to Mark. "Within five minutes I can be out windsurfing when the conditions are good."

"I've never tried that," Mark confessed.

Homer looked him up and down. "You appear athletic. I'll

have to get you out while you're on Maui. This is one of the best windsurfing locations in the world. But back to the matter at hand—tell me about your situation."

"I stumbled upon a body, and Detective Puna Pa'a is trying to link me to the murder."

Homer laughed. "Don't take it personally. Our Detective Pa'a thinks everyone is guilty of everything. He's basically a competent cop. Possibly overly zealous at times. What evidence does he have?"

"I was the one who reported finding the body, and my room key was found near the body."

"And how'd it get there?"

Mark's neck grew warm. "I had a hole in my swim trunk's pocket. The card apparently fell out while I was leaning over to see the body."

"That's not enough to prove anything. I suppose Puna threatened you and told you not to leave the island."

"That's right."

Homer laced his fingers together. "His routine doesn't vary much. Any other suspects so far?"

"I don't know if they're suspects, but three people were playing pickleball with George Tanabe—"

"George?" Homer interrupted.

"Yes, he was the murder victim."

"I'll be damned."

"You knew George?"

"Yes. He was a witness against a client of mine a year ago. Claimed my client tried to sell him some cocaine. I always thought it was the other way around. Trouble was my client got picked up with the powder in his possession."

"The police did make a comment that George may have been involved with drug dealing."

"I tried to discredit him, but he came across as squeaky clean. Never been convicted of any drug-related activity, although he seemed often to be somewhere near deals going down. Where there's smoke and all that."

54

Mark looked out the window at a coconut tree swaying in the breeze. "So even though the police never caught him, maybe someone he dealt with did."

"It's possible." Homer frowned. "Who else was with George the night of the murder?"

"There's Ted Franklin, a tennis pro who lives in a guest cottage on the Reinholt estate. He's the one who invited the others over to play pickleball the night of the murder."

"I've heard of Ted, but never met him."

"And the other two were Lefty Kalama and Keone Ahuna."

Homer sucked on his lip for a moment. "That's interesting. Lefty could be involved as well. He's another whose name has come up in several cases I've had. He's on the fringe of the drug trade in some way from what the grapevine says. Looks like you've been around some suspicious characters."

"I heard a comment about Lefty being suspected of growing marijuana."

"That's quite a local industry. With the economic slowdown, some of our island entrepreneurs have planted patches in undeveloped areas. You have to be careful when hiking off the main trails. You can get shot for getting too close to someone's *garden.*"

"And this is common here?"

"Yes. There are too many small plots hidden in too many places and too few police too busy with domestic quarrels to do much about it. Many people want to live off the land. In the old days that could be a grove of coconut trees and a taro patch. Now the most lucrative business involves pointy-leaved plants. Part of our local culture. People grow enough for their own use and to supplement their income."

"And Keone Ahuna," Mark said. "Do you know anything about him?"

"No. Haven't heard his name before." Homer tapped the eraser end of his pencil on the desk. "When we put it together, Puna's fishing for evidence. He'll be working his routine with the three guys who played pickleball the night of the murder and will check up on you every several days, but he doesn't have anything specific."

"What happens when it's time for me to go back to the mainland?"

"If he gets additional information linking you to the murder, it could get sticky, and he could arrest you. But with nothing else, he can't stop you from leaving. Stay clear of our local crime scene, and you should be fine."

"Should we get back together?"

"Let's set up another appointment tomorrow. I'll meet you at the beach for a windsurfing lesson and to check in."

"So what's higher, your legal fee or your teaching fee?"

"They're both the same."

* * * * *

Mark left Homer's office with mixed feelings. He understood that Puna couldn't do anything to him right away. But there remained a threat hanging over his head, and he wanted to get it resolved by the end of his vacation. Maybe he could speed along the investigation on his own. Might be worth several stops on the way back to the hotel. But first, he drove to the car rental agency at the airport to replace the tire.

* * * * *

In Kihei, Mark spotted the sign for the Gateway Plaza and turned off the highway. He found a small shopping center and after cruising through the parking lot located the sporting goods store. Mark got out of the car and went into the shop.

A bell rang, and Lefty looked up from stringing a tennis racquet in the back of the store. "Hey, Mark, what brings you here?"

"I was passing through and thought I'd stop and buy pickleballs to contribute the next time we play."

Lefty stretched his arms and ambled out from behind the

stringing machine. He reached up on a shelf and pulled down two boxes.

"I have a good supply. Grab what you want."

Mark made his selection and forked over a twenty dollar bill for Lefty to make change.

There was no one else in the shop, so Mark asked casually, "How long have you known Ted?"

"For over a year. Why do you ask?"

"He seems to live in pretty good style at the Reinholt place."

"Yeah. He swung a sweetheart deal there. Free place to live. Doesn't have to do much for it, either. Give a few tennis lessons to Mrs. Reinholt when she's on Maui, and keep the gate locked so no one breaks in. These rich people go to the trouble of buying that place and hardly use it. Go figure."

"A young guy like Ted must be making out well. Tennis pro salary and no housing expenses. I bet there are other perks as well."

Lefty winked at Mark. "He does supplement his income."

"Oh?"

"A good looking guy like Ted. There are enough rich widows and divorcées who stay at the Maui Queen. They take tennis lessons, get to know the smooth Ted Franklin, and then spend money on their favorite tennis pro."

Mark winked back. "Bet he gets a lot of free meals."

"And presents. Plus investment money."

"Investment money?"

"Sure. These widows and divorcées have money to burn. Often ready to throw a little away for one of Ted's schemes. They never get anything back, but have a good time in the process. They don't need the money and consider their loss an entertainment expense."

"I've heard there's a lot of drug activity on Maui. Ted doesn't get involved in that does he?"

Lefty stopped smiling. "Where'd you hear that?"

"When Puna was questioning me. He accused me of being involved in drug deals. Seemed to think George had some link there."

Lefty's demeanor changed as if a black cloud had blocked the sun. "I wouldn't go around asking who's involved in drug deals on this island. Nosy people end up dead for that. I need to get back to work."

"I won't take any more of your time, but now that I'm armed with some pickleballs, how'd you like to set up a game?"

The smile returned to Lefty's face. "You bet, Bruddah. How about tonight?"

"Fine by me."

"I'll line up Ted and Keone. I was planning to meet them at the Maui Queen for lunch in a little while."

Then it struck Mark. In his haste to continue his investigation, he had committed to another event away from Sophie. He'd have to dedicate the next few days only to her.

* * * * *

Drugs sure hit a nerve with Lefty. Mark realized there was more below the surface in this island culture where he had only tapped the tip of the iceberg so far. He strolled through the shopping center until he found a public phone booth. A phone book dangled from a cord. He looked up Tanabe and found a listing for George and Muriel Tanabe in Kihei. He memorized the address and phone numbers. It was a good thing he had an excellent memory. One of the skills that had helped him during his business career.

Time to meet the widow.

* * * * *

After stopping at a gas station to ask directions, Mark found the small one-story wooden house on a street with no sidewalks. He pulled up on the grass behind a dented green Ford pickup truck and got out.

Looking around to find no neighbors in sight, he approached

a woman watering a row of flowers along the front of the house. "I'm looking for Muriel Tanabe."

The woman straightened up. She was attractive with the island blend that was hard to exactly determine, but could have included any combination of Filipino, Chinese, Japanese, Portuguese and Hawaiian. Her eyes flared. "What do you want?"

"I was the person who found George. I want to pay my condolences."

"Were you one of his druggy friends?"

Mark flinched. "No. I happened to be walking by and spotted his body. I'm very sorry for your loss."

"Well, he's dead. I don't want to talk about it." She turned her back on him and continued to water the flowers.

"I'm trying to help find the murderer," Mark raised his voice above the sound of running water.

She turned back to face him again. "You police?"

"No. I'm a tourist."

She gave a bitter laugh. "What makes you think you can do anything our incompetent police can't do?"

"I take it you don't have a high opinion of Detective Puna Pa'a and his department."

She spat in the grass. "He harassed George for years. Then when George gets assassinated, he does nothing."

"Assassinated?"

"Yes. My poor dumb husband was killed because someone thought he knew too much." A tear trickled down her cheek.

"I heard several comments that the police suspected George of drug dealing."

"They tried to pin something on him. His problem was that he had the wrong kind of friends, and I use the word 'friends' loosely. His drinking buddies were involved in drugs. I tried to get him to give them up, but he was too stubborn or loyal or stupid." She reached for the faucet and turned off the water.

"I've met the people he played pickleball with. Are they part of that crowd?"

"Lefty is." She stopped and stared at him again. "You're asking a lot of questions, aren't you?"

Mark opened his hands toward her. "Here's my situation. Detective Puna Pa'a has been harassing me as well, and I'm trying to clear my name."

Muriel took the hose and coiled it in a neat circle. "If you keep poking around, you'll probably end up like George." She stalked up the steps, went into the house and slammed the door.

★ ★ ★ ★ ★

Mark sat in his car thinking. Two suggestions within an hour that he might get killed if he kept snooping around. And the warning note attached to his tire. Maui, the Valley Island. Just stay out of their valleys.

He slapped his palm against the dashboard. He hadn't handled the interview with Muriel Tanabe very well. She was obviously very bitter over her husband's death, but there was probably more he could have gleaned from her. If he kept up with this new alternative career, he'd have to hone his interrogation skills.

In spite of everything, he had learned one useful piece of information.

Chapter 9

As Mark drove away, he thought over how Muriel had confirmed the suspicion that Lefty was connected to drug activity. That fit in with the reaction he had elicited in Lefty's shop earlier and the hints from Homer Nagano. The drug theme kept emerging over and over again. He would have to figure out a way to carefully explore that link, the emphasis on *carefully*.

When he entered the hotel lobby, he found Ted Franklin in his tennis whites and blue UCLA baseball cap, speaking to a woman.

Ted spotted him and waved him over.

"Arlene. I'd like you to meet a buddy of mine, Mark Yeager." Ted put his arm around Mark's shoulders. "Mark, this is Arlene Henrick."

She offered a wrist covered with enough gold bracelets to settle the national debt. "How do you do?"

Mark shook her hand, sensing the warm slender fingers.

"Arlene is staying here and becoming quite the tennis player." Ted put his arm around Arlene's waist.

She laughed. "Ted is being overly kind. But he is helping me improve my tennis game, particularly my weak backhand. You should see the shots I can make because of Ted's instruction. My tennis friends back home will be so amazed next summer. Where are you from, Mr. Yeager?"

"You can call me Mark. I'm from Boulder, Colorado. And you?"

"Boston. I've come all the way from the East Coast to Maui to learn how to hit a topspin backhand, rather than my puny slice." She swished her arm to demonstrate. "Now if you'll excuse me, it's time for my massage."

As she sashayed away from them, Ted smacked his lips. "Quite a woman. Owns more real estate than she knows what to do with."

Mark winked at him. "Being a tennis pro here must be quite an opportunity for a young guy like you."

"Can't complain. Widows and divorcées come here looking for adventure and ways to improve their tennis game. I understand we have a pickleball game lined up tonight."

"Yeah, I ran into Lefty this morning."

"Lefty and Keone are in the bar. Want to meet them for a quick beer?"

"Sure," Mark replied. "I'll see if Sophie wants to join us as well."

* * * * *

Mark found Sophie relaxing by the pool. He sneaked up behind her and planted a kiss on the top of her head.

She looked up from her thriller. "Oh, it's you. I thought it was my cabana boy."

"Very funny. And I thought *I* was your cabana boy. Have I lost my job?"

"Well, you haven't been around that much."

"Ouch. I'll have to change my priorities."

She set her novel down on the ground. "So, does the lawyer think the police are going to arrest you? Will I be stranded on Maui on my own? Will I have to spend all my time with the cabana boy rather than you?"

"No. He feels this is typical of how the detective operates and I shouldn't worry. He did express suspicions about the victim being linked to drug dealing. I even met the victim's widow."

"Young and attractive, I bet."

"She is. But very angry. Blames the police and friends of her late husband. I'm sure drugs are involved. One of the other players, Lefty Kalama, seems connected to the drug scene. But I don't have anything definite yet."

She picked up a towel and wiped the perspiration off her face. "The circumstantial evidence against you is pretty weak. I agree with the lawyer that you should have no problem."

"By the way, my lawyer also gives windsurfing lessons. Tentatively, tomorrow. You interested?"

"I'll come watch."

"I also received an invitation to play pickleball again tonight."

She stood, picked up her towel and shook it out. "So you're going to leave me unattended while you run off for another game with the suspected local drug dealers. I really will have to replace you with the cabana boy."

"Before you do that, put on your muumuu and come meet my new pickleball buddies. They're in the bar. You can assess them for yourself."

"Why not? I need to see what kind of criminals keep dragging you away."

* * * * *

They strolled into the bar and sat at a table with the three men.

After the introductions, Lefty turned to Sophie. "How do you like our island?"

"I'm having a relaxing time. A little swimming. A little snorkeling. And a local boy named Kea has been selling me all kinds of souvenirs."

Keone wrapped the table with his hand. "I know that kid. Or I should say I know his mom, Leilani."

"That the gal you were dating last year?" Lefty asked.

"Yeah. We broke up." Keone took a long swig of beer. "Things didn't work out."

Lefty faced Sophie. "You mentioned snorkeling. If you want the best snorkeling around, you should go to Molokini. Incredible variety of fish."

"That would be interesting," Sophie said. "We've been looking at that island out our window since we arrived here. What do you think, Mark? Should be try to go out there?"

"I'd enjoy that," Mark replied. "I'll have to look into it. I saw some advertisements in the auto rental brochure."

Lefty snapped his fingers. "Let me set up a trip to Molokini. I have a friend with a boat I can line up."

"Let's do it," Sophie said. "How soon?"

"I'm not working at the store for the next two days. Either tomorrow or the next day."

"We have plans for tomorrow, but the day after would work," Mark said.

"You make the arrangements, Lefty," Sophie smiled. "Mark will pay for it."

They discussed snorkeling, fishing and pickleball. Finally, Ted raised his hand. "Let's play liar's poker to settle the bar tab. Everyone grab a dollar bill, except Sophie."

"No, I'm going to play, too." She graced them with her most winning smile.

"You guys better be careful," Mark said. "She's apt to take all of us."

"Here's the rule," Ted said. "Whoever wins picks the person to pay for the drinks."

They nodded in agreement.

True to Mark's prediction, Sophie snookered the four guys and won.

"Now," she announced, "I'm going to make Mark pay because he's such a tight wad."

Mark scowled. "I'm not tight. I just don't waste money."

The guys cheered and slapped him on the back.

Mark asked for the tab and signed his name and room number. As he handed the leather holder to the waitress, Keone abruptly stood up, bumped her and the bill fell to the floor.

"Sorry, I'll get it." Keone bent over to retrieve the bill. He looked at it, dusted it off and handed it to the waitress.

★ ★ ★ ★ ★

Back in their room, Mark asked Sophie what she thought of the group.

"Ted tries to be too smooth. I see him as a wheeler dealer. Not one to be trusted."

"Your observation is right on. He has a rich *divorcée* in tow. I met her earlier. Arlene Henrick."

Sophie raised her eyebrows. "The tennis pro hustler."

"But he's been very hospitable. Taken good care of us at the pickleball court. Provides the equipment for the game and beer afterwards."

"Lefty seems friendly enough, and even though you suspect he's involved in drugs, he did offer to set up a snorkeling expedition for us. He may be hiding something though. There was a sense of unease about him."

"Yeah, I really noticed that when I brought up drugs in his shop earlier today. He was like a thundercloud blocking the light. Really shut down."

Sophie put a finger to her cheek. "Keone is a little strange."

"He's the quietest."

"That goatee of his. Reminds me of the actor playing Don Quixote in *The Man of La Mancha* we saw in Denver last year."

Mark laughed. "There's a ring to it: Keone, Quixote."

"Fits right in with the purchase I made today." Sophie pointed to a windmill standing on the dresser. "You wouldn't expect to find anything like that on Maui."

Mark strolled over to the windmill, which stood a foot high with weathered cloth sails. "You didn't get this from Kea, did you?"

"No I found it in the hotel gift shop. It caught my eye, and I had to have it."

"You mean you're not buying everything from Kea?"

"I don't believe he carries this type of item."

"Don't assume anything. That kid can probably get you anything you want on this island."

Sophie picked up the windmill. "What do you think of my purchase?"

65

Mark took it from her and inspected it again. "Very attractive, but how will we get it back to the mainland without breaking it?"

"The vanes come off so I can easily pack it. I'll get some bubble wrap to protect it. I think it will be perfect on our mantle at home."

"How much did this cost?" Mark asked.

"You don't want to know. But the good news is—you can afford it."

★ ★ ★ ★ ★

Sophie expressed an interest in doing some exploring and shopping. Mark decided to try the exploring first and suggested Iao Valley.

"You'll like that," Sophie said. "It's free."

Mark smiled at his wife. "That's my kind of price."

They parked and ambled over to look at the twelve-hundred foot spire of the Iao Needle.

"Quite a sight." Mark snapped a picture with Sophie in the foreground. Then she took a picture of Mark.

Mark put his camera away. "We have this site memorialized. Do you know why they call this the Iao Needle?"

"No, why?"

"Because the first person to scale the top and sit on the pointy peak shouted, "Eeow!"

Sophie gave Mark a well-deserved swat. "Because of that horrible joke, you're going to drive me to Lahaina so I can spend lots of money." She held up a business card she had received from Kea, identical to the one Mark had. "I want to visit Kea's cousin, Abe, who has a photo gallery."

They enjoyed the view along the rugged coast. The road leveled off, and Sophie pointed to the buildings of a town ahead. "Our destination awaits us."

"That kid is going to cost me my life savings," Mark said.

"Don't sweat the small stuff. Besides, it's *our* life savings."

"I suppose you'll also want to visit his other cousin's shop in Kaanapali?"

Sophie hugged Mark's arm. "Eventually, but today I want to see Lahaina. We'll make a separate trip to Kaanapali later on. That way I'll have another shopping trip to look forward to."

Mark groaned.

"Suck it up, big guy. Shopping is good for you."

"I wouldn't go so far as to say that, but I suppose I can stand half an hour or so."

"Are you kidding? We have the whole rest of the afternoon."

They found a parking spot in town and wandered around viewing the huge banyan tree with its aerial roots that formed multiple trunks. Kids scampered around through this natural play area.

Sophie waved toward the giant banyan. "I read that this tree was planted in 1873, covers over two-thirds of an acre and is a quarter mile in circumference."

"You're a wealth of information. Did you memorize the whole Auto Club Hawaii Tour Book?"

"Practically. You can consider me your local tour guide."

Mark looked up toward the mountains covered by thick clouds. The sloping hills showed lush green. He turned one-hundred-eighty degrees to look out to sea at the island of Lanai. Then they proceeded through town, the brightly painted old wooden buildings adding color to the island paradise.

Next, they visited The Wo Hing Museum built in 1912 that showed movies Thomas Edison made of Hawaii in 1898 and 1906. The flickering black and white silent films captured a culture long lost to all the current tourist business.

After they left the museum, Mark said, "I feel like I'm an official Maui resident with what I've seen."

"If that's the case, it's time for shopping."

Mark groaned again.

They walked along the waterfront with Sophie stopping to admire every shop window until they located Abe's Photo Gallery and entered a shop with a wonderful display of local landscape, seascape and underwater photographs mounted on the walls.

"We're looking for Abe," Sophie said to a young man behind the counter.

"That's me. Photographer and owner of the shop. How can I help you?"

Sophie graced him with her award-winning smile. "We were referred to you by your cousin, Kea."

"No kidding. In that case you can get anything you want for a twenty-percent family discount."

Sophie poked Mark in the ribs. "Look at all the money Kea is saving you."

Mark rolled his eyes. "Look at all the money Kea is *costing* me."

"You have no complaints. You've purchased some high quality kukui nut necklaces and conch shells, and today we're going to buy some photographs." She stepped over to a scenic view of coastline. "Where was this taken?"

Abe joined her. "That's along the Hana coast, near a place called Shark Cove."

"So I assume there are sharks in the ocean there."

"Yep. Not a place I'd want to go swimming. I do underwater photography, but I stick to places like Molokini Island."

"We're going there the day after next," Sophie said.

"You'll love it. Some of the best fish viewing in the world." Abe pointed to another picture. "And here's one of my favorite spots. 'Ohe'o Gulch. At one time it was called the Seven Sacred Pools, but there are actually twenty-four pools. Have you had a chance to go there yet?"

"It's on our planned list." Sophie continued around the gallery while Mark focused in on a seascape with sunlight reflected off the water and an island in the background.

Abe stepped over to where Mark stood and tapped the frame. "That's Molokai in the distance from Napili Beach."

Mark realized they still had a number of beautiful spots to visit on this island. He only needed to get Detective Puna Pa'a off his back, and he and Sophie would be free as myna birds.

Sophie decided on a picture of Iao Valley and the 'Ohe'o Gulch picture.

Mark leaned over her shoulder. "But we already have pictures of Iao Valley."

"True. Those are for our scrapbook. This one is professional quality for our living room."

As Abe wrapped the prints up in protective brown paper, Sophie said, "Tell me more about your cousin, Kea."

Abe chuckled. "Hey, he's the best business person in the whole family. He worked for me here last summer. Said he wanted to earn some money and learn how to run a business. Within a day he knew every picture in the shop and had an interesting story to tell when someone asked. That kid can sell. My revenue doubled over the previous summer. I had to keep going out to take new pictures because he kept selling through my stock. Has he told you any of his Hawaiian stories?"

"Not yet," Sophie replied.

"You ask him the next time you see him. In addition to his sales skills, he's quite the storyteller. He's read up on Hawaiian history and mythology and even come up with some of his own new stories."

"I noticed storytelling listed as one of his areas of expertise on his business card," Mark said. "The one that had your gallery address on the back."

Abe shook his head. "That kid. Always promoting. He'll have the whole family working for him in a few years."

★ ★ ★ ★ ★

After stashing the purchased photographs in the trunk of the car, they decided to enjoy an early dinner at the Pioneer Inn. They strolled along the yacht harbor with the green wood, white trim, second story balconies and red roof of the Inn evoking a picture of the town a hundred years ago.

Inside, a *holoku* clad waitress seated them.

After a quick perusal of the menu they ordered, and food soon arrived.

Mark took a sip of iced tea and set the glass down. "How's your mahi-mahi?"

"Delicious. If you had deserted me for another evening without a good dinner, you'd be in real trouble."

"I'm not planning to play pickleball every night, but the opportunity presented itself."

"Don't make it a habit."

* * * * *

On the ride back to the hotel, they stopped along the coast and Mark took several photographs at dusk while Sophie remained in the car.

When he returned, Sophie nudged him, "I bet you decided to try your hand at photography after you saw the prices Abe charged."

"You know me so well. Since you like photographs, I thought I'd get some large prints made to complement the two you bought."

"Anything to save a few dollars, my tightwad husband."

"Hey, that's why we have money in the bank. I don't spend it all."

"No, that's my job."

* * * * *

As Mark drove to the pickleball court that night, he reviewed the activities of the day. For being on a vacation, he had been on the run since seven in the morning, dealing with the nail in the tire, the lawyer, trying his hand at his so-far-unsuccessful investigation and taking Sophie on the trip to Iao Valley and Lahaina.

When he reached his destination, he held up his purchase from earlier in the day and announced: "New balls from Lefty's store." Mark knew his pickleball friends back in Boulder would be surprised to hear how willingly he provided new balls. They always kidded him over his reluctance to produce a new ball as if he were giving up a valuable jewel.

"Let's get going," Ted said. "I have a date at ten with a rich *divorcée*." He gave a conspiratorial wink to Mark.

Keone seemed distracted during most of the match. In the third set when he was teamed with Mark, out of the blue while changing sides he grabbed Mark's arm. "You live in a big house in Colorado?"

Mark scratched his chin, wondering where this comment came from. "Reasonable amount of space."

"Probably worth a lot."

"Houses are expensive in Boulder. We bought it ten years ago. Prices have gone up since then. We also put in some improvements my wife wanted."

Keone sucked on his lip for a moment and proceeded to the other side of the court with a furled brow as if trying to solve the country's economic problems.

On the next point, Mark was receiving on the forehand side, and Ted and Lefty played each shot to Mark. After over ten successful dinks, Mark started to feel his arm getting heavy.

Finally, Ted hit a shot that angled sharply crosscourt, out of Mark's reach.

Mark put his hands on his knees and bent over. "The humidity and heat are getting to me." He didn't mention his age as another factor.

"You'll get used to it," Ted replied. "When I first came here I couldn't teach tennis more than four hours a day. Now I can go from nine to five and still do this at night."

When the match was over, Ted announced: "One quick beer, and then I'm kicking all of you out."

As they sat there, Keone turned to Mark. "I hear you used to have your own company."

"Yes. I started a company six years ago and sold it last year."

"Must have made a lot when you sold it."

Mark stared at Keone. "I did okay."

71

"Hey," Lefty said. "I meant to tell you. I have a boat lined up for ten o'clock day after tomorrow to go to Molokini with Mark and his wife. Who else wants to join the expedition?"

"I'm fully booked with lessons," Ted said. "Count me out."

"How about you, Keone?" Lefty asked.

"No. I need to work on some plans."

"Sophie and I are looking forward to it," Mark said. "Where do we meet?"

"Kihei Boat Landing. I'll give you directions."

"Okay, everybody out." Ted lifted Keone out of the chair and gave him a push. "Time to hit the road."

"Since Ted is being so inhospitable, anyone want to stop for another beer?" Lefty asked.

"What do you have in mind?" Mark asked.

"There's a little place between Wailea and Kihei. Kamaina Tavern. On the right side of the road."

"Yeah, why not," Keone said.

Mark thought for a moment. He should get back, but maybe this would be an opportunity to learn more about Lefty and Keone. Keone in particular had been acting squirrelly this evening. He took the car keys out of his pocket. "I'll join you for one more beer."

* * * * *

Half an hour later, the three of them sat at a table at the tavern sipping bottles of Primo. A waitress dropped a basket of peanuts on the table.

Mark grabbed a peanut and shelled it. "This one of your regular hang outs?"

Lefty reached for a peanut as well. "Damn straight."

"This is the regular meeting place, this side of Kihei," Keone added. "Excuse me a moment. I need to visit the john."

As he walked away, Mark leaned toward Lefty. "Keone was asking kind of strange questions tonight. Kept inquiring about my house and job."

Lefty laughed. "He's suffering from money problems again. When he gets that way he always wants to know how rich everyone is. You only have to worry when he hits you up for a loan of a thousand dollars. He's probably sizing you up. My advice—don't give him squat."

Two large men entered the building. Mark watched them approach the bar as if they owned the place. One of them spoke to the bartender. Lefty went pale and slunk down, obviously trying to hide. His movement had the opposite effect, catching the eye of the second man.

They came over to the table. Both were dressed in jeans, boots and short sleeve blue working shirts. They looked like refugees from a weight training camp.

Mark guessed they must be in their early thirties and noticed that one had a scar on his right cheek.

Scar Cheek pointed a callused finger at Lefty. "Oana hasn't received anything from you recently."

"I've been m-meaning to leave him a message," Lefty stammered.

"He doesn't like to be kept waiting." Scar Cheek leaned over and grabbed Lefty by the shirt.

"I'll take care of it first thing in the morning. I p-promise."

The man waved his hand toward Mark. "Who's the *haole?*"

Mark met the malevolent gaze. "I'm his lawyer."

"Yeah, right." Scar Cheek snarled. "Lefty doesn't need a lawyer. He needs an undertaker. You got one more day." With that, he knocked over one of the beer bottles, spilling liquid onto Lefty's lap, turned away and marched toward the door. His companion followed him.

"Who's the guy with the scar?"

"He's called Malo."

Mark noticed that Lefty's hands were shaking. "What's that all about?"

Lefty held his head in his hands. "I'm in deep shit."

"That guy seemed serious with his threat."

"He is. I need to take care of some business tomorrow otherwise

73

he'll be after me."

"Who's this Oana he mentioned?"

Lefty took a deep breath. "You don't want to know."

"This have something to do with drugs?"

Lefty's eyes widened. "What makes you ask that?"

"Those two looked like enforcers, and you seem to owe Oana something you haven't delivered."

"This conversation is over." Lefty threw a five dollar bill on the table, staggered to his feet and stumbled toward the door.

Mark sat there stunned.

Shortly, Keone returned, smoothing his hair. "Where's Lefty?"

"He had to go. Two guys came and threatened him. Something to do with Oana."

Keone looked from side to side, then whispered to Mark. "He's a bad dude. You never want to piss off Oana."

"Lefty didn't want to talk about Oana. You know anything about him?"

"Oana runs drugs and loans on this side of the island. Dangerous guy."

"Since he's so well known, how come Detective Puna Pa'a hasn't done anything about him?"

"People mention Oana, but no one ever sees him. He runs a ring of people who work for him and take care of his business."

Mark watched the bartender mix a concoction and put a cherry on top. "Either a recluse or an invention."

Keone grabbed a peanut and removed the shell. "Whatever he is, people are afraid of him and do what his stooges tell them."

Mark's gaze returned to his companion. "Is Lefty involved in drugs?"

Keone regarded Mark warily. "Lefty has his own little agricultural business. I'm not going to discuss it. You want another beer?"

"No, this is fine for me. I need to get back to my wife soon."

"You left her alone?"

"She's in the room reading. She knows I like to play pickleball, but I don't want to press my luck by staying out too late."

"Yeah. I know what you mean. I was married once."

"Didn't work out?"

"No. I guess I like being on my own too much. A few girlfriends now and then but nothing permanent. Have my place up in the hills. That's fine for me."

"I don't think I'd like living away from people," Mark said.

"It's quiet, and no one bothers me."

The waitress came over and asked if they wanted more beer and peanuts. They both shook their heads.

Mark leaned toward Keone. "I never did hear what you do to support yourself."

"Odd jobs. Do some maintenance work at the Maui Queen and some other hotels in Kihei and Wailea. Sometimes help Ted at the tennis courts."

Mark scraped his chair away from the table. "Let's get another game going in a few days."

"I'll talk to the guys. Plan on evening after tomorrow."

★ ★ ★ ★ ★

As Mark drove away he considered what he'd heard. Lefty was in some kind of trouble probably linked to growing marijuana, Keone was a semi-recluse who had money problems, and Ted was hitting on rich widows and divorcées. Along the way, George got knocked off. Quite a cast of characters—he had his suspicions concerning each of them, but nothing concrete yet. He needed to find the right link.

Chapter 10

The next day Mark and Sophie drove to Kahului to meet Homer Nagano for a windsurfing lesson.

Sophie sat on the beach with her hair tied up in a scarf while Homer showed Mark how to stand on the board, first on the sand and then by holding the board for him in the water. Mark put his arms out to the side to gain equilibrium. When Homer let go of the board, Mark stayed up for a few moments before tumbling into the water.

"Merely a matter of balance. You let the wind pull you and use your body as a counter balance."

Mark looked out to sea, where windsurfers swooped back and forth. He thought back to his misadventures one summer as a kid while trying gymnastics. "They make it look so easy. I've never been good at balance sports. I prefer racquet and paddle sports."

"You'll get the hang of it," Homer assured him.

Homer held the board while Mark mounted it again. After five tries he was able to sail out a hundred yards, but would lose his balance when he tried to turn, plunging into the bright blue ocean.

When he managed to make one successful turn, Sophie applauded from the shore. Mark waved, promptly lost his balance and tumbled into the water.

Not to admit defeat, he kept at it for another hour.

Sore and tired, Mark finally decided he'd had enough and sat next to Sophie on the sand. "I started this sport thirty years too late."

Homer plunked down to join them. "Not bad for the first time.

Usually takes three or four outings to get the feel for the board and sail. Sophie, you should try it as well."

"No thanks. I'll leave the sore muscles to Mark. But I could stretch my legs. I'll leave you gentleman to discuss how to keep my husband out of jail. I'm going for a walk."

After Sophie left, Mark took a handful of sand and let it run through his fingers. "You indicated that Lefty Kalama might be involved with drugs. I was having a beer with Lefty, and two guys came in who looked like local gangsters. They threatened Lefty on behalf of a guy named Oana. Know anything about him?"

Homer's face darkened. "That's a name out of the past."

"You've met him?"

"I had the unfortunate experience of representing him several years after I started my practice on Maui."

"What kind of case?"

"He was accused of being part of a protection racket that threatened a store owner. It got down to his word versus the store owner's. At the last minute, the store owner withdrew the complaint. Probably feared for the lives of his family members."

"Did you have any other dealings with Oana?"

"The problem was he liked the way I handled his case. Approached me afterwards to sound me out on becoming a kind of 'consigliari' for his business. I refused."

"A good decision."

"Yes and no. I retained my integrity, but Oana was persistent. He kept after me for six months. When I finally said, 'Hell no,' he got mad. The next night when my family and I were visiting friends, my house mysteriously burned down."

Mark's head jerked. "Were you able to prove anything?"

"Nope. No witnesses, no clues. No one saw nothing. That was my last dealing with Oana. Good riddance."

"I've heard that no one sees him anymore."

"That sounds like him. Have someone else do his bidding. Distances himself from the crimes and lets others take the heat. He's not going to do anything directly that could get him arrested."

"But wouldn't the police eventually be able to tie criminal activities back to him through his stooges?"

"You'd think so, but he's smart. So far no one who's in contact with him has dared to double-cross him. He must keep them loyal with a combination of rewards by sharing the proceeds and threats. He operates at enough distance from the street-level dealers that he's been safe so far. Wily cuss."

"Have you heard anything about him lately?"

"I suspect his business is growing. There is a rumor that some boys from the mainland are trying to move in on him."

"Do you think that's real?"

Homer crinkled his forehead. "Whenever someone is as successful as Oana, there are attempts to take over the territory. He's smart and established so I think it would be difficult for someone to unseat him. He has enough support infrastructure that he could put pressure on any competition. I think he's in control for now."

"What's he look like?"

"As I said, I haven't seen him in a number of years. *Haoli* guy with a dark complexion. He's lean, approximately five-ten, your age, large nose and piercing dark eyes. He has a tattoo of a shark on his left hand."

* * * * *

When Mark and Sophie returned to the hotel, Sophie went to the room, but Mark decided to walk up to the tennis courts to find Ted. He passed a hibiscus bush and thought of picking a flower for Sophie, but he didn't want to destroy the colorful display of yellow and orange.

He sat on a bench and watched Ted hitting balls to Arlene Henrick, working on her volley. She was an attractive woman, obviously keeping herself in good shape. Ted barked out instructions, and Arlene dutifully followed his directions, leaning forward to punch decisive shots to one side of the court and then the other.

When they were done, Mark walked down to the edge of the court. "You were hitting some good volleys, Arlene."

"Thanks, Mark. Ted brings out the best in me." She winked at Ted. "I'll catch up with you in a minute. I need to freshen up." She dashed up the sidewalk and disappeared into the lady's restroom.

"I understand we may have a game tomorrow night," Mark said.

"Yes. Keone set it up. He and Lefty want to challenge us. Best two out of three. Losers buy beer."

"A serious grudge match." Mark laughed.

"That's right. This one will be for the island championship. We'll make them sorry they even thought of challenging us."

They continued to joke about the upcoming match as they walked into the pro shop to wait for Arlene.

Ted put his racquet down on the counter. "You and I are going to clean up. We'll show them who's best."

They gave each other high fives, and Mark said, "Yeah. I think you and I can close the deal tomorrow."

Mark looked up to see that Arlene had come into the shop through the open door. She placed her hands on her well-formed hips. "What kind of scheme do you two have going on?"

"Nothing," Ted replied putting his arm around Arlene's shoulders. He winked at Mark. "Only a little opportunity Mark and I are working on."

* * * * *

That evening Mark and Sophie drove along the same road they had traveled earlier in the day for windsurfing. They arrived at the home of Dexter and Harriet Kwan in Spreckelsville. After introductions, they settle in for glasses of wine out on the lanai overlooking the ocean.

Mark shielded his eyes and stared out at a fishing boat in the distance. "Quite a view you have here."

"We don't get the sunsets like you do on your side of the island."

Harriet took a sip of wine. "Dexter, remember the sunsets when we used to eat at the Pineapple Hill Restaurant?"

Dexter let out a deep sigh. "That was our favorite restaurant, up in the hills on the west end of the island. Unfortunately, they went out of business in the mid-nineteen-nineties. Had a terrific shrimp dish, and the view was stupendous." He kissed his fingers. "We even saw a green flash from there once."

Sophie furled her eyebrows. "Green flash?"

Dexter leaned toward Sophie. "Right when the sun goes down, it you watch the horizon carefully, once in a while you can see a green flash at the moment the sun disappears. I've looked many times but only seen it on three occasions."

"I usually miss it," Harriet said. "If you blink at the wrong time there's no second chance."

"We'll have to watch for that," Sophie said. "Dexter, on the plane you mentioned another sight we shouldn't miss. Hana."

He pulled himself up to his full five-foot-seven. "Absolutely. The best winding road on the island. There are over six hundred curves in the first thirty miles from Kahului. The whole trip to Hana takes over three hours. I love the drive, but it isn't Harriet's favorite."

She scrunched up her nose. "All those turns make me car sick. We have to stop every half hour so I can get out of the car and breathe some fresh air. That really makes it a long journey. You wouldn't think in terms of long car trips on our little island, but Hana is a challenge."

Dexter took a sip of wine. "I also affectionately call that road the mango squish highway because of all the mangos that fall and get run over. The highway is lined with very productive mango trees."

Mark winked at Sophie. "That reminds me of the trip we took with our kids to Yellowstone one summer. We went on a highway in Wyoming that was covered with jackrabbit carcasses. Our son labeled it the 'bunny squish highway.'"

"Nearly the same thing," Dexter said. "But in addition to the scenic, if daunting, drive, Hana is a quaint town. A picture of

80

old Hawaii. Be sure to visit the Hasegawa General Store. It's been there since 1910 and is a local legend. There's even a song written about it. You can find anything you want, as well as many things you don't need."

"Sounds like my type of store," Sophie said.

"Uh-oh, don't get my wife started on shopping."

"Oh, pooh. I've hardly done any shopping . . . yet."

"The 'yet' is what I'm afraid of."

Sophie flicked her hand toward Mark as if dismissing a pesky fly. "Harriet, have you ever considered living anywhere besides Maui?"

Harriet nudged Dexter. "There's a saying here, Maui *no ka 'oi*—Maui is the best. We wouldn't like to be in any other place." She waved toward the ocean. "The view, the trade winds, the friendly people. Our two kids live on the mainland but come back every chance they get, towing along spouses and our grandkids. As long as they keep visiting regularly, we're set. And we do go to the mainland to visit them once or twice a year as well."

"Do you have other family on the island?" Mark asked.

Dexter and Harriet gave each other knowing looks. "That's an interesting story," Dexter said. "I'm Chinese, and Harriet's Japanese. You *haoles* may think that doesn't matter, but our parents were very upset when we told them we were getting married forty-five years ago."

Harriet laughed. "My mom wanted me to marry the son of her best friend in Wailuku. My dad did business with lots of Chinese but badmouthed them at home as being crude and unscrupulous."

"It was just as bad on my side of the family," Dexter continued. "My parents left China in the late 1930s and settled in Kahului and had a real problem with how the ruthless, invading Japanese soldiers treated people in China. My dad threatened to disown me if I considered a Japanese wife. I told him he could do whatever he wanted, but I was going to marry Harriet. After much posturing, he eventually came around because who could resist Harriet?"

"After all that outrage at the beginning of our marriage, our parents became good friends. Nothing like grandkids to bring them together."

Mark raised his glass. "A toast to world peace through the diversity of Hawaii. Are your folks alive?"

Harriet bit her lip. "Both of our dads have died, but are moms live a block from each other in Wailuku. They take walks together every day. Best buddies. Now they're inseparable. Who would have imagined that forty-five years ago?"

Over dinner Dexter described the real estate business that he and Harriet started right after they married.

Mark tried to imagine starting a business on this island. It would be important to have local contacts and to know the traditions. Much different from running a high tech business in Boulder.

Harriet ushered them out to the lanai again before going into the kitchen to fix dessert. She returned, carrying a tray with four cups of vanilla ice cream covered with macadamia nuts and coconut syrup.

Mark brought up the names of the people he had met playing pickleball. "Do you know any of them?"

Dexter threw his napkin down on the table. "I don't spend much time on your side of the island and have never met the tennis pro you mentioned or Keone Ahuna."

Mark noticed that Dexter had neglected to mention Lefty but picked up a tension in his demeanor. He decided not to follow up on the subject for the moment.

After desert, Dexter offered to show them the shoreline of his property. Sophie declined, and Harriet said she'd stay with Sophie, so the men headed outside for a stroll.

Mark watched the waves break over the reef, white showing in the final moments of dusk. "Quite a place you have."

"We've lived here for twenty years. We wanted property along the coast. This house came up for sale, and I snapped it up."

"I noticed that you didn't respond earlier when I mentioned playing pickleball with Lefty Kalama."

Dexter came to an abrupt stop. "I didn't want to discuss him in front of your wife. I've heard some bad things about Lefty."

Mark leaned forward. "How so?"

"One of my friends is a dentist who treated a patient for missing front teeth. The guy was punched by Lefty over some questionable business transaction."

"What kind of deal?"

"I never got a straight answer but suspect it had something to do with drugs. There's a lot of that taking place on this island."

* * * * *

As they drove back to the hotel, Sophie leaned toward Mark. "I sure liked the Kwans. I have a much better feeling about them than your pickleball buddies."

Mark tapped the steering wheel. "That's only because you met Dexter on the plane."

"No. It's because they're honorable people. I'm not sure with your friends. My intuition tells me each of them has a shady side."

"I have some of my own suspicions, but they've been friendly so far and included me in the pickleball games. And Lefty did offer to take us snorkeling tomorrow."

Sophie snuggled closer. "That's true. We'll see how that adventure turns out."

* * * * *

Back at the hotel, they walked toward the lobby, and Kea emerged from the darkness. "Hey, I have a fresh plumeria lei for the pretty lady. Only ten dollar." He held it up for Mark and Sophie to see.

"Does everything you sell cost ten dollars?" Mark asked.

"Pretty much. Makes it easy. Tourists always seem to have a ten dollar bill." Kea held up the lei again. "You want this one?"

Mark inspected the merchandise. "Kea, I'm spending more money with you than on the hotel."

"Hey, only fair. I have best merchandise on the whole island. You can't go wrong when you buy from Kea."

Sophie rubbed her hands together. "I'd like to get that, Kea."

Mark sighed and opened his wallet. "I'll give you nine dollars."

Kea shook his head. "Nope, ten dollar."

Sophie put her hand on Kea's arm. "I'm your best customer. Can you lower it to eight dollars?"

Kea looked up at Sophie with a large smile. "For you, pretty lady. Eight dollar. You get the super duper *wahine* discount."

Mark sputtered. "What? You wouldn't accept nine dollars from me?"

Kea handed the lei to Sophie. "She's a better negotiator."

Mark resisted the urge to strangle the kid but pulled out his wallet and forked over a ten dollar bill.

Kea pulled a wad of cash out of his pocket and peeled off two one-dollar bills. "Keep the lei in a cool place and it will last for two or three days."

Mark put the change back in his wallet. "Hey, Kea. I have a question for you. I understand you know a man named Keone Ahuna."

Kea spat on the ground. "Not nice man."

"How so?"

"He beat up my mom one time. But I fixed him. I put a nail in his tire."

Mark remembered the deflated tire on his rental car. "You didn't happen to do that to my car as well, did you?"

"No way. You my good customer. I never do bad things to good customers. I only do bad things to bad people."

"That's a relief. Sophie told me you want to eventually start your own company."

Kea's eyes lit up. "You bet. I've been checking out the souvenir shops around this side of the island. I can do much better— provide higher quality products at lower prices. You should see the junk they sell in this hotel. I saw a windmill last week that would easily fall apart."

Sophie and Mark exchanged glances.

"I ran my own company and would be happy to discuss my experiences with you, Kea."

"That would be great. I've been studying equity financing and could use some help on how to structure an IPO."

Mark held up a hand. "Whoa. You're getting a little ahead of yourself. Sophie said you want to get a business degree at the University of Hawaii."

"Sure. But I can start my company first. That way I have a little practical experience along the way. I think I'll form a LLC. I figure I can also find some angel investors at the hotels around here. How much would you like to invest?"

Mark laughed. "You need a business plan first."

"No problem." Kea took off his backpack, opened it and pulled out a bound document. "Here you go."

Mark leafed through it and arched an eyebrow. "You put this together yourself?"

"Yep. I've been checking out sample business plans on the Internet and been doing a lot of reading. Let me know what you think, and tell me how much you can invest. I'd suggest around ten thousand dollars."

Mark gulped. "I'll definitely read it. By the way, we went to your cousin Abe's photo gallery in Lahaina yesterday."

"Good. You got the twenty percent discount, right?"

"That we did. He also said you're quite the storyteller. I saw that on your business card as well."

"Yep. I tell you the best story about the islands for only ten dollar."

Mark rolled his eyes. "Here we go again."

Sophie winked at Mark and faced Kea. "Let's go sit by the ocean and you can tell us a story. But I expect the *wahine* discount."

"You got it. Only eight dollar. You still get the best story for that." Kea held out his hand, and Mark once again opened his wallet and provided the fee.

Mark thumbed through the remaining bills. "I'm running low on cash."

"I can set up a credit account for you." Kea gave his gap-toothed smile.

They walked along the side of the hotel and sat in beach chairs looking out at the ocean, which reflected the gibbous moon.

"You want a regular story or a scary one?" Kea asked.

"We need a good ghost story." Sophie snuggled up against Mark. "Something creepy."

"Okay. Since you've been to Lahaina, I tell you a story of two *haoles*, Stubby and Luke, and the trouble they got in during the whaling times. As you know Lahaina was where the whaling ships came into port to get supplies. So often there were *haole* sailors who didn't understand the Hawaiian ways. This is a story that my great grandfather told me and is true. It's a story about the *Menehunes*."

Sophie grasped Mark's arm. "I'm ready."

Chapter 11

Kea waved toward the moon. "On a night like this with the moon reflecting off the ocean, a sailor named Stubby, named for the little finger torn off his right hand when it got tangled in a line during a fierce storm, leaned close and whispered to his friend Luke, 'I hear there's treasure in the mountains above Lahaina.'

"'Who told you that?' Luke asked.

"'I overheard two seamen getting ready to ship out. Said the natives know all about it.'

"Luke felt that special warmth in his chest. Treasure! 'I could use a little more cash than the measly pay for sixteen months of raising and lowering sails.'

"'Right you are, me son.'

"'Let's ask that gal, Melani, we met.'

"They found Melani sitting on the seawall, polishing kukui nuts. As Luke sat down beside her, he noticed a tall Hawaiian man with a cape on his shoulders strolling along the waterfront. Luke admired the bright red and yellow feathers of the garment.

"'Who's he?'

"'That's one of the *Alii*, the royal family,' Melani replied.

"'Quite an outfit.'

"'Yes, made from feathers of the little birds found in the mountain forest. And no one else can wear those, only the royal family.'

"Luke smiled. 'Do you ever go up in the hills above Lahaina?'

"'Yes.'

"'Ever hear of treasure up there?'

"Her eyes got big. 'Could be, but big trouble from *Menehunes*.'

"'What's that?'

"'Little people. They guard *heiau*, sacred place where royalty buried.'

"'Burial caves,' Luke said. 'Do you know where to find them?'

"'My brother Kula does, but no one goes inside. *Kapu*, keep out. *Menehunes* make plenty *pilikia*.'

"'What could they possibly do?'

"Melanie's gaze shifted downward. 'Very bad. Stay away from *Menehunes*.'

"'Like back home.' Stubby laughed. 'In me land the leprechauns guard the pot o' gold. Let's get some natives to guide us.'

"The next day they lined up Melani's brother Kula to take them up in the hills.

"After an hour hike they came to a place where the trail split.

"'We go this way,' Kula pointed to the left.

"'What's the other way?' Stubby asked.

"'*Heiau. Kapu.* No can go.'

"'Why not?' Luke asked. 'We're here to explore.'

"'Forbidden for anyone but chief to go near the cave.'

"'Luke here is a chief. Right, me son?' Stubby poked him in the ribs with the stub of his missing finger.

"'We want to see the cave,' Luke explained to Kula.

"'Crazy *haoles*. You no listen?'

"'Let's take one look.'

"Kula shook his head. 'No break *kapu*.' With that he started back toward Lahaina.

"'Well, he led us to the right place,' Stubby said. 'Let's go find the treasure.'

"They marched on and came to a stone wall in front of a cave. Stubby was ready to climb over the wall when a two-foot tall man in loin cloth appeared and held up his hand. 'This land *kapu*. Go 'way before bad things happen to you!'

"Stubby laughed. 'It's only a midget no bigger than a kid trying to scare us away.' He climbed up the wall and held out his good hand to drag Luke up with him.

"'Look,' Stubby shouted. 'There's something shining in the cave. See, I told you. There's treasure here, and the midget's trying to scare us away.'

"They scrambled down the wall and entered the cave.

"As his eyes adjusted to the dark, Luke saw instead of treasure, two skeletons lying on a yellow and red feathered cape.

"At that moment a stomping-mad *Menehune* appeared at the mouth of the cave. 'I give you one last warning to leave, so go now or else you never return from here.'

"A trickle of sweat rolled down Luke's forehead. 'Let's get out of here.'

"'No way,' Stubby said, rubbing his hands together. 'We've come for the treasure.'

"Luke knew he had to leave. He raced out of the cave and climbed over the wall. He turned around once, but Stubby wasn't coming.

"Suddenly, lightning flashed, followed by an immediate roar of thunder."

Kea clapped his hands together, and both Mark and Sophie jumped. Kea spread his arms wide, "Luke ran all the way back to Lahaina and arrived at the hotel, soaking wet. His stomach ached and his head hurt. He trudged to his room and collapsed on his bed. He was sick for two days, unable to eat or move. The town doctor came to see him.

"'What happened to you, young man?' the doctor asked.

"'I went into a cave up in the mountains. Ran back here. Something made me sick.'

"The doctor shook his head. 'I keep getting these cases of sailors who go into the hills and get ill. I can't find anything wrong with you.'

"After the doctor left, Luke got dressed and staggered downstairs. He asked the barkeeper if he had seen Stubby.

"'Not a sign of him since you two were last here together.'

"Luke was worried. He hired a group of Hawaiians to help him search for Stubby. When they got up to where the trail split, the Hawaiians, knowing better, refused to go on.

"Luke held out a handful of money. 'I'll pay you to go to the cave with me.'

"They shook their heads. No way would any of them go. They too smart, not like the dumb *haoles*.

"'Please. Come as far as the wall, and I'll give you this money.'

"No one moved. Finally, Luke sucked up his courage, told the men to wait for him there and headed to the *heiau* by himself. Arriving at the wall, he saw no *Menehune*s, so he climbed over and sneaked into the cave. There on the floor of the cave lay three skeletons.

"Luke looked carefully at the third skeleton. It was spread out on the cave floor, not on the yellow and red cape like the two older skeletons. Then he saw the right hand. There was no little finger.

"Luke's heart raced. He stood up. In front of him stood a *Menehune*, picking his teeth with a spear.

"Luke pivoted and dashed out of the cave. He ran so hard, he knocked over two huge Hawaiians back at the trail junction. Within a day he shipped out never to come back to Lahaina again. The end."

Sophie let out a loud sigh. "That story was worth at least eight dollars."

"Any time you want another story, you let me know. I have plenty more stories of Hawaii that you will enjoy. Next time I tell you how Madam Pele, the goddess of the volcanoes, caused trouble for one unsuspecting *haole* on the Saddle Road on the Big Island." Kea jumped up. "Uh-oh. Got to go." He scampered off into the bushes.

Sophie waved toward the disappearing figure. "That was an abrupt departure."

Mark turned his gaze toward the hotel and saw the assistant manager stalking toward them. "There's the explanation—Kea's nemesis just showed up."

The assistant manager strode up to them. "Has that kid been bothering you again?"

Sophie put the lei over her neck. "Not at all. We enjoy his

company. He adds so much to the enjoyment of our stay at your hotel."

Chapter 12

On the way back to their hotel room, Sophie grabbed Mark's hand. "What did you think of his story?"

"Once again I've contributed to the health of the local economy by financing our friend, Kea. But I have to admit his story was an interesting blend of history and local lore. Are you going to have nightmares tonight?"

"I don't think so, but if I do, you'll have to protect me."

He held her tightly. "It will be my pleasure."

"His story provides a good warning to stay out of burial caves."

"Fortunately, we won't be traipsing around in the tropical jungles where we'd find burial caves."

* * * * *

Back in the hotel room, Mark read Kea's business plan and marked it up with suggestions on how to improve it. After finishing the document, he dropped it onto on the nightstand. "That kid is pretty sharp."

Sophie regarded him over her mystery novel. "Of course. He out negotiated you for both the kukui nut necklace and the conch shell."

Mark's cheeks grew warm. "I'll have you know I'm a good negotiator."

"I'm not saying you're not. Kea is better."

He let out a resigned sigh. "Bested by a twelve-year-old."

"Don't take it personally. He'll probably be running the island in another twenty years. So, tell me your specific thoughts on his business plan."

"He's covered a lot of the bases. A solid executive summary and a good description of the opportunity. He's realistic in starting small and then building up, so as not to become overextended. He intends to use his family and friends to produce kukui nut and shell necklaces at the outset. I've seen too many business plans that are too ambitious at the start and doomed to failure."

Sophie put her book down on the nightstand. "He acts very grounded. Very mature for his age."

"That's for sure. Not many twelve-year-olds have this much business savvy. The strongest part is the marketing plan. As we both know he's an excellent sales person. He knows his prospective customers and what appeals to them. He nailed the competitive analysis of the hotels with their gifts stores—inferior quality and high prices. He intends to provide good quality goods at a fair price. He plans to put together discount coupons to give away to tourists but needs to work on how he will distribute those coupons. He's not clear on how people will get the coupons. The hotels aren't going to give them away so he has to find some publication or other tourist businesses that will work with him."

"He has a start with his cousins' network. Abe and Nora can give out coupons in their shops."

"True, but he'll need more than two places supporting his business. I'm sure he'll work that out since he already understands cross-promotion."

Sophie yawned. "And other things he needs to improve?"

"Two areas, really. First, supply chain. He'll eventually need to have additional suppliers beyond his friends and family. As the business grows, they won't be able to keep up with demand. He needs to give that more thought. Second, financing. He'll have to identify how much funding he needs and what share of the business he's willing to give up for the investment. He definitely knows more about business than I did when I was twice his age. He's street smart and also writes well."

"Maybe his home schooling works."

"I'm sure he directs his studies to things he finds important to develop and run a business."

★ ★ ★ ★ ★

The next morning Mark threw Kea's marked up business plan in the trunk of the rental car, figuring he could give it back to the kid the next time he was accosted in the parking lot, and he and Sophie arrived at the Kihei Boat Landing five minutes before ten for the trip to Molokini.

On the small cabin cruiser, Lefty announced, "We're all set. Beer, chips, sweet sour seeds and snorkeling equipment."

"Sweet sour what?" Sophie asked.

"Cracked seed. Dried plum that makes a great snack. You'll either love it or hate it."

Sophie scrunched up her nose. "Sounds awful."

Lefty was a confident skipper, and they took a direct course toward Molokini. The constant breeze caused white caps to form on wave peaks and led to a choppy ride.

Mark watched Sophie's hair blowing in the wind. She smiled back at him and wasn't turning green. He decided not to broach the events at the Kamaina Tavern with Lefty, who seemed in a good mood. No sense bringing up a sore topic. And for Sophie's sake he wasn't going to discuss the report of Lefty knocking out a man's teeth.

Half way there, Sophie announced, "I'm getting a little queasy."

"No problem," Lefty said. "I'll slow down. We have lots of time."

They anchored off the crescent moon shaped rock formation that formed the island of Molokini. Only one other boat, moored approximately two hundred yards away.

Sophie said she felt a little better but decided to stay in the boat and not go snorkeling.

Mark donned the flippers and grabbed the mask and snorkel. "Let me at those fish."

94

"Follow me," Lefty said. "I'll show you the best place."

They jumped in. Mark adjusted his mask and inserted the snorkel in his mouth and blew water out to clear it. The mask fit snuggly. As they bobbed in the water, he noticed another boat had anchored nearby—a large cabin cruiser. Then he put his head in the water.

The wonders of the ocean opened to him as a school of silver stick fish skimmed by, two feet below the surface. There were fish of varying colors: yellow and black angelfish, the bright orange and green of the *humuhumunukunukuapua'a*. A tuna flicked its tail and shot in front of him.

Lefty pointed ahead and they swam toward a large school of orange fish that Mark could not identify. He took a deep breath and dove down ten feet to get a better look at another school of fish.

Back up at surface level to catch his breath, Mark spotted a sea turtle and followed it while it stroked its flippers through the water. What a beautiful creature. The shell reflected sunlight coming through the water. He floated along keeping far enough away to avoid disturbing the turtle but close enough to watch its graceful motion.

Out of the corner of his eye he saw a large object. He flinched before realizing it was a scuba diver, a man in a wet suit, holding a spear gun. The man cut right in front, and Mark saw on the back of his hand a distinct tattoo of a shark.

When he surfaced, Mark tapped Lefty on the shoulder. They both floated while removing their masks.

"I thought this was a fish preserve," Mark said.

"It is. No fishing allowed."

"I saw a scuba diver with a spear gun."

"What? That's not allowed in these waters."

Mark wiped water off his face. "Apparently that guy doesn't know or doesn't play by the rules."

"We should report it. Any description?"

"I noticed one distinguishing feature. A tattoo of a shark on the back of his hand."

Lefty jerked his head, swallowed water and coughed.

"You all right?" Mark asked.

"Must have got some water in my mouth."

"So should we do anything regarding the guy with the spear gun?"

"We'll worry about it later. Let's move to another part of the island."

*   *   *   *   *

It was only later when they headed to a new location, that Mark remembered what his lawyer, Homer Nagano, had told him. Oana, the elusive crime kingpin, had a tattoo of a shark on his hand.

Mark wondered if that was a common tattoo or the signature of Oana.

*   *   *   *   *

Lefty anchored the boat again, and this time Sophie was feeling well enough to join them. Whenever she spotted a new type of fish, she waved her hand wildly. After an hour they returned to the boat.

They sipped beers and ate snacks.

Lefty waved his can of Primo at Sophie. "You seem fully recovered."

"The trade winds and the boat not rocking so much as before helped. Then a swim with the beautiful fish. No way I would miss that."

Lefty packed up and fired up the engine.

As they headed back to Maui, Sophie tossed her wet hair to the side. "That was amazing. Thanks for taking us there."

Lefty saluted. "All part of the service."

*   *   *   *   *

After they retrieved their car and drove back to the hotel parking lot, Mark asked, "Do you feel better about Lefty now?"

"He certainly was a gracious host on the boat trip, but there's something that doesn't strike me as genuine about him. He put on a good show, but there's an underlying menace to him that I can't exactly put my finger on."

"Your intuition at work?"

"Yes."

"I'll keep that in mind." Mark came to an abrupt stop right under the portico of the hotel. "Did you notice something unusual just now?"

"No, what?"

"Kea wasn't here to accost us with his sales pitch to buy something. He usually pops out of the bushes when I'm in the parking lot."

"Maybe he's off replenishing his supply of souvenirs to sell to us later."

* * * * *

Inside the hotel the answer to Kea's presence became known. The assistant manager held the boy by the arm. "I'm calling the police. You can't keep harassing our guests."

"I no harass nobody. I only ask lady if she want to buy seashell bracelet."

Sophie approached the assistant manager. "What's wrong if I may ask?"

He shook his free hand at Kea. "This delinquent has been bothering another guest. It's time to put a stop to his bad behavior."

"Did she complain?" Sophie asked.

"No, but he's always harassing people. He jumps out of the bushes and tries to sell his cheap merchandise."

"I think his presence adds to the atmosphere of this hotel." Sophie stomped her foot. "If you don't release his arm immediately, my husband and I are going to move to another hotel."

"But... but," he sputtered.

"We'll take him outside and speak with him, so release him immediately."

The assistant manager let go, and Sophie and Mark led Kea out into the parking lot.

Kea wiped his forehead. "That one close call. Thank you for saving me. I give you twenty-five percent discount on anything from now on."

Sophie knelt in front of Kea. "You need to take a break for a few days. Don't you have another location where you sell your goods?"

"Yeah, I go to the hotels in Wailea, but this is my favorite spot. And you my best customers."

"We'll buy more from you, but let the assistant manager cool off for a few days. It'll be best for your business that way."

"Okay, for you, pretty lady, will do. Here's a present." He reached in his backpack, pulled out a large shiny spotted cowry and handed it to Sophie. Then he tapped Mark on the arm. "What did you think of the business plan?"

"It's a good start. I have some written comments for you."

Kea pointed to the lobby. "Uh-oh, here comes that guy again. You show me what you wrote next time." Then he disappeared into the bushes.

★ ★ ★ ★ ★

That night Mark arrived at the pickleball court ten minutes early to stretch and hit practice serves. He first lay on the court and brought his feet to his chest to stretch his back. Next, he put his right foot on the net post and leaned forward. He repeated this exercise with his left foot. After half a dozen serves from the deuce and ad sides, he was ready for the big match.

When everyone arrived they agreed to play best of five games.

Ted and Lefty set the tone for the showdown while they warmed up.

"You're going down." Ted blasted a forehand at Lefty who

deftly volleyed it back.

"Oh, yeah. You and that old *haole* think you can beat us? No way, man. Keone and I will rip you apart like gutting a mahi-mahi."

Mark waved his paddle. "Hey, watch who you're calling old."

Nothing like a friendly grudge match with the prerequisite trash talk. Keoni stayed out of the fray, a frown on his face, as if he were the Secretary of State trying to solve a delicate diplomatic problem.

Ted served first and hit a hard, deep serve cross court. Lefty played the backhand shot equally deep to Mark.

Mark tried to hit it short down the middle, but popped it up too much in Keone's direction. Keone volleyed the ball down the middle.

Ted stabbed at it, but the ball went high and Lefty stepped in to put it away right at Mark's feet.

In the second game, Lefty slammed a shot that missed Mark's head by inches and sailed long.

Ted pointed to his chin. "Keep aiming for our heads all night. You'll lose the point every time."

Mark hoped Lefty didn't follow that advice. One of those times he might connect.

The third game ended up going to fifteen to thirteen before Ted put away two shots while serving. It was a hard fought see-saw battle, but Mark and Ted prevailed three games to two.

Ted turned off the court lights, and they sat on the patio courtside in metal chairs around a circular table with the only ambient light coming from the guest cottage. A gentle breeze rustled the leaves of a nearby hibiscus bush. Mark looked up and could see a few stars amid the passing clouds.

Ted licked his lips. "This beer tastes so much better when it's being paid for by the losers. You local boys did pretty good but not good enough."

Lefty slammed his can of Primo beer down on the table. "You're lucky I missed a couple of shots at the end of the third set. Otherwise you'd be paying for it. Hey, Keone, you think that old *kahuna* can put some kind of curse on these stinkin' *haoles*?"

Keone burped. "Not worth the effort. They'll eventually go back to the mainland and leave us in peace."

"Then who will play pickleball with you?" Ted asked.

"We'll round up some local boys who have proper respect." Lefty raised his can toward Keone, and they clinked them together.

Ted sighed and gave a satisfied smile. "I could sit here all night drinking beer paid for by someone else. This is the life."

Mark decided it was time to address the elephant on the patio. "Anyone hear anything new about the investigation into George Tanabe's death?"

It was as if he had dumped a bin of rotten vegetables on the table. His question was met with three scowls.

Ted spoke for the group. "Nope."

No one else ventured a word.

Keone had been restless. He squirmed for a moment and announced, "I have to get going."

"You seem distracted, Keone," Ted said. "Can't take the pressure of the big match?"

"I have a lot going on." He jumped to his feet abruptly and jogged to the gate.

"I've never seen him like that." Lefty scrunched his eyebrows. "And he was the one who set up the match."

"That in itself is unusual. He typically waits for one of us to arrange it." Ted smacked his lips. "Let's have another beer."

Lefty excused himself to go into the guest cottage to use the bathroom. While he was gone, Ted turned to Mark. "A funny thing happened this afternoon."

"Oh?"

"Yeah. I approached Arlene with a business deal, but she got real upset."

"Maybe she's not looking for that kind of relationship."

Ted laughed. "She acted suspicious. Before, she was interested in my little investment proposals. This time she put the kibosh on my idea immediately."

Mark flicked a piece of lint off his shirt. "Stuff happens."

"Yeah, women. You can't live with them, and you can't live without them."

Lefty returned, and the three of them talked for half an hour. Mark avoided bringing up the subject of George Tanabe as that seemed to be off limits. Instead, he told Ted about the snorkeling expedition while Lefty sat back in his chair and sucked on his beer. Finally, Lefty stood. "Time to hit the road. I have some business to take care of."

Mark stretched. "I better get back as well. Thanks for the game."

"We'll do it again in a few days. As soon as Lefty and Keone have finished licking their wounds and are ready to buy beer again."

Mark reached his car first and drove away quickly. He hadn't picked up anything useful from the other three, but one more idea occurred to him to try. He found an opening in the brush a half mile along the road, pulled in, flipped off his lights and watched in his rearview mirror.

Within minutes Lefty's old Honda Civic chugged by.

Mark waited a moment, pulled out and followed at a safe distance.

Lefty drove through Wailea Beach and continued onto the Pi'ilani Highway toward Kihei. Mark followed, blending in with another car he let cut between them.

Mark thought Lefty might stop at the Kamaina Tavern, but he continued north to the outskirts of Kihei. Then he turned right into a parking lot.

Mark stopped, half a block back and doused his lights. He watched Lefty walk into a building. After a moment, he checked his watch, determining he had a few more minutes before getting in the dog house with Sophie, clambered out of his car and crept toward the entrance.

A sign in front said, "Valley Island Realty." A handful of cars were scattered through the parking lot—a mix of old trucks, beat up sedans and Lefty's Honda.

Mark prowled along the side of the building until he found a window that was open a crack to let in the trade wind.

He heard Lefty's voice.

"I've come with the stuff. That settles what I owe Oana."

A deep voice replied, "We'll see. Let me weigh it first."

Mark was listening so intently to the conversation inside that he failed to pay attention to where he was.

Suddenly, there was a crunch of gravel.

He spun around. Too late.

Chapter 13

A strong hand grabbed Mark's arm and wrenched it back. He gasped from the sharp pain and pitched forward hitting the ground chin first. The impact made his head spin.

His other arm was thrust behind and something was wrapped around his wrists. Then the toe of a shoe struck his ribs.

"Get up," a voice commanded.

Mark tried to get to his knees but fell forward again from lack of leverage.

Two hands seized his shoulders and roughly lifted him up.

"Move." A push in the center of his back propelled him forward. He tripped, but regained his balance.

Inside the building, he caught sight of four men and Lefty seated at a table. Mark recognized two of the men as the ones who had accosted Lefty at the Kamaina Tavern. One had the distinctive scar on his cheek.

"Found this *haole* snooping around," the voice behind him announced.

Lefty blinked and turned pale.

"Hey, Lefty, looks like your lawyer's in the wrong place at the wrong time." Scar Cheek, who Lefty had previously identified as Malo, laughed.

"Maybe we should feed him to the sharks," another man said.

"Lefty, what do you think we should do with your lawyer?"

Lefty looked around wild-eyed. "I don't know."

"I hear there's a drug problem on this part of the island." Malo slapped his hand on the table. "Maybe we should consider helping out. Give Detective Puna Pa'a someone to arrest. New wave of *haole* crime, in from the mainland, corrupting our fair island."

One of the men leaned back in his chair. "Yeah. A police raid finds him with some shit. Give them someone to lock up. That should end the island crime wave for good."

"His fingerprints all over the place, a stash in his pocket. An anonymous tip brings in the police. That's the least we can do to clean up the community."

"Hey, LeRoy. Get out your needle."

One of the men rummaged in a bag and pulled out a syringe.

"Give him enough to knock him out for half an hour so the police can get here."

LeRoy jabbed the needle in Mark's arm.

Mark saw the room spinning and collapsed.

* * * * *

When Mark awoke, he heard sirens. He raised himself to his knees. He remembered the group around the table. His hands were no longer tied. He brushed his hand against his pocket, noticed a lump, reached in and lifted out a plastic baggie containing white powder. Shuddering, he dropped it on the floor.

Footsteps approached the building.

He had to get out of here. He looked frantically into the hall and saw a back door. He stumbled across the short distance, turned the knob and peered out.

No one there.

He heard the front door knob turning. He staggered out into the dark parking lot. Straight ahead was a shrub-covered hillside. He disappeared into the undergrowth.

He went in far enough to provide cover and collapsed onto the ground, gasping for breath. Once his ragged breathing and heart rate returned to normal, he looked back to determine if anyone had seen him. Apparently not. Just the flashing lights from the police cars reflected off a building across the street.

He realized his predicament. His fingerprints were on the

plastic bag he'd dropped. They'd match the prints taken when he'd been at the police station.

He probably had an hour or so before the connection was made. He forged through the undergrowth and skirted the parking lot. No police on the street. He stepped out of the bushes near his car, quickly unlocked the door and dropped onto the seat.

Still groggy, he took several deep breaths to overcome nausea. No one paying any attention to his car yet. He clicked on his seatbelt and drove back to the hotel, glancing periodically in the rearview mirror to see if anyone was following him. When he arrived, he scanned the circular driveway in front of the Maui Queen to make sure no police cars were present.

As he entered the lobby, he was accosted by Arlene Henrick. She marched right up to him and shouted, "Have you seen Ted?"

Mark took a step back. "I played pickleball with him earlier."

"Well, he's not at his place and doesn't answer his cell phone."

"I have no idea what time it is." Mark looked at his watch for the first time since being knocked out. "He was there two hours ago."

"He tried to sell me some completely worthless property," Arlene said, glaring at Mark.

"What?"

"You heard me. And you're part of this scam. I overheard the two of you plotting at the tennis courts yesterday. I'm going to have you both arrested."

She turned on her heals and stomped away.

What did Ted do? Mark had no time to find out. He needed to go talk to Sophie about his predicament.

When he entered his room, he found the reading light on and the bed cover rumbled on Sophie's side. She must be in the bathroom.

"I'm back," he called.

No answer.

He looked in the bathroom. No Sophie.

That's strange. He looked more carefully around the room. Her book was splayed out on the bed. She only left a book that way if she was getting up for a moment. And she always turned the light out when she left. He couldn't think of a reason that she'd leave the room.

He looked in the bottom dresser drawer to see if her purse was stashed there, and found it neatly tucked under a T-shirt.

He wondered why it was here. She left it in this drawer when she was in the room, but took it with her unless she was going to the beach. And she wouldn't be going to the beach in the middle of the night.

Something didn't make sense.

He looked around the room again. No message light flashing on the phone. He searched through the room, checking the drawers, closet and bathroom. Nothing to indicate where Sophie had gone. If she went down to the bar for a drink, she would have left him a note.

He double checked the bed and nightstand. No note.

He slid open the sliding glass door and stepped out on the balcony. A gentle breeze rustled through the coconut trees between the hotel and the beach. He squinted into the darkness, punctuated by several floodlights that reflected on the grass lawn. No sign of Sophie.

He heard the room phone ring. He dashed inside. Maybe Sophie was calling him. She probably had gone for a walk and was checking in with him. He put the receiver to his ear and said, "Hello."

A muffled voice growled in very precise, slow words, "If you want to see your wife alive leave two hundred thousand dollars in twenties in the dumpster at the Kihei Boat Landing by eleven P.M. this coming Wednesday night. Don't contact the police or your wife dies."

"Who is this?" Mark shouted.

There was a click.

Sophie. A constriction seized his chest. Kidnapped. Two days.

He slammed his fist on the nightstand. Questions were spinning through his head. Who had kidnapped Sophie? How could he save her? Who could help him? He couldn't meet with the police.

They wouldn't believe him, and besides, he'd be arrested for drug possession as well as being a suspect in the murder of George Tanabe and probably a fraud complaint from Arlene Henrick.

He took a deep breath to calm his heightened heart rate. Had he recognized the voice? No. Obviously disguised.

He had to prepare himself. He couldn't stay here. He slid open the drawer, reached in Sophie's purse and found the envelope where she kept her mad money. He'd need some cash for what he had to do. He lifted out five one hundred dollar bills. That plus the fifty or so dollars he had in his wallet would have to see him through for a while. He also took Sophie's credit card, although he'd have to be careful if trying to use it.

He packed his toilet kit and stuffed it along with a pair of jeans, swim trunks and a handful of T-shirts, socks and underwear in a beach bag. He took a quick shower and changed into hiking shorts and a clean shirt, before double checking to make sure he had his cell phone.

He surveyed the room once more. One item caught his attention. The windmill on the dresser. One of the vanes was broken.

Chapter 14

Mark told himself to stay calm. He had to think this through and not do anything rash. What else would he need? He glanced around the room. He'd have to establish a new base of operations. Grabbing the Maui driving map from the dresser and a phone book from under the nightstand, he threw these into the beach bag.

He considered again going to the police, but he'd get arrested and wouldn't be able to do anything to save Sophie. Still, he could enlist their assistance. He pulled out Puna's card, picked up the room phone and punched in the number. He got voicemail.

"Detective, this is Mark Yeager. My wife has been kidnapped. Please come check our room at the Maui Queen Hotel for any clues. I don't know who did this." He hung up without mentioning the drop site and timing. He needed to handle that himself.

He had to get out of here.

After taking one last look at the room, he crept down the hall and took the back stairs, not wanting to encounter Arlene or anyone else in the lobby.

In his car he opened the map and with the assistance of the parking lot overhead light, located the Kihei Boat Landing. Although he had been there to get on the boat for the snorkeling trip, he hadn't paid much attention to the surroundings. It was five miles north. Several hotels were listed nearby. He'd drive through the area and check it out.

When he reached the landing with its boat ramp and small harbor, he surveyed the nearby structures and located a single dumpster. Now he knew what he had to deal with. After cruising through several side streets, he settled on a small, older hotel a few blocks away. The Oceanview Palms had one other advantage: an indoor parking structure so his car couldn't be seen from the street. He couldn't spot the ocean and didn't notice a palm tree on the premises, but it would do. He prepaid in cash for two nights, registering as Michael Andrews. Fortunately, the sleepy clerk didn't ask for an ID.

In his small room he turned on the light and sat down at the desk to make plans. In the morning he'd call Homer Nagano, and he had some items to purchase. He checked his map and located the Kihei Mall just up the road. After that, he settled into a fitful sleep.

★ ★ ★ ★ ★

The sunlight glaring through the opening in the curtains jarred Mark awake the following morning. He rubbed his eyes and reviewed the events from the night before. This was not a good situation. He felt a pain in his gut from what had happened to Sophie. He had to act quickly but keep his wits about him.

He placed a call and was informed that Homer wasn't expected for another hour.

Damn. He needed to make contact with Homer. Instead, he jogged down the road to the boat landing to further inspect the area. He stopped next to the large dumpster on the edge of the parking lot, away from the water. Nearby was a clump of kiawe trees and some overgrown brush that could provide cover. He reconnoitered until he had a plan in mind then returned to the hotel.

Next was a trip to the shopping center to make his purchases. He found everything he needed. Back in the car, he pulled out his cell phone and tried Homer again.

"He's on the other line," the receptionist said.

"Tell him it's an emergency. This is Mark Yeager."

"Just a minute."

Mark tapped his fingers on the dashboard while waiting. Finally, Homer came on the line.

"What's the panic?"

"I need to see you right away," Mark said. "I have some major problems."

"If you come to my office, I can meet you in an hour."

"I'll be there." Mark pushed the end key.

★ ★ ★ ★ ★

When he reached Kahului, he noticed that the gas gauge read close to empty. Risking the use of Sophie's credit card, he figured it wouldn't give away any useful information about his whereabouts, and he wanted to conserve his cash.

In the law office he had to wait ten minutes before Homer came out to greet him.

Once they were behind the closed door, Mark burst out, "I've been set up in a drug deal, and my wife's been kidnapped."

Homer put up his hand. "Hold on. Take your time and tell me everything."

Mark recounted following Lefty, listening through the open window and getting captured.

"Did you recognize any of them?"

"Yeah. There were the two thugs who accosted Lefty and me two days ago in the Kamaina Tavern. One of them is a big guy named Malo."

"Oana's enforcer."

Mark recounted the message delivered to him on the hotel phone demanding two hundred thousand dollars. "And one other thing. I'm also being accused of some sort of fraudulent deal that the tennis pro, Ted Franklin, foisted on a *divorcée* named Arlene Henrick."

"Sounds like you got yourself in all kinds of *pilikia*."

"Unfortunately, that's the case. I have a plan to deal with the kidnapping, but I need to stay free from arrest for two days to execute it."

"Let me make a phone call. I'll find out what's happening with the police." Homer reached for the phone.

Mark listened to Homer saying "Anything been filed against Mark Yeager?... uh huh... yeah... timing?"

Five minutes later he reported back to Mark. "Bad news. There's a warrant out for your arrest."

"Great. Just what I need." Mark jumped up from his chair and paced the room. "What am I charged with?"

"They've thrown the book at you. Murder of George Tanabe, drug possession, drug dealing and fraud. Ted Franklin's also been listed on the fraud charge."

"Ted's little deal with Arlene Henrick."

"And one new charge as of this morning. Kidnapping."

Mark slapped his forehead. "You've got to be kidding."

"I'm afraid not. You're accused of kidnapping Sophie."

"What! I left a message for Detective Puna Pa'a last night that Sophie had been kidnapped. Now he suspects me?"

"Yep. As your lawyer, I'd advise you to turn yourself in. As a husband, I'd advise you to ignore my advice."

"I need to get a gun," Mark said.

"I didn't hear that." Homer covered his ears.

"How easy is it to buy one here?"

"Last year I bought a gun that I keep in the office just in case I have a problem with a client. But I had to show identification and go through a background check to get it."

"Oana probably deals in illegal weapons, but I'm not exactly popular with his people at the moment."

The receptionist buzzed Homer. "Your ten thirty appointment has arrived."

"Wait here, Mark. I'll need to spend a few minutes with this client, but he and I can use the conference room."

Homer went out and closed the door.

Mark leapt to the desk and started searching. In the bottom drawer he found a Smith and Wesson. It was loaded. He tucked it in the belt of his jeans and smoothed out his T-shirt to cover it.

When Homer returned, he asked Mark, "Do you have enough money to get by?"

"I'm fine for now."

"Do you think Oana's responsible for the kidnapping?"

Mark wrinkled his forehead. "No. I think they're separate events. The kidnapping took place at nearly the same time I was following Lefty, so Oana's thugs weren't concerned about me until after Sophie disappeared."

"If you have any trouble with the police, call me right away. I'll give you my home and cell phone numbers." He jotted on a pad, tore off the top sheet and handed it to Mark. "You'll have to deal with the kidnapping and avoid Oana's boys on your own."

"One favor."

Homer arched an eyebrow. "Yeah?"

"Call Puna. Inform him I did not kidnap my wife and that the police should look for the real kidnapper and try to locate Sophie."

"Will do. And you?"

"I have my own plan to find Sophie, but the police should be working on it as well."

Homer bit his lip and stared at Mark. "Let me give you a little bit of unsolicited island advice."

Mark narrowed his gaze at Homer. "Okay."

"Do you ever collect shells on the beach?"

"Yes, I've been doing some of that since we came to Maui. What's that have to do with my predicament?"

"Bear with me a moment. If you're walking down a beach and want to find shells where do you look?"

"In a pile of material that's been washed up at the high tide mark."

"Right. The current and waves tend to force rocks and shells into clumps. That's where you'll find the most shells. But what if you want to find the largest, most unique shells?"

Mark scratched his head. "Obviously not there. You're trying to make a point."

"Exactly. You either have to dive for them or find them in an isolated place away from where everyone else is looking."

"So if I'm going to find clues for locating my wife and getting the police off my back, I should look elsewhere than in the expected places."

"You said it, not me."

"Sounds like advice from some inscrutable Asian ancestor."

"That's mainly for Chinese, but my mom claimed we were related to the famous seventeenth century haiku poet, Basho. You'll have to be very resilient to get out of this mess. Here's a translation of one of Basho's poems: 'Broken and broken again on the sea, the moon so easily mends.' Take it for what it's worth."

As Mark left, he thought over what he'd heard. He needed to first follow up with all his contacts in regards to the kidnapping and stay resilient. Finding Sophie was top priority.

* * * * *

Mark drove back to Kihei, monitoring his speed. No sense tempting fate.

His next step was to call Ted. It took three tries over an hour to make a connection.

"Ted, what's the deal with Arlene? She accused me of being involved in some sort of property scam with you."

"She's merely acting overly emotional. I tried to get her to make an investment."

"She claims it was a fraud."

"After checking out the adjoining property, she thought the price was too high. It was a lack of understanding on her part of the advantages of this particular lot."

"It's worse than a misunderstanding. She's filed a complaint against both of us with the police."

There was a pause on the line. "I'll see what I can do."

"You better take care of it quickly before both of us land in jail. Have you heard from either Lefty or Keone today?"

"Only Lefty. I saw him earlier. He was beat up pretty bad last night."

"What happened?"

"Said he got into a bar brawl. Looks like someone worked him over."

"Probably hanging out with the wrong kind of crowd. Do you know where I can find Keone?"

"He's probably at his cabin today."

"Where's that?"

"I don't know exactly. He's never had us over. Somewhere up in the hills above Waikapu."

"You must have some general idea where it is."

"That's as much as I know. Lefty might have an idea. He'd be in his shop now."

Mark tried to decide how much to tell Ted. "There's one other thing you should know. Someone kidnapped Sophie."

"What?"

Mark listened to the tone of his voice very carefully.

Ted sounded genuinely surprised. Either a very good actor or it was news to him.

"When I got back to my room last night she was gone."

"And you two hadn't been fighting or anything?"

Mark clenched his fist. "No. She was kidnapped. Someone left a ransom message."

"Maybe the police can find fingerprints on the note."

Mark felt better. Now he was sure that Ted wasn't involved.

"I have this little problem with the police. Thanks to your activities with Arlene, the cops won't exactly welcome me except to lock me up."

"As I said, I'll get that cleared up."

"You better."

*　*　*　*　*

Mark next drove to Lefty's shop. Spotting someone else inside, he waited until the customer left. Then he entered.

When Lefty looked up and noticed Mark, he flinched. "What are you doing here?"

"I have a few things to discuss with you."

"Well, I don't want to talk to you. You've caused me enough shit already."

"Me get you in trouble?" Mark slammed his fist on the counter. "It seems like your drug dealings have caused me endless grief. Your friends set me up, and the police are after me."

"Turn yourself in. We'll both be safer with you in police custody."

"Is that so? It happens that I don't want to be held in jail. I didn't do anything, and you, for one, know it. I want you to help clear my name."

"I can't do that. They'll kill me."

"Maybe I'll do the task for them." Mark pulled out Homer's gun and pointed it at Lefty. "I want some straight answers."

Lefty's swollen eyes bulged.

"First, what do you know about the kidnapping of my wife?"

Lefty's bruised forehead wrinkled. "Kidnapping?"

"Yes, while your friends were setting me up, someone kidnapped Sophie. I know it wasn't you because you were at Valley Island Realtors doing your little deal, but maybe some of your friends were involved."

"They don't go in for that." A drop of sweat fell from Lefty's forehead. "Kidnapping causes too much of the wrong kind of attention. But they're not above killing people who cross them."

"Any other ideas?"

Lefty shook his head. "No. I don't have a clue."

"One other thing. How do I find Keone?"

"He's probably at his cabin."

"Why don't you give me directions?"

Lefty mopped his forehead with the back of his wrist. "I've never been there. Keone never invited me."

"How come both you and Ted are such good friends of Keone's, but neither of you has ever been to his place?"

"You have to understand Keone. He's a loner. No one goes

to his cabin. All I know is it's somewhere in the hills above Waikapu."

"Good. You're coming with me to show me the approximate location."

"I can't leave the shop."

"Yes you can." Mark went to the front door and turned the sign so "Closed" faced outward. He waved the gun at Lefty. "Let's get in your car. You drive, and I'll sit in the back seat."

Lefty scowled. Then he threw his hands in the air in resignation and marched toward the door.

* * * * *

Once they were in Lefty's aging blue Civic, he asked, "Where do you want me to go?"

"First, let's drive to the place closest to where you think Keone lives."

After a twenty-minute ride, Lefty pulled off the Hanoapi'ilani Highway onto a side street and stopped.

"This is the place I've seen him turn. That's all I know."

"Drive along here, and we'll see what we find."

After a quarter of a mile the road divided into two branches.

Lefty scratched his head. "I have no clue which way to go."

"We'll explore around. Take the road to the left first. We'll see if we can find Keone's truck."

"You can't miss that old, beat up pickup, although it looks like so many on the island."

They passed a number of small wooden houses and came to another divide in the road.

"Keep to the left," Mark commanded.

They passed a number of houses, and the road eventually dead-ended with only overgrown forest ahead.

"Go back to the last divide and we'll follow that road."

They continued to wander through the hills, but nowhere spotted Keone's truck nor any hint of him.

"Does Keone have a phone?"

"Nope. No phone line, and he doesn't have a cell phone."

"How do you contact him for pickleball games?"

"He stops by my shop regularly. That's our method of communication."

After following several more fruitless routes, Mark realized that he wasn't going to achieve anything by driving through the countless streets. "Let's head back to your shop."

"Keone always shows up within a few days. You have to be patient."

Mark slammed the heel of his hand into the back of the front seat, causing Lefty to lurch. "I don't have any patience left."

Chapter 15

When they got back to the shopping center, Mark sat for a moment in the back seat. "There's one other thing you're going to help me with."

"What's that?"

"I want to arrange a little meeting with your friends who tried to set me up last night."

"Are you crazy? You don't want to mess with those guys. I don't want to mess with those guys. That's suicide."

Mark tapped the muzzle of the gun against the back of Lefty's head. "You don't have to be involved. I only want you to help set up a meeting."

"How do you expect me to do that?"

"You must have a way to get a message to one of Oana's cohorts. Just arrange it, and I'll show up instead of you. Let's go into the shop, and you can make a phone call right now."

Lefty was sweating profusely. "They beat me up because you showed up last time. I can't get away with scheduling a meeting with you."

"I'll explain that you were under coercion. Let's go make the call. Set it up for this afternoon. A nice public place like the Kamaina Tavern."

Lefty reluctantly agreed. Inside the shop he picked up the phone, and Mark stood close by with the gun in his hand.

"I have some information for Oana," Lefty said into the phone.

"No, I can't talk now. I'll meet you in one hour at the Kamaina Tavern."

He hung up with his hand shaking.

"That was very good," Mark said. "I'll wait here with you. Then we'll both drive our cars to the bar. You can go on from there, and I'll fill in for you at the appointed time."

"Okay, but I can't keep my shop closed all day."

Mark went over and turned the sign around. "You're open for business for twenty minutes."

Mark sat in a chair at the back of the shop watching Lefty string a Yonex MP Tour-1 XF 98 tennis racquet.

Lefty didn't set the clamp right, a string slipped and he had to start over again.

The bell rang, Lefty jumped as if he had been jabbed with a red-hot poker. A customer entered the shop to buy some tennis balls. After a short discussion, the man made a selection, paid and left the shop.

Lefty returned to his stringing job.

Finally, Mark checked his watch. "Okay, time to close the shop. I'll follow you."

They both climbed in their respective cars and drove toward the Kamaina Tavern.

When they reached the parking lot, Mark pulled alongside and lowered his window. "You can go. I'll take it from here."

Lefty drove in a half circle and took off like a shot.

Mark parked next to two beat up pickup trucks. He locked his cell phone and Homer's gun in the glove compartment and entered the tavern, taking a deep breath to build his courage. He would need to use all his negotiating skills and then some for this encounter. Too bad he didn't have Kea working with him, but he wouldn't want to risk the kid being exposed to these thugs. Mark had dealt with some pretty tough people in the business world. A number were sociopaths, but they tended to force people out of business not kill them.

As he had expected, Malo, the enforcer with a scar on his cheek, and his companion were seated at the bar.

Mark gave a casual wave. "Gentlemen, would you care to join me at a table?"

119

Malo looked at him. "What the hell are you doing here? You're supposed to be in jail. Where's Lefty?"

"Lefty had a little accident. I'm filling in for him."

Malo sneered. "Maybe it's time for you to have a little accident as well."

Mark clenched his teeth and stared at Malo. "Maybe Oana wouldn't be too happy if you failed to let him know that his business is going to be seriously disrupted."

Mark walked over to a table and sat down.

Shortly, the two men joined him.

"What kind of shit are you trying to pull?" Malo asked.

"I think this is important enough that Oana will want to hear it directly."

Malo slammed his fist onto the table. "Oana doesn't meet with people like you. You're nobody."

"Well, this nobody escaped from being arrested. I expect Oana won't be very pleased with an employee who doesn't prevent a serious loss to his business."

Mark turned to Malo's companion. "Be sure to let Oana know that Malo didn't want to stop a takeover of his business by a mainland syndicate."

"What mainland syndicate?" Malo grabbed Mark's shirt.

Mark knocked his hand away. "I'll explain it to Oana. Set up a meeting."

The two men looked at each other.

"Stay here," Malo instructed his companion. He pulled out a cell phone and walked out the door.

Mark studied the man. "You have a name?"

"Kimo."

"Your friend doesn't seem very willing to protect Oana."

Kimo leaned over the table toward Mark. "Bullshit. He's Oana's best man."

"If he doesn't act on this, he's apt to be Oana's ex-best man."

Mark hoped that he could put enough doubt in the man's mind to convince him that it was important for Oana to see Mark.

Malo stepped through the door and signaled to Kimo, who

ambled over to join him. They conferred in hushed tones, and Malo put the phone to his good cheek.

At least it's not a quick "no," Mark thought. If he could get to see Oana, he could pursue his next step. He was pretty certain Oana wasn't involved in the kidnapping, but he had to close out that possibility. The link to the murder of George Tanabe was a more realistic possibility. If he could get with the head man, he was sure he could get a reading. That was the objective: meet with Oana and stay alive.

Finally, Malo and Kimo returned.

"We're going for a ride," Malo said.

"Does that mean Oana will see me?"

"It means that we're going for a ride."

Mark's heart beat faster.

This clearly was a veiled threat, but Oana couldn't ignore the message he'd sent. He'd have to check it out first.

Mark would have to take his chances. "Your truck or my car?"

"Funny man," Malo said. "Kimo, you drive. We'll squeeze this guy between us in the cab."

They climbed in one of the pickup trucks Mark had seen before. He was firmly pinned between the two large men. He remembered a similar situation on the flight from Denver. At that time he only dealt with impolite seat companions not killers.

"One more thing." Malo reached beneath the seat and extracted a burlap bag, which he pulled over Mark's head.

"I can't breath very well," Mark said.

"Good practice for what will happen if you disappoint Oana." Malo laughed.

The truck jolted forward. From where it was parked, Mark surmised they were heading north. After fifteen minutes, the truck turned to the right, and Malo leaned into him.

He swayed back and forth during a series of turns and tried to picture a map of the island and where they might be going.

He heard passing traffic. They came to a stop for a short time. Must be a traffic light. Then a right turn. He could sense a slight incline. Must be heading up the side of Haleakela.

A series of turns and the truck started bumping over a rutted road. Several more turns, and they came to a stop.

He heard the doors open and the pressure on both sides of him disappeared.

"Time to get out."

A hand grabbed him and dragged him out of the truck's cab.

Mark stumbled but kept his balance.

A strong arm guided him, and he staggered forward.

"Up three steps."

Mark lifted his shoe tentatively and found the stair step.

The arm guided him, and he heard a door open and then close behind him.

"Sit down."

The arm thrust him down, and he struck a hard wooden chair seat.

Mark reached for the burlap bag.

A hand slapped the back of his head. "No. You keep that on. You can talk, but not see anything. Understand, *haole*?"

Mark hesitated. He felt at a distinct disadvantage not being able to make eye contact with Oana. This was not the situation he had envisioned. He took a breath, stifled by the burlap bag. Dust in the material caused him to cough. He cleared his throat. "Thanks for the opportunity to meet with you. How do you want me to address you?"

"You can call me Oana. Why the insistence on this gathering, Mr. Yeager?"

The voice was calm and cultured with no hint of local accent. Mark pictured an art curator in his fifties or a college professor wearing a bow tie.

"Oana, as I'm sure your associates have informed you, I've had several encounters with them."

"Yes. They aren't exactly fans of yours. You seem to have a knack of rubbing people the wrong way, Mr. Yeager."

"Through a variety of circumstances, I've witnessed the results of a murder, and my wife has been kidnapped."

"Kidnapped?"

Mark listened carefully. He detected a genuine tone of surprise.

"I don't think your people are involved in the kidnapping, but thought you might have heard something about it."

Oana laughed. "Mr. Yeager, kidnapping is a federal offense. I can assure you that my associates wouldn't be involved in such activities. I do find it humorous that you would come to me seeking assistance."

"I'm checking out all the possibilities. Since you are well-connected on this island, it seems logical that you might have picked up some hints about the kidnapping. I'm trying to follow any leads I can."

"I appreciate the backhanded compliment, but this is news to me. You'll have to take care of it on your own."

"What about the murder of George Tanabe?"

"George was a man who flirted with death. He probably became involved in a transaction he shouldn't have... enough chitchat. You're reported to have some information for me."

Mark had learned everything he was going to. He needed to make a graceful exit and stay alive.

"I picked up a report that a syndicate from the mainland was getting ready to move into Maui. I thought it was important that you receive this news."

"I've heard those rumors for years. Nothing new. I was anticipating that you had something specific for me."

Mark expected that if he could see, Oana would be glaring at Malo.

"That's as much information as I have," Mark said. "You can check it out through your other sources."

Oana's tone changed. "I don't appreciate having my time wasted." Mark heard the sound of fingers snapping. "Show Mr. Yeager the view from the cliff."

"Right boss," came the eager reply from Mark's right side.

A hand grabbed his shoulder and spun him around. He received a shove and stumbled forward. The hand roughly guided him down the stairs and back into the pickup truck.

Once again pinned between the two large men, Mark asked,

"What's the view from the cliff?"

"It's a surprise," Malo's deep voice answered.

Mark shivered. This wasn't turning out the way he wanted it to.

After what he estimated to be a forty-minute drive with numerous twists and turns, ending with a ride over a bumpy road, they came to a stop. The burlap bag came off his head, and Mark blinked at the unaccustomed sunlight. They were at the end of a dirt road on a cliff overlooking the ocean. Waves crashed over jagged rocks.

"This is a place few tourists get to see. Out of the way. Not even many *kama'ainas* come here. Too many sharks."

After they got out, the two men reached in the back of the pickup and extracted automatic rifles from under a blanket.

Malo motioned. "Walk out to the point."

Mark stumbled forward, coming to the edge. He peered down to see waves crashing into the base of the cliff thirty feet below. He was right over rugged water. It reminded him of the cliff divers in Acapulco. Someone could sail right off and land in the water. He flinched. His dream on the flight to Maui. A premonition? A small cove was bounded by a rock outcrop across a short stretch of foaming ocean. Turning away from the ocean, he saw that the ridge he stood on was separated from another ridge by a gully that led to the outcrop. Inland, both ridges met in overgrowth a half mile away.

Out of the corner of his eye he saw the two men had not moved. They were checking their weapons. He had to delay them.

He took two steps toward them. "Hey, guys. This isn't a smart thing to do."

Malo punched his companion in the shoulder. "Hey, Kimo, did you hear what the *haole* said. This isn't a smart thing to do."

They both burst into laughter giving each other a high five with their free hands.

In a split second, Mark knew what he had to do. With his heart beating wildly, he pivoted and ran toward the edge of the cliff. He leaped out as far as he could.

As he approached the water, he took a deep breath and heard from above a surprised, "Shit!"

Chapter 16

M ark hit the water feet first and shot downward. It was a good thing he had been snorkeling and practicing holding his breath. When his momentum stopped, he pulled himself to the surface pushed his mouth out of the water far enough to gulp in a lungful of air. He began swimming as fast as he could. A wave slapped his face. He eyed where the waves hammered the cliff and stroked away so as not to be dashed into the rocks.

The sound of automatic fire rattled from above.

He ducked under the water again and gave several long arm pulls to gain purchase and to move away from his attackers. Surfacing again, he took in a breath of air and re-submerged. He continued this pattern for several minutes until he came up and spotted the rock outcrop nearby. This would provide a barrier from the shooters. After he swam behind it, the surf buffeted him. A wave smacked the rock outcrop sending a plume of spray shooting skyward. The turbulent ocean rocked him, like a leaf caught in a maelstrom. Good thing he was in shape from the swims he had taken on this disastrous vacation.

He bobbed his head out of the sea and spotted three fins protruding from the water. Malo hadn't been kidding about sharks. He tried to find a place to climb on the rocks, but the surf was too rough and the rocks too shear. He continued to swim around the small peninsula until he found a place he could hold onto. Grasping for the rock, a wave knocked him forward gashing his elbow and spewing blood into the ocean. Not good with sharks in the area. He had to get out of the water.

A fin moved toward him. Another wave jolted him, lifting

him onto the rock. He grabbed hold, barely clinging to a small handhold. He reached upward, and another wave hit.

Almost losing his grip, he lunged as hard as he could for another small protrusion. He inched upward until he was out of the surf.

After resting momentarily to catch his breath, he clambered up to the top of the rock. As he raised his head, bullets began to strike the rocks around him. He ducked back down behind the crest.

He'd have to climb along the side away from the shooters.

He surveyed the ocean along the point. Fins were circling five feet away. Not worth risking getting back in the water. He'd have to work his way as best he could along the side of the rocks, high enough to not get washed away, but low enough to avoid being a target for the men on the next ridge.

Right now he was not in the line of sight of his attackers. He took several deep breaths. Then it struck him again. The dream on the plane. Not identical to this situation but close enough. He shivered, and it wasn't from being wet.

Hand over hand, he slid and grasped along the rocks toward the coastline. If he could get a little farther, there was undergrowth to hide in.

To his dismay, he saw an opening in the rocks. A stretch of gravelly beach separated him from the safety of the trees.

He ventured a glance toward the ridge. The men would have a clear shot at him if he went out there. His only hope—they were too far away to shoot accurately.

It was starting to get dark so he waited. His hands hurt from holding onto the rough lava rock. His elbow wound had coagulated into a reddish brown. He shivered, not from cold, but from the tension of his predicament.

As night surrounded him, he ventured out and started across the stretch of sand. Halfway there, the nearly full moon burst through an opening in the clouds. He froze. Then he ran.

A burst of bullets ricocheted off the gravel, and he plunged head first into the undergrowth. He landed hard, hitting his chin on a protruding root. Pulling himself up, he scrambled farther into the trees. It was a tropical jungle. He proceeded far enough so that he was sure bullets couldn't reach him. It would be impossible for anyone to find him in the dense tree cover and tangled vines.

He sat down on a rock to assess his situation. Good thing there were no snakes and poison ivy in Hawaii. He'd have to wait out the night, but he had to get back to Kihei. There was a meeting with a kidnapper to keep the following night. He had to be there.

Who could have kidnapped Sophie? He ran scenarios through his mind. One of his pickleball buddies? Possible but it couldn't have been Lefty. He didn't think it had been Ted, and he hadn't been able to locate Keone yet. Someone associated with George's murder who had been following him and put a nail in his tire? Could be, but who was that person? Someone connected with Oana? The crime gang definitely tended toward murder rather than kidnapping. Nothing fell into place.

The darkness now protected him from Malo and Kimo, but eventually he would need some daylight so he could make his way out of this jungle. Caught between the devil and the deep blue sea, so to speak.

Rain started to fall. That's what kept this island so green. Didn't help when you were out in the forest though. He huddled against the trunk of a hala tree to gain some protection from the downpour.

After twenty minutes the rain stopped. These tropical showers. They came and went.

Mark pushed farther into the undergrowth for several hours until exhaustion overcame him. When he had traveled far enough to prevent his attackers from finding him, he hunkered down to catch his breath. Good thing it was warm here. To be out at night and lost in a cold climate would be a disaster.

He had to try to make a little more progress, although it was difficult in the dark. He continued by heading uphill. A dark shape emerged to the edge of his vision ahead. In his imagination, he thought it resembled a house, but as he approached he saw it was a well-organized pile of rocks. Then it struck him. A *heiau*. He skirted the side and came to a cliff face with a cave entrance. His first thought was this would provide shelter for the night. He heard scurrying sounds through the vines. That couldn't be *Menehunes*. His imagination was running wild. After the story Kea had told, he had no desire to go into the cave. He continued his journey.

It began to rain again. Although soaked, he could stand it given the warm air temperature. Drops cascaded down his face. He wiped them away with the back of his hand. He squished through puddles that accumulated on the jungle floor. The only consolation was that while it rained, the mosquitoes didn't bother him. What a mess he must look like. He stepped on a large ti leaf, almost slipping. *Take it easy.* He heard a snapping sound in the brush ahead. He came to an abrupt halt. A shape dashed in front of him, missing by inches. In the ambient light he caught the sight of a tusk—a wild boar. That's all he needed. To be impaled by a pig.

After another hour of pushing aside branches and vines, too tired to continue and unsure if he was making progress or not, he selected a spot where he could pat down vines and leaves to make a bed. He sat down but something hard poked into the back of his thigh. He ran his hand through the cover of leaves and picked up a round object. Although he couldn't see it well, he fingered the object. A kukui nut. He wiped it on his shirt and wondered if he could polish it to a sheen similar to Kea's kukui nut necklaces. What the heck. He put it in his pocket. It could be his lucky kukui nut.

The memory of the movie, *Castaway*, flashed into his mind. He and Sophie had seen it when it first came out. The character Chuck Noland, played by Tom Hanks, had adopted a volleyball, called it Wilson and had spoken to it. Mark could do the same; he'd live off the land, call his kukui nut, Kui, and tell it all his woes. What a minute. He had been off on his own for only a few hours, not stranded on a deserted island for months. *Get a grip.* Besides, he had to find his way out of here and deal with the kidnapper the next night.

Swatting mosquitoes, he listened to the faint sound of waves crash into the distant rocks below and settled down to the buzzing of flying insects. Every time he almost squirmed into a comfortable position, images of Sophie being tied up somewhere flashed through his mind. The kidnapping was his fault. He couldn't be sure, but he had made an enemy on this island, and that person had taken it out on Sophie. And through his carelessness and being off playing pickleball, he had not been there to protect his wife. He had to get back for the money drop. He reviewed his priorities: stay out of reach of Oana's henchmen, work his way out of this jungle, hitch a ride back to get his car, track down the kidnapper, find Sophie. Simple as that. *Right.*

Eventually, fitful sleep overtook him.

★ ★ ★ ★ ★

At daybreak, Mark awoke, stiff, wet and covered with mosquito bites. Somewhere above him in the forest canopy he heard the cooing of a dove. He had no idea where he was or where to go, or if the two men were pursuing him or had given up. His stomach rumbled. He realized he hadn't eaten since breakfast the day before. His mouth was dry.

He remembered his kukui nut and took it out of his pocket to inspect. A dull brown, not the bright polish of Kea's necklaces. Maybe if he kept it in his pocket long enough, the cloth would shine the outer surface. He placed it back in his pocket.

Listening to the distant waves crashing, he figured if he walked in the opposite direction, he'd eventually find a road. Then he'd have to determine if anyone was waiting for him or not.

Raising his sore body, he tentatively stretched his legs. He moved uphill feeling like a walking mosquito breakfast feast.

He pushed his way through vines and shrubs for a few minutes and stopped to listen to the sound of the ocean. It was fainter now and still behind him. He pushed on.

He heard the sound of running water ahead and struggled through a thick clump of brush to find a small stream. Dropping to the ground, he guzzled the cool water. In the mountains of Colorado, he'd worry about Giardia, but he wouldn't concern himself with that here.

When he raised himself and wiped the water off his mouth, he listened again to the barely perceptible sound of ocean waves in the distance.

He moved away and up an incline. Pushing aside some branches, one snapped back and slapped him in the face. He put his hand to his cheek and found blood. After struggling through thick vines, he came to a small break in the undergrowth that overlooked a ravine.

No sign of civilization, but also no sign of the two men.

He continued up the incline, reaching a point where the tangle of vines falling from trees formed a web too thick to penetrate without a machete.

He moved laterally until he came to a break in the dense mass of growth and then resumed his upward progress. A variety of birdcalls punctuated the morning stillness. A rustling in the brush. He froze.

Scurrying sounds and a small rodent shot in front of him. Maybe a mongoose. Like the time camping as a boy when a squirrel had tried to raid his tent.

Moving forward, he came upon a slight indentation in tall grass between shrubs. It could have been a hiking trail or an animal path. He decided to follow it.

The ground leveled out so it was necessary to pay close attention to the direction he traveled. Abruptly, the trail disappeared. One moment it was there, and then he couldn't find it anymore. He sighted a tree ahead and lined up another tree in approximately the same direction. He wasn't sure if he was moving away from the ocean because he could no longer hear the sound of waves.

Coming to another impossible tangle of vines, he headed to the side in a vain attempt to find an easy opening in the undergrowth. He pushed through plants up to eye level and suddenly emerged into a clearing. After traipsing through the jungle, this area seemed like an oasis, a square of approximately a hundred feet on a side.

He looked more carefully. Plants grew in rows in the middle of the clearing. He strolled into the open space and inspected a plant. *Uh-oh.* Pointy leaves. Marijuana.

Chapter 17

Mark heard sounds on the opposite side of the clearing, and a man emerged from the jungle, holding a shotgun. He wore a ragged straw hat, old dungarees and work boots.

"What are you doing in my patch?"

"I'm lost. Trying to find the road."

The man raised his shotgun. "Damn poacher. I'm not going to let you steal my crop."

"I don't want it."

"I can kill you now or let you die the hard way. Then you'll never let anyone know where I've planted."

"Since I have no idea where I am, I can't tell anyone where it is."

The man glared at Mark from a dirty face with equally dirty black and gray beard. "Especially if no one ever finds you."

Mark blinked as sunlight glared off the barrel of the shotgun. He considered running into the jungle, but this guy could shoot him in the back before he made it into cover.

The man reached behind his back and extracted a coil of rope from a backpack. He pointed the shotgun toward the trees to Mark's left.

"Walk that way."

Mark complied.

"Straight ahead."

Mark parted the brush and stumbled forward, feeling the shotgun against his back.

"Turn right."

Mark staggered in the direction indicated, again parting foliage to make a path.

"Stop," the man commanded. "Put your hands behind your back."

He proceeded to tie Mark's hands.

"Sit down against that tree."

Mark tried to lower himself, but the man shoved him down. Mark struck the ground, and pain shot through his tailbone.

"Back against the tree."

The man took the rope and wrapped it tightly around the tree so that Mark was thoroughly bound and unable to move.

"You'll make a good snack for the mongooses." He laughed.

With that he disappeared into the undergrowth.

Mark struggled, but his hands and arms were immobile. The one positive—the man hadn't shot him. How was he going to get out of this rope, and when he did, what direction was the road? He had to get back to Kihei to keep the appointment with the kidnapper.

He moved his body from side to side to see if there was any slack in the rope. Nothing. He struggled until he exhausted himself and then sat still, breathing heavily.

His lucky kukui nut certainly wasn't doing its job. *Think.* There had to be a way to get out of this. He tried lifting himself up. He detected a small amount of give in the rope. He lowered himself down as low as he could go. Again, a small amount of movement. His hands touched the ground. He tried scooting down farther. His fingers brushed a rock. He tried moving the rock. It was imbedded in the ground. He dug into the moist soil. A fingernail broke. He continued digging, trying to get a grip on the rock. It moved slightly. He thrust his fingers into the dirt, tearing another nail.

Sweating profusely, he pushed his left palm against the rock. It budged. He gripped it and wiggled. Ever so slowly it came loose from the earth. He moved it around in his hand. Smooth on one side, but jagged on the other end. He positioned it so that he could rub the jagged edge against the rope binding his wrists. He began to work it back and forth.

His hand cramped and he dropped the rock. Breathing heavily, he ran his fingers along the ground as far as he could reach until he located it again.

He rested before resuming the task of cutting the rope. When his hands cramped again, he stopped in time so as not to drop the rock. He waited until the cramp disappeared. Then back to scraping the rope.

The morning progressed. Mark knew he didn't have much time if he was going to get untied, find his way out of the jungle and somehow get back to Kihei to prepare for the encounter with the kidnapper.

He licked his dry lips and tasted salt evaporated from the perspiration dripping from his forehead. Bugs kept getting stuck on his face. His cheek itched, but he couldn't do anything but suffer.

Taking a deep breath, he resumed scraping the rock against the rope. As he cut through strands of the tough rope with the jagged rock, he could periodically feel the rope give a millimeter.

Finally, he was down to one last strand. He heard a final "snap" and the pressure on his wrists loosened.

Although his hands were still bound, he was able to reach one end of the frayed strand of rope with his fingers. With a slight tug, a loop of rope came free. Then another loop. His hands were free, but he remained connected to the tree.

He wiggled and felt a small amount of give. With his hands he pulled at part of the coil and was able to release some rope from around the tree. Then it got stuck.

Sliding back and forth he was able to free the tangle. Moments later he had enough slack to wriggle out of the remaining loops of rope.

He stood up stiffly and shook his arms. Opening and closing his hands, he worked the circulation back into his numb fingers.

For the first time he took in where he was. Trees everywhere, no sunlight, no indication of which direction led away from the ocean. He heard a bird call and listened after the caw died away for any sounds of waves crashing. Too far away.

He had no clue which direction to try. No time to lose. He found a small indentation in the undergrowth. Maybe that was the way he and his captor had come. Should he go that way or avoid it? He decided to take his chances in that direction. Pushing through the undergrowth he immediately lost any sign of where he had come from.

Mark had the sudden image of being stranded here and never finding his way out. His gut clenched, and his throat tightened. He couldn't allow negative thinking. He had to persevere and get himself out of this situation. He remembered the haiku poem Homer had told him. Resilience. He took another deep breath and allowed his heartbeat to slow. *Onward.*

He pulled vines aside and kept moving through the undergrowth, finding himself going downhill. He retraced his steps.

The ground leveled off again.

Mark picked what appeared to be a continuation of the uphill direction, looked back for a landmark and then sighted a tree ahead. Once he reached this tree, he lined up another using the previous landmark. With this crude navigation approach he continued on.

He came to a rise and headed upward until the brush broke away to reveal a ravine. He resumed walking up the ridge, hoping he'd eventually have to cross some road, but having no clue how long it would take.

He parted the vines and spotted a distinct trail. His heart beat faster.

The trail grew wider and eventually turned into a four-wheel drive road. He could see the overgrown ruts once formed by vehicles. It seemed that no one had driven this route for years.

The road wound upward until Mark saw an opening ahead. Rather than continuing straight ahead, he entered the undergrowth and cautiously navigated his way alongside the trail. The clearing gave way to a paved road. It was a two-lane highway that must be the major road for this part of the island, wherever he was.

Mark again pictured a map of Maui. He had to be either on the road to Hana or on the northwest part of the island. He didn't know if he should travel left or right to get back to Kihei. He also didn't know if someone might be waiting for him around a bend.

He paused, partially hidden in the undergrowth. A passenger car raced by. Mark sat motionless on his haunches listening. Another car drove slowly past in the opposite direction. He sucked up his courage and stepped out toward the highway. He could see fifty yards in each direction before the road disappeared around bends. If he saw a pickup truck, he'd duck back into the bushes.

An old black clunker rounded the bend from the left. Mark thrust out his thumb. The car slowed, the driver made eye contact and then sped up.

Mark looked down at his wrinkled shirt and blood stained elbow. He reached up and ran his hand through his disheveled hair. He must look like the hitchhiker from hell.

Returning to the undergrowth, he pulled a wet ti leaf out of the ground to wipe the dried blood off his arm and face. He smoothed out his shirt as best he could and put some jungle moisture on his hair to tame it and on his face to give it a spit polish.

He was ready to face the traffic again. A car drove past every few minutes, but for fifteen minutes none gave an indication of stopping. No signs of Oana's thugs. Eventually, an aging blue Chevrolet Cavalier coming from the right pulled to a stop. Looked like his rental car.

"Where you going?" a middle aged man in a baseball cap asked.

"I need to get to Kihei."

"You'll have a long walk if you come with me. I'm headed to Hana."

"Thanks anyway."

Mark now knew he was on the Hana Road and needed to head to the right. He only put his thumb out for cars going that direction. The sporadic traffic yielded no results until a white Toyota Camry jerked to a stop.

"Hop in," a young man said.

Mark climbed in and asked, "Are you going anywhere near Kihei?"

"No. But I can take you as far as Kahului."

"That would be helpful."

Mark realized he could go to Homer's office in Kahului to get some assistance.

"Don't see many hitchhikers along here," the man said.

"I was hiking and got lost."

The man glanced sideways at Mark. "You should be better prepared when hiking around here. I was visiting my brother in Hana. Great hiking trails there."

"I'll have to try it some time." Mark gave a feeble smile.

He was dropped off three blocks from Homer's office and walked the rest of the way.

Homer was working at his desk and waved Mark in. "What happened to you? You're a mess."

"Oana's enforcers tried to kill me. I jumped off a cliff, swam with the sharks and ducked some bullets. But I couldn't escape the mosquitoes and branches."

"Clean yourself up in the bathroom."

Mark went in the restroom, looked in the mirror and recoiled in disgust. He was lucky the one driver had picked him up. There's no way Mark would have given a ride to someone who looked like a crazed jungle escapee. He splashed water on his face, wiped off blood and moisture with a paper towel and declared himself as presentable as he was going to get.

He noted that Homer hadn't mentioned the missing gun. If he hadn't noticed that it was gone yet, then when he did, he wouldn't be able to connect it with Mark. He ran his fingers through his hair as a makeshift comb and returned to Homer's office.

Homer slipped a sheet of paper into a manila folder and dropped it onto the desk. "I had a phone call from Detective Puna Pa'a. You became the subject of a major rant."

"What'd you tell him?"

"I mentioned I had suggested to you turning yourself in. He laughed and said he'd have you locked up within days."

"As long as I can stay free until I get Sophie back. Tonight, I'll contact the kidnapper."

"And about the kidnapping. I assured the good detective you had not abducted your wife—"

"And?"

"He thinks it's a diversionary stunt you've pulled to take attention away from your other crimes. He still has those charges against you for murder and fraud. He's not letting up on you one iota."

"Good grief. He's not taking the kidnapping seriously."

"I'm afraid not. But he will look for Sophie. He thinks that's the way he'll find you."

Mark put his hands to his head. On top of his other discomfort, a raging headache pulsed through his forehead. He had to find Sophie, and his attempt to have Homer contact Puna had only backfired.

"Don't look so glum. We'll get this cleared up, and you can get back to windsurfing."

Mark returned his gaze to Homer. "It's going to be a long time before I have the freedom for that. I have to get back to my car. It's at the Kamaina Tavern between Kihei and Wailea."

Homer looked at his watch. "I'll have my admin, Andrea, give you a ride. It's lunch time, and she can take a little longer break than usual."

Andrea led Mark to her car, but before they had gone a half mile, Mark insisted that they stop to get something to eat. He treated her to a sandwich and ravenously ate two cheeseburgers, fries and a milk shake before they continued on toward Kihei.

On the drive, she discussed the six months she had worked for Homer after finishing high school.

"You plan to go to college?"

Her dark eyes shone. "Yeah, after working for Mr. Nagano I want to become a paralegal. I like assisting people with their legal problems."

Mark only hoped Homer could help him with his long list of crime accusations.

When they reached the Kamaina Tavern, Mark was relieved that his car remained where he left it. He thanked Andrea and waved to her as she drove away. It was only when she was out of sight that he turned toward the car. His heart sank. All four tires were as flat as squished mangos.

Chapter 18

Upon closer inspection, Mark discovered that someone had slashed the tires on his car. Not merely a few puncture holes but as if someone had been on a rampage to shred rubber. Oana's boys made sure that he didn't have transportation. He looked wildly around. No one appeared to be waiting for him.

He quickly unlocked the car and glove compartment and retrieved his cell phone and Homer's gun, which he tucked in his belt and covered with his shirt. He couldn't exchange the car at the rental agency; the police would be watching for that. He didn't want to risk using Sophie's credit card again, and he lacked enough cash to buy tires. Besides, someone might get suspicious if he were to buy tires for a rental car. His first priority was to give the appearance of dropping off a bag of money for the kidnapper that night. He'd have to walk the five miles to his hotel.

He kept an eye out for police cars, but didn't see one until he reached the hotel. He immediately recognized the car. It was the one he had ridden in before, driven by Akahi, Detective Puna Pa'a's assistant.

Mark crossed the street and entered the lobby of another small hotel. The receptionist smiled at him and returned to her work. He sat down facing the front window so he could watch. Akahi and the manager came out of the lobby and walked along the building to the unit Mark had occupied. The manager opened the door, and Akahi went in.

Mark snorted in disgust. His options were even further limited. No transportation and no place to stay. He'd have to avoid his room. The idea of a shower and nap had seemed so appealing.

He waited until Akahi drove off, sure that the manager was under instructions to call as soon as Mark showed up. He'd have to get his shower and nap another way.

Walking toward the ocean, he found the Kamaole Beach Park. He ducked into the restroom and found a shower and the remains of a bar of soap. He waited until he had the place to himself, pulled several brown sheets from the paper towel dispenser, wrapped these around the gun, wallet and cell phone and hid the bundle in a corner. Then he stripped, washed himself and scrubbed his jeans, shirt and underwear.

After wringing out his clothes, he put them back on, retrieved his valuables including his lucky or unlucky kukui nut and located a sunny, grassy spot, not visible from the parking area. He lay down to rest and dry his clothes. What a predicament he had got himself into. His wife had been kidnapped, the police sought him for a whole laundry list of crimes, and the local crime syndicate wanted him dead. On top of this he had no car and no place to stay. Other than that, all was fine in paradise. In spite of his trouble, the exertion and tension of the last day made his body heavy. He closed his eyes.

★ ★ ★ ★ ★

Mark awoke with a start and sat up. The sun was intersecting the horizon. His clothes were still damp, but not soaking as before.

Stretching his stiff limbs, he ambled over to the Rainbow Mall to purchase an early dinner of a rice plate with teriyaki steak. He chugged a cup of iced tea and settled in to finish his meal.

After it was dark, he returned to the park. There were several families roasting hamburgers and hot dogs on hibachis. The aroma tickled his nose. Good thing he'd had dinner. He found a spot to sit, leaning against a coconut tree and watched a group of kids have a flashlight war, their beams darting back and forth across the grass.

Sophie. A pang surged through his chest. He had to make

142

this one chance work with the kidnapper. The police might be looking for her, but he had no confidence they were trying very hard, and the odds were they weren't going to save her. It was up to Mark to do that.

He checked his watch. He'd head to the Kihei Boat Landing at nine o'clock.

* * * * *

He raided a dumpster and found a large plastic bag of trash. He carried this with him to the boat landing. To anyone watching, he would appear to be a homeless man carrying his possessions in a plastic bag.

At his destination, he made a complete turn to check for any suspicious looking people. He didn't pick up any signs of the kidnapper but threw the trash bag in the designated dumpster just in case the kidnapper was watching. He walked up the road, then cut back through the undergrowth to a place he had previously found with an unobstructed view of the dumpster. He sat down and surveyed the scene. Two cars were parked near the water. No one appeared to be in either.

Around ten forty-five a pickup truck drove by, circled around and left. Mark squinted but couldn't discern the color or any distinct features of the vehicle.

Mosquitoes continued to feast on his neck. He swatted again and shifted his position to try to get comfortable. He had no idea how long he would have to wait.

He checked his watch periodically. Eleven came and went. Nothing.

He shifted his stiff legs and hunkered down for a long night. He was a bright guy. He should be able to figure out who the kidnapper was. *Think*. He reviewed what had happened. He could eliminate Oana and his gang as suspects, given the timing of his encounter with them. Likewise, he had followed Lefty, and Lefty had been preoccupied with Oana's thugs. What about Ted? Possible, but not likely. He had been cleaning up after the pickleball game and would have been hard pressed to get to the hotel to kidnap Sophie before Mark showed up.

Then it clicked. He remembered the broken vane on the windmill in his room. Sophie had sent him a message. He slapped his forehead. So simple. Quixote. Keone. They had joked about the similarity of names.

And how squirrelly Keone had acted. And the questions regarding how much money Mark had. And Keone had left first after the pickleball game. He would have had adequate time to get to the hotel and kidnap Sophie. He punched his right fist into his left hand. Of course. It made sense in a weird sort of way.

He didn't think Keone was a killer. The guy must have needed money for some reason and resorted to kidnapping. He could only hope that while being held hostage, Sophie had not been hurt or assaulted. His gut clenched. He had to believe that.

At eleven fifteen a pickup truck entered the parking area. Mark looked closely. It could have been the same one he saw earlier. It slowly circled the lot and pulled up next to the dumpster. The engine stopped and the lights went out.

The hair on the back of Mark's neck stood on edge. He reached in the waistband of his jeans and removed the gun, nervously gripping it in his right hand.

The truck door opened, and a man got out. The light in the cab showed no passengers. The man approached the dumpster and opened the lid.

The squeak caused Mark to flinch.

With the dumpster uncovered, the man leaned over to peer inside.

Mark made his move. He emerged from the undergrowth and crept up on the man who was intent on examining the contents of the dumpster.

"Hold it right there," Mark said in a steady voice. "I have a gun pointed at you."

The man extracted himself from the dumpster.

Mark gave a clipped order. "Turn around, Keone."

The faint reflected light outlined his goatee.

144

"How'd you know it was me?"

"Process of elimination. Where's my wife?"

A look of terror appeared on Keone's face.

Mark waved the gun at him. "I want some answers. Now."

Chapter 19

Keone visibly slumped. "Your wife's at my cabin."

Mark brandished the gun. "She better be unharmed or I'll kill you."

"Sh-she is."

"You're going to take me there. Get in." Mark motioned at the pickup truck as he edged toward the passenger side, not taking his eye or the gun off Keone.

Keone slowly reached for the door handle. "Stay cool."

They both got in the cab of the truck.

"As I said, if you want to live, I better find my wife in good shape. Understand?"

A bead of sweat glistened in the dim light on Keone's forehead as he started the engine. "Yeah."

Mark kept the gun pointed at him. "Why'd you do it?"

Keone rested his head on the steering wheel for a moment and mumbled, "I needed money and thought you could afford it."

"You're going to need a lot more than money. Let's get going."

Keone put the truck in gear, and they lurched from the waterfront, shortly reaching the main road. Then after driving twenty minutes, he turned onto a side street.

Mark watched intently as they passed through the area he and Lefty had unsuccessfully explored days earlier. After several twists and turns, Keone pulled up in front of a cabin set back off the road, not easily visible.

Mark reached for the passenger side door handle. "Let's get out. You open the cabin. I'll be right behind you. No sudden moves."

146

Keone followed the instructions and once the door was open, lit a hurricane lamp.

Sophie sat in a chair with her hands and feet bound and a handkerchief over her mouth.

Mark brandished the gun. "Untie her."

Keone fiddled with the ropes and in a minute freed her feet and hands. Sophie removed the handkerchief.

"Mark," Sophie shouted and limped over to give him a hug.

He clasped her fiercely. "I was so worried about you."

Momentarily distracted, Mark heard running footsteps. He raised his gaze to see Keone rush out the door.

Mark released Sophie. "Stay here." Then he raced off in pursuit.

Outside the cabin, Mark scanned the truck and nearby woods. *Where could he have gone?*

A twig snapped.

Mark twisted to the side and caught a glimpse of motion.

Keone had disappeared into the forest.

Mark fired a shot into the air. Thrashing sounds reverberated from within the woods followed by a scream and a thud.

Mark returned to the cabin.

Sophie sat on a chair shivering. "I heard a shot. Did you kill him?"

"No. It was a warning shot in the air. He ran into the woods, and something happened. I need to find a flashlight."

"Try over there." Sophie pointed to the small kitchen.

Mark rummaged through drawers and cupboards until he found a flashlight. It gave off a dull glow. "Wait for me again. I'll go check where he went."

Mark located the point where he had seen Keone enter the undergrowth. Following a faint trail, Mark proceeded into the woods.

The flashlight illuminated a small indentation in the tall grass between the trees. He spotted several broken twigs.

Running the beam back and forth, Mark followed the trail of crushed grass stalks.

147

Abruptly, he came upon a clearing. Shining the light ahead, the beam disappeared into darkness. Cautiously, he inched forward pointing the light at the ground. In two steps the light no longer reflected on dirt. He was standing at the edge of a cliff.

His shoe brushed some dislodged rocks, which tumbled down and reverberated along the face of the cliff.

He pointed the beam down and saw rocks giving way to level ground fifty feet below. Peering more carefully, he spotted a human form with splayed limbs at the base of the rocks.

Mark searched along the side of the clearing and found a place where he could climb down. When he reached the bottom, he found Keone's body. His head was crushed on one side, and his neck lolled awkwardly. There would be no more pickleball for Keone.

Mark might never learn more to understand the motives of this strange young man. The important thing—Sophie was safe.

He climbed back up, retraced the path he had taken into the woods and emerged by the cabin. He took several deep breaths to calm his rapid heartbeat and entered the cabin.

Sophie jerked her head up from where she sat in the chair. "What happened?"

"It's over. Keone fell off a cliff and is dead."

Her face hardened. "He deserved it. This whole thing was so unnecessary."

"Did he hurt you in any way?"

"No. That was the strange part. He actually apologized for kidnapping me. He gave me plenty of beef stick, salami, cheese and water. Not my favorite meals, but I didn't go hungry or thirsty. Still, it was an awful situation to be in. He kept me tied up in a chair whenever he went out at night."

"Did he discuss why he kidnapped you?"

Sophie nodded. "He babbled constantly of his need for money but didn't mention any details."

"How did Keone think he would get away with the kidnapping and not be caught by the police?"

"After he got the money he told me he would release me and

disappear into the jungle and live off the land." She pointed to a backpack leaning against the wall of the cabin. "He had his supplies prepared and stored there."

"Odd logic."

"Yeah, he really wanted you to leave him the money. He kept asking if you'd get the cash and follow the instructions he'd given you. I said of course you would."

"I wasn't going to let him get away with it. I had to find out where he was hiding you."

Sophie patted his hand. "Although it would have been hard for you to give up that money."

Mark's face went warm. "That's not the point. I was going to find you any way I could."

"I know."

Mark went over and looked at the backpack. "How did he kidnap you in the first place?"

"He came to the room. Identified himself as your friend and said you had left your driver's license in a drawer and had asked him to retrieve it."

"Which, of course, I didn't."

"I didn't realize that. I should have been suspicious, but I had met him before, and you had been playing pickleball with him. Unaware of his real intentions, I opened the door."

"What then?"

"He had a gun. He told me to leave quietly and I wouldn't be harmed."

"But on the way out, you broke the windmill vane to give me a hint to recognize the kidnapper's identity."

She smiled. "That was the only thing I could think of. I'm glad you picked up on it."

Mark let out a deep sigh. "It took me until tonight to put it together. I should've been quicker to get it. Then what happened?"

"He drove me up here, and I've been in this cabin ever since."

Mark hugged Sophie. "I'm so sorry you had to go through this. My main objective was to find you. Now I have to figure out how to deal with my other predicaments."

"Oh?"

"While you've been relaxing here, I've been set up on a drug charge, am wanted for George Tanabe's murder and have a fraud complaint from one of Ted's *divorcée* friends, Arlene Henrick. The Maui crime mafia is also after me."

Sophie gasped. "What are you going to do?"

"First, we need to get you back to the hotel. We'll take Keone's truck. From there you can call the police and report what happened. I have to stay in hiding until I can clear myself."

"Why don't you turn yourself in?"

"You sound like Homer. The problem is, Detective Puna Pa'a has already decided I'm guilty. I need to remain free to clear myself."

"Couldn't Homer get you out on bail?"

Mark shook his head. "With all the charges, I don't think I'll have a chance to post bail. I have to work this out on my own."

"How long do you think that will take?"

"I have no idea. I'm still searching for the motive for George's murder. That's the key. In the meantime, I'll have to avoid the police."

"I'm not going to sit around waiting for you," Sophie said. "I'll pitch in since I have the flexibility of not being wanted by the police."

Mark squeezed her hand. "That would be great. I need help, and we could be quite a team."

"If we could raise two kids through their teenage years we can handle anything."

Mark only hoped she was right. "I'll keep Keone's truck. You can get a rental car in the morning and go to an ATM to get lots of cash." He handed her back her credit card.

"You took my card?"

"Had to. Since mine was compromised early in our trip. You paid for some gasoline is all. I also raided your mad money."

"You weren't supposed to know I had that."

"Come on. How long have we been married?"

She bit her lip for a moment. "You're right. I'll get some cash after some sleep. Where are you going to stay for the rest of the night?"

"Although I'd like to continue our second honeymoon, I'm sure our room is being watched. I'll sleep in the truck somewhere and find a new hotel in the morning. We can meet at noon at the Grand Wailea."

"Once you get settled in your new hotel, maybe I'll come visit." Sophie winked.

"You'll have to make sure no one follows you."

As they drove back to the hotel, Sophie grabbed Mark's arm. "Did you see any hint that Keone would do something as crazy as stage a kidnapping?"

"He had been acting strange. He kept asking questions about our house and how much money I made. Apparently, he was sizing me up as someone who could pay a ransom for whatever reason."

"And how did you catch him?"

"I made a fake money drop and hid to wait for the kidnapper to show up. Fortunately, he hadn't really thought through the plans."

When they reached the hotel, Mark stopped to let Sophie get out and scanned the parking lot. "No sign of a police car, but I can't risk being seen here."

She kissed him. "Don't get too stiff sleeping in the truck. I'll see you at noon."

He drove off. A mile away, he found a dirt road that led into the undergrowth. He pulled in, out of sight of the main road, and turned off the engine. What a weird set of events. He let out a loud sigh of relief. Sophie was safe. Now he had a whole chain of crimes to deal with. Tomorrow.

After wriggling around, he got as comfortable as possible and soon fell asleep.

* * * * *

Mark awoke to the cawing of myna birds. His neck was stiff,

and his kukui nut had made a dent in his upper leg where he had laid on it. He considered chucking it out the window but upon further consideration decided he needed any luck he could muster. He was deep enough in the trees that he couldn't see any sunlight, but the surrounding vegetation came alive with more chirping birds and the scurrying sounds of small creatures. This was better than large ones.

He checked his wallet. He had enough cash to pay for one day in a hotel. Driving toward Kihei, he found an inexpensive place and parked several blocks away on a side street under a banyan tree. He found a coffee shop and bought a cup of coffee and two malasadas to go. Then he strolled to the hotel, checked in using a different name and paid in cash.

Once in the room, he gobbled the pastry, guzzled the coffee and took a long hot shower. Once dried and dressed, he picked up his cell phone and called Homer, who fortunately answered.

"You're in your office early today."

There was the sound of papers rustling. "Yeah. I'm getting ready for a court appearance and need to file some documents."

"Some good news. Sophie's safe."

Mark could hear a loud breath being released. "That's a relief."

"My next task—I have to clear my name."

"You've now on the top of Maui's ten most wanted list."

"Are you joking?"

"No. You've also been accused of pushing Keone off a cliff and stealing his pickup truck."

"Didn't the police believe Sophie that she was kidnapped?"

"I don't know about that. I'm only reporting what you're officially charge with as of half an hour ago."

"I need to get to the bottom of this. Obviously Detective Puna Pa'a is convinced I'm a one-man crime wave. Oana's thugs don't even have to set me up anymore. It's happening automatically."

"Here's one other tidbit for you. George Tanabe's wife was cleaning out the garage and she found a hidden packet of jewelry. She called the police. Turns out it was reported stolen by a woman staying at the Maui Queen two weeks ago."

Mark thought back to the scene that had started this fiasco, George's lifeless body lying next to the pickleball court.

"George got in over his head. In addition to drugs he must have been mixed up with someone dealing stolen jewelry. I've only been focusing on the drug connection and its relationship to Oana."

"Be careful. You've been linked to enough crimes. No sense adding jewelry theft."

Mark laughed. "Why worry about one more. After being an upstanding citizen for over fifty years, I seem to have gone bad."

"Only fifty years? I thought you were fifty-seven."

"I stole a candy bar when I was five. My mother turned my backside purple. I've never strayed since. Unfortunately, Detective Puna Pa'a wouldn't be impressed."

Homer indicated he needed to get to court and signed off.

* * * * *

Mark spent the rest of the morning trying to figure out his next move. He would strategize with Sophie over lunch, but he had to find some way to gain more understanding of the various crimes that someone else had committed. He turned on the television and watched a news report. Fortunately, no pictures or reports of him showed up. He watched an old *Love Boat* episode, only wishing he were on a cruise ship rather than being pursued by the police and the local mob.

He checked his watch and determined he could soon leave the room for the lunch engagement with Sophie. He looked forward to seeing her and hearing what she had to report. He stretched, stood and headed for the door when his cell phone rang. He paused to answer.

Sophie's voice came in a whisper, "I'm being followed."

Chapter 20

Mark plunked down in the chair by the one table in the room and picked up the sound over the phone of traffic in the background. "Sophie, you can speak up. They won't hear you. What's going on?"

"One of the hotel staff gave me a ride to the car rental. After I picked up a car, I noticed a man sitting in a vehicle across the street. When I pulled out of the parking lot, he followed me. He's been behind me ever since."

"Did you get a look at him?"

"Skinny guy; looked part Hawaiian and part Chinese. Slicked back hair."

"Sounds like Akahi, Detective Puna Pa'a's sidekick."

"I don't know if I'll be able to lose him."

"Don't worry about it. We'll have to postpone our lunch together. I can't risk getting caught by him. What happened last night when you called the police?"

"Puna himself showed up. Very intense. He asked more questions related to you than to Keone."

"I've become his favorite suspect for any crime on this island. Did he believe you when you told him Keone had been the kidnapper?"

"I don't know. I showed him the rope marks on my wrists and ankles. I described what happened and he listened attentively. Then we drove to Keone's cabin, and I showed him the chair I'd been tied to."

"And Keone?"

"I pointed to the path he had taken. After you followed him

154

and returned, it was well marked."

"Homer says I'm a suspect in Keone's death."

"What?"

"Puna thinks I pushed him off the cliff."

"That explains one of Puna's questions. He asked if you had been chasing Keone. If he believes that Keone had kidnapped me, he must think you killed Keone out of revenge."

"Homer also said that George Tanabe was involved with jewelry stolen from a woman who stayed at the Maui Queen." As he said this, an idea struck him. "You could help by getting some background information about that theft."

"Doing what?"

Mark tapped a ragged tattoo with his fingers on the table. "You report some jewelry missing. Speak to the hotel manager. Say you've heard that this had happened before. See what he says."

There was a silence on the phone. "I could hide my diamond and ruby necklace and report it missing."

"Do that when you get back to the hotel. See what you can learn."

"And what are your plans?"

"I think I'll make a call on George's widow again."

"What is it with you and Ted Franklin? All these divorcées and widows."

Mark rubbed his chin. "That's another path we need to pursue since I've been blamed for Ted's actions. Why don't you strike up an acquaintance with Arlene Henrick. See what she has to say about Ted."

"Well at least you're not volunteering to talk to the *divorcée*."

Mark stepped over and peeked through the curtain. No police in sight. "I'm not very popular with her at the moment. She wants me locked up."

"I'll see what I can find out."

"And I'm also going to have a conversation with Ted. Should be able to catch him at the tennis court or at the Reinholt estate. I better get started. Let's talk this evening. I love you."

155

"I love you too. Let's get this resolved quickly. I don't like telephone romances."

★ ★ ★ ★ ★

After hitting the disconnect button on his phone, Mark looked through the curtains again to make sure the coast was clear, left the motel, walked the two blocks to Keone's truck and drove to Muriel Tanabe's house. There was no answer to his knock. Disappointed, he returned to the truck and headed south. He checked the gas gauge. Keone had been kind enough to have a three-quarters full tank. Next stop the tennis courts.

Ted didn't appear to be there so Mark strolled into the office and found a young man in tennis whites sitting at a desk.

"Ted around?" Mark asked.

"No. He's taking the rest of the day off. I'm filling in for him."

Mark resisted the urge to ask if this guy played pickleball. "Any idea where he'd be?"

"Probably at his place."

★ ★ ★ ★ ★

When Mark returned to the truck, he considered the time he was wasting. He'd try the Reinholt estate before giving up for the day. And each time he drove around in Keone's truck, he risked the police spotting him. One thing in his favor—Oana's gang didn't know what he was driving. And there were a lot of beat up brown pickup trucks on Maui.

At the Reinhold home, the gate was locked. Mark pulled the truck over against the stone wall, partially blocking the narrow road. He lowered himself out of the cab and ambled over to push the button on the speaker box.

A voice crackled with static, "Yes?"

"Ted, this is Mark Yeager. I need to talk to you."

There was a pause. "Okay. I'll open the gate."

Mark jumped back in the truck, and once the gate had slid far enough, drove into the driveway."

Ted strolled out of the bungalow.

"Why are you driving Keone's truck?"

"I borrowed it. Have you heard about Keone?"

"Lefty called and said there had been some kind of accident."

"Not exactly. He kidnapped my wife, and after I caught him, he ran away and fell off a cliff."

Ted's eyes widened. "What?"

Mark watched the gate close. "I need some information."

Ted looked from side to side. "I don't have too much time. I'm meeting someone in half an hour."

"This won't take long. There are a few things I don't understand that maybe you can clear up."

Ted gave him a blank look. "I'll help if I can."

"First, about Keone kidnapping my wife. That's a major crime. Do you know if he's been in trouble with the police before?"

Ted looked thoughtful. "No. He's always been a loner, but no crime-related problems I'm aware of."

"Seems like a big step from no trouble to kidnapping. Money problems?"

"Keone kept running short of cash. His only possessions consisted of the cabin and the truck." Ted pointed to the beat up pickup.

"Could he have gotten into serious debt recently?"

Ted paused. "That's possible. Several weeks ago he bragged that he had come across a big opportunity. He did like to gamble when he had some money."

"Did he discuss this opportunity with you?"

"No. He tried to borrow money from me, but I refused. He also hit up Lefty and George, but they knew it was pointless to loan Keone money. He didn't have many other friends, and he never mentioned if he found a source of money."

"And the gambling. How extensive was that?"

"He liked to bet on sports teams."

"How does that work on Maui?"

"It's easy. There's a bookie in Kahului. Lays bets off through a connection in Las Vegas. I've even placed a few."

"Where would I find this guy?"

Ted stared at Mark. "Actually it's a woman, Ginger Fong, who runs a bar called The Lost Castaway. Off Kaahumanu Avenue on Kane Street."

"So Keone must have thought he had a sure winner, went into debt and probably lost. Then he turned to kidnapping to solve his financial problem."

Ted wrinkled his forehead. "Could be."

"He'd have to be pretty worried about the debt to go to that extreme."

"Depends on who he owed money to. Some people get pretty violent when money's not paid back."

Chapter 21

Mark left the Reinholt estate, drove a mile north and pulled over to the side of the road to call Sophie.

"Anything new on your end?" he asked.

"I reported the necklace missing and spoke with the hotel manager."

"Did he share anything?"

"Opened up like a jack-in-the-box. He was very apologetic and admitted there had been an earlier incident."

"What happened?"

"A woman was taking a shower. She left a set of jewelry on the dresser and when she came out it was gone."

"Any suspects?"

"Half a dozen."

"What?"

"There had been a problem earlier that day with the air conditioning in her room. A whole crew had tromped through working on it."

"So one of them could have cased the room and come back later."

"Exactly. According to the manager, the police questioned everyone, but found nothing concrete."

"Any of our friends involved?"

"Good question. Same one I asked. Turns out both George Tanabe and Keone Ahuna performed maintenance work at the Maui Queen and were questioned."

"That's interesting. George steals jewelry, and his wife found some of it. Then the Keone connection. He obviously needed money. Maybe he was also involved in selling stolen jewelry but didn't make enough or George didn't give him a cut and Keone killed him." Mark's mind swirled with possibilities. "Did he say anything while holding you captive that would link him to George's murder?"

"No. He was only obsessed with getting ransom money from you. While you're trying to figure it out, here's one other tidbit for you."

A car cut around the parked pickup truck missing the left fender by inches. Mark flinched. Island drivers. "Go ahead."

"The victim was a *divorcée* and tennis enthusiast."

"How did you learn so much?"

Mark could practically hear a smile over the phone. "The manager was concerned that he'd have to contact the police again. I said I'd hold off reporting it until I looked thoroughly. After that he was very cooperative."

"And later you called to say you'd found the missing necklace after all."

"Of course."

"Any luck with Arlene?"

There was a pause on the line. "Not yet. I haven't been able to find her but will keep trying."

"I hope you two will hit it off."

"I'll find a way. Maybe we both can complain about you."

★ ★ ★ ★ ★

As Mark headed toward Kihei, he chuckled to himself. Sophie was an amazing woman. With her helping, he had hope. He only had to avoid the bad guys and the police and stay alive. Simple as that.

He pulled into Gateway Plaza, parked and marched into Lefty's store. No one else was there.

Lefty looked up from behind the counter, a can of tennis balls in his hand and a hint of fear in his eyes. "What are you doing here?"

"I have a few questions for you. About Keone."

Lefty hung his head like a guilty child and said nothing.

Mark clapped his hands together to gain Lefty's attention. "Keone once told me that he did maintenance jobs around the Maui Queen."

Lefty regarded Mark warily. "That's right."

"I heard that George Tanabe also did similar jobs."

"Sure. The hotel paid well for part time work."

Mark placed both hands on the counter and leaned toward Lefty. "It seems that one or both of them might have been involved in stealing jewelry. Ring any bells?"

A drop of sweat glistened on Lefty's forehead. "I don't think Keone did anything like that."

"But what about George? It so happens his widow found a piece of stolen jewelry hidden in his house."

Lefty shifted his weight. "Could be."

"If he was stealing jewelry, could it be tied to Oana?"

Now Lefty looked really uncomfortable. "Don't know anything about that."

"I think you do."

A glint of anger showed in Lefty's eyes, and he clenched the can of tennis balls as if trying to crush it. "Look. You've seen the type of people who work for Oana. Both you and I have had trouble with them. Leave well enough alone."

"I wish I could, but I can't live a normal life because I'm accused of things I haven't done. I need to find out what's going on so I can clear myself. I'm not trying to get anyone after you. But I will get answers."

Lefty gave a resigned sigh. "Okay. Maybe George might have gone too far, and if he sold stolen jewelry, it might be through Oana."

"What about Keone? I understand he liked to gamble and might have been in debt big time to someone."

"Keone never could save anything. He loved to bet on professional football and basketball."

"Did he mention a big opportunity recently?"

Lefty set down the can of tennis balls he had been holding and relaxed. "If you mean did he hit me up for money, yes."

"And what did he say he wanted the money for?"

"Someone gave him the lead on a sure thing. He was trying to scrape up a large amount of cash to make it once and for all." Lefty waved his arm. "You know. The big payoff that would sit him pretty and he wouldn't have to worry about money all the time."

"And if you or his other pickleball friends wouldn't help him, where would he go for a large amount of money?"

Lefty tensed again. "To Oana."

★ ★ ★ ★ ★

As Mark left the shop, he thought over the things he'd learned. All roads led to Oana: drugs, stolen jewelry, loan sharking, murder. What had seemed like a friendly game of pickleball at the outset had enmeshed him in a wide variety of criminal activities, spiraling around the elusive Oana, the unseen man with a cultured voice. That didn't fit. What kind of guy was this Oana, anyway?

Mark pulled up in the front of Muriel Tanabe's house. An old blue Ford Escort was parked in the driveway.

She must be back. Composing himself and not sure if she would even talk to him, he trudged to the door and knocked.

Muriel opened the wooden door and stared at him through the outer screen. "What do you want?"

"Since we last talked, I understand that you've found some stolen jewelry?"

Her dark eyes bore in on him. "What of it?"

"I know none of this is easy for you, but I'm trying to find out who killed your husband and clear my own name."

She pointed an accusing index finger at Mark. "Look. I don't want you around here, and I'm not going to talk about this anymore."

"My wife was kidnapped, I've been threatened by a thug named Oana and like George, Detective Puna Pa'a is harassing me. I know you don't have to, but you might be able to provide information that would help."

"What do you mean your wife was kidnapped?"

"One of George's pickleball buddies, Keone, kidnapped my wife and held her for ransom. She's safe now."

"I knew he was crazy but didn't figure he was that bad." She looked at Mark carefully. "All right. I guess I can listen to what you have to say."

He released a burst of air from his lungs, realizing he had been holding his breath. "Thank you. Let's start with George. The jewelry you discovered may have been stolen from a woman staying at the Maui Queen."

Her eyes widened. "George often worked there."

"I think someone murdered George because of the stolen jewelry. Did he ever give any hint about what he was involved in?"

She looked down. "George didn't mention what he was doing. I guess I was pretty naïve. I took his side, but after finding the necklace, I have my doubts."

"Have you found any other jewelry around the house?"

"No. I searched everywhere as did the police. Nothing."

"Anything else that might be linked to George?"

She thought for a moment. "I did get a strange phone call yesterday."

"Oh?"

"It was a man's muffled voice. Asked if I wanted to donate any old clothing or shoes to charity."

"What'd you say?"

"That I didn't have anything at this time. Then the voice said he'd check back again. Weird voice."

Mark rubbed his chin, then snapped his fingers. "Shoes. George's body didn't have any shoes on when I found it. Lefty said later that George had tender feet and didn't go barefoot."

Muriel's eyes widened. "That's true. He had *haole* feet."

"Would you mind showing me any of George's shoes that you have?"

Muriel gave a resigned sigh. "Why not? Come on in."

She opened the screen and led Mark into the bedroom and pointed to the closet with shoes littering the floor. "Take a look if you like."

Mark bent down, picked up a work boot and inspected it. He started sorting through the shoes. On the first pass he didn't notice anything unusual. Then he looked more carefully at a tan loafer.

"Could I borrow a screwdriver?" he asked.

"I guess."

Muriel left the room and returned to hand him a long wooden handled tool.

He inserted it between the heel and sole and twisted. There was a snap and the heel flew off, dumping a strand of emeralds on the floor.

They both looked at it in silence.

"I'm afraid George was involved in serious theft and fencing. Someone killed him over it."

Muriel sat down on the bed and put her head in her hands.

Mark could hear the sobs as her chest heaved.

"I'll leave you alone. Call the police and give them the latest evidence. You might put in a good word for me."

She looked up briefly and nodded.

* * * * *

As Mark drove toward Kahului, he considered the latest set of events. George hiding stolen jewelry in his shoes and someone murdering him. Again, it seemed tied to Oana, but why would someone have to kill George? They could take the jewelry and leave it at that. It didn't make sense.

He found the Lost Castaway Bar and pulled into the small parking lot, taking one of the remaining spots.

Inside, loud Hawaiian music met his ears. The smell of sawdust mixed with the musky aroma of spilled beer. After his eyes adjusted to the dim light from several hurricane lanterns, he noticed that the place was busy for a weekday afternoon.

Mark sat at the only open stool at the bar and surveyed the scene. Mostly men. A wide variety of locals, some in shorts and flip flops and others in overalls and work boots.

A mid-forties woman with a red hibiscus in her short black hair, attractive in a tomboy way, joked with customers from behind the bar. She swiveled and leveled her gaze at Mark. "What'll you have?"

"Coors Light."

Sitting next to him, a large man with stomach protruding from beneath a too-short Hawaiian shirt shouted, "Ginger, how come my glass is empty."

Ginger parried back, "Because you've had enough. Leave before I tell your wife that you're here rather than at work."

The man on the other side laughed. "Randy, she's got your number."

"Ah, come on, Sammy. I'm her best customer, and she treats me like crap." Randy swayed on the stool.

Mark had a vision of the three-hundred pound man falling over on him. Like being covered by a beached whale. Or like the men he was trapped between on the flight to Maui or being pinned between Oana's enforcers on the way to the cliff overlooking shark-infested water.

"If you're my best customer, how come you never pay your bar tab?" Ginger asked. "Always waiting for someone else to pick it up."

"I give the place local color. Also, think of the business I bring you, Ginger. All my buddies come to your bar."

"You don't have any buddies except for Sammy here." She swatted a towel at the man sitting next to Randy.

Sammy raised his glass in salute and chugged the remains.

Mark waited until Ginger came back to check on him.

"Another beer?" she asked.

"No. I'm fine. But there's something else you can help with. I want to place a bet on the Broncos-Colts playoff game."

"Who says you can make a bet here?" She threw the bar towel

over her shoulder.

"Friend of mine. Keone Ahuna. Told me this was the place."

"How do you know Keone?"

"We played pickleball together near the Maui Queen. Since we're both sports enthusiasts, the subject came up about where to place bets. That's why I'm here."

She looked at him warily. "Haven't seen Keone lately."

"He told me he placed a big bet here a while back. You remember that?"

She smiled. "Too big. He stayed here to watch the game on TV. Almost had a heart attack when the Lions beat the Packers."

"I can't understand why he bet so much on that game." Mark picked up his beer.

She grabbed the towel and gave a swipe at a puddle of beer on the bar. "He told me he had a hot tip. Sure thing."

Mark took a sip from the inch of remaining beer in his glass. "From the way Keone talked he must have bet at least $50,000 on that game."

"Even more than that."

Mark shook his head in mock surprise. "Not like him to place that much."

"No. It had never happened before. He showed up and plunked down this big wad of cash."

"Beats me where Keone got that kind of money."

"Said he had a benefactor."

"I'm not in that league. I'll put twenty bucks on the Broncos. What's the point spread?"

Chapter 22

As Mark drove away, he wasn't sure where the investigation would go next. Keone got in debt, and for that much money he must have borrowed it from Oana's syndicate. He kidnapped Sophie in an effort to recoup a significant amount of money, probably fearing he'd get killed if he couldn't repay Oana. From what Sophie mentioned, Keone must have intended to repay the gambling debt with the ransom money and then disappear into the wilds of Maui. Figured he could hide from the authorities but didn't think he could elude Oana. When the ransom didn't work out and faced with the prospect of both prison and the enforcers coming after him, he took off in fear. Now he was dead, and Oana couldn't be repaid. That wouldn't sit well with the local mob boss, but what could he do?

Back at his hotel, Mark called Sophie.

She whispered into the phone, "I can't talk. I'll call you back in an hour."

The line went dead.

Mark didn't know what to make of it. He went out to grab a quick hamburger before returning to the hotel.

As promised Sophie called back.

"Mark, you're even in deeper trouble now."

"How can I be in any worse shape?"

"The police have been grilling me for the last two hours. Muriel Tanabe was found murdered in her home this afternoon."

Mark's stomach clenched. "What happened?"

"They wouldn't say. But they indicated your fingerprints were found, and a neighbor saw Keone's truck driving away. Even

167

remembered the license plate."

Mark dropped down on the bed as if someone had punched him in the gut. No one had noticed another vehicle, but some snoopy neighbor had seen *his* truck. "I must have been followed when I visited her. But why would someone kill Muriel?"

"I don't know, Mark, but I'm scared. There are too many things lined up against you. Detective Puna Pa'a was very angry. He threatened to arrest me as an accessory. Wanted to find out where you were hiding out."

"What'd you tell him?"

"I said I had no clue. I could be absolutely truthful since I have no idea where you're staying. There's no way I can see you. They'll follow me wherever I go. How are you going to get out of this?"

"I don't know. I learned why Keone kidnapped you and found out that George Tanabe stole jewelry, but I haven't figured out who murdered him or how to clear myself."

"Can Homer help?"

"I'm not sure what he can do, but I'll call him."

"And you better be careful when driving Keone's truck. Every policeman on the island is looking for it."

"I'm surprised they haven't pulled me over yet. Fortunately, it looks like so many other beat up pickup trucks around here."

"Puna thinks you're some kind of mafia figure from the mainland. He told me you killed George, Keone and Muriel to send a message to Oana that you're taking over his territory."

In spite of the situation, Mark laughed. "That's all I need. Oana is already after me. Now he'll hear from his sources about Puna's theory. It will be a race to see who gets me first, Oana or the police."

"I'm wondering if you should turn yourself in to the police. That might be safer than remaining on the lam."

"I've thought of that, but the murderer or murderers are free, and Puna's following the wrong path in going after me. Once he has me in custody, he'll be done, and nothing more will happen to find the real killers. It's up to me to work this out since no one else will search for the real perpetrators."

"I have another piece of news for you."

"I hope it's good news. I could use something on the positive side."

"Depends on how you look at it. I had a chance to talk to Arlene Henrick before the police arrived."

"And she told you she's filed a complaint against Ted and me."

"Actually, she was very cordial once I told her I was divorcing you."

Mark's chest tightened. "What?"

"Don't worry. It was merely a means to get her to open up. That way we had a common enemy."

"And did she mention Ted?"

"She hasn't seen him. He apparently took a leave of absence. Must be waiting for the situation to blow over and for Arlene to leave."

"But she's sticking around."

"Yes. She says she'll stay until both of you are nailed."

"Nice to be thought of so highly."

"She thinks you and Ted have this nice little scam you work together. I assured her that you only recently met Ted. Next, she speculated that you both must have common crime connections. She has no trouble believing you're linked to organized crime. She gave me a ten minute monologue regaling you as the worst type of scum."

Mark couldn't believe what he was hearing. "She hardly even knows me. In her mind she's built me into this criminal because she took one conversation between Ted and me out of context. Also gives Puna more ammunition."

"I read her as the type who once she makes up her mind she's hard to convince otherwise. She gave me the rundown on her ex-husband. He was the greatest guy she had ever known until he showed interest in one of her friends. From then on, he was a slimebag."

"And now I have a 'bad guy' label on my forehead."

"Absolutely. Don't mess with her. She showed me a derringer

169

she carries in her purse. She indicated if the police don't get some results she will. And she means it."

"I should arrange for Arlene, Puna and Oana to be in a room with me at the same time. If they're bad shots, maybe they'd shoot one another."

"Very funny. Stay away from Arlene."

"Don't worry. I'm trying to avoid all of them. I need to piece the puzzle together. There has to be a solution here, although it's eluding me."

"You'd better hurry before someone catches you."

Mark thought for a moment. "There is one other thing you can do for me. Since you've made friends with the hotel manager, see what you can find out about Ted. You might also snoop around the tennis courts and ask the guy who's covering for him."

"Anything specific you're looking for?"

"Arlene's can't be the only complaint about Ted. I heard mention of another problem he had with a hotel guest. See what else he may have done."

"And what's your next step?"

Mark tapped the nightstand. "I think I'll check in with Homer. See if he's heard any more from the police concerning my one-man crime wave."

★ ★ ★ ★ ★

Later, Mark tried Homer. He was busy, but his receptionist, Andrea, told him to call back in thirty minutes.

Mark paced the room, trying to figure out his next move. He had to solve George's murder, clear himself from the drug charges, prove that Keone's death was an accident, show that he had not stolen Keone's pickup truck, find Muriel's murderer and clear himself from involvement in Ted's scam. If he could accomplish that, he'd be back to where he was the morning he first found the pickleball court. What his sport had led him into.

After checking his watch, he picked up his cell phone and called Homer again. This time Andrea put him through.

"Mark, I've been concerned about you."

"I've been worried about me, too. Things seem to be getting worse rather than better."

Homer cleared his throat. "I checked with our mutual friend, Ben Quentin. I asked him if you had a criminal past. He told me you had been involved in a murder investigation in Boulder, helped solve it and were as honest as they come. Amazing the trouble you've gotten into here. Maybe the island air doesn't agree with you."

"Yeah, I can't believe everything that's going on. Did you hear what happened to Muriel Tanabe?"

"Yes. Puna called earlier. He's really pissed. I've never heard him so mad. I felt like saliva would shoot out of the phone."

"He just finished grilling Sophie about me."

"Puna feels he has an air-tight case against you on this one. Demanded that I have you turn yourself in."

"Yeah. Then I'd never have an opportunity to prove my innocence. What did you hear about the murder?"

"Only that she was bludgeoned. Puna wouldn't say what the weapon was."

Mark felt sick to his stomach. Such an unnecessary death. "Sophie says the truck I'm using was spotted driving away."

"That's right."

"But no one else was seen in the area?"

"Not that's been reported."

"One or more people arrived after I left. Someone in the neighborhood must have seen something."

"I think Puna has all the evidence he wants."

"That's the trouble. He thinks he has it wrapped up in a big Christmas bow without doing the necessary open-minded investigation necessary to find the real culprit." Then the realization struck him. "I'll have to check out the surrounding area. Any idea who saw the pickup truck?"

"No. Puna wouldn't say. Someone near Muriel's house. But you have a bigger problem."

Mark's stomach tightened. "Now what?"

"Oana called me."

"Why would he do that?"

"He found out that I'm representing you. He gave me a message for you. To net it out: 'Give me the one hundred thousand dollars Keone owes by noon tomorrow. Then leave the island or you're a dead man.'"

"Why the money?"

"He says since you killed Keone, you're responsible for his debt."

Chapter 23

At the news of Oana expecting that Keone's debt be paid, Mark tensed. "Strange logic."

"That's the way Oana operates. The money must be repaid, no matter what. In his mind that means you."

"And his comment to leave the island?"

"He wants you out of his territory. Otherwise, he said he'll find you and take care of you personally."

Mark couldn't help himself and actually chuckled. "He'll have to wait in line. Puna and a derringer-toting *divorcée* are also after me. I've become a very popular guy."

"This isn't a joking matter. Oana is coming out of his lair himself to kill you. No one ever gets away when Oana wants him."

"So I've really irritated the big guy. That might mean I won't have to worry that his henchmen will kill me if Oana wants to do it himself."

"I'd recommend getting off the island quickly."

"I can't leave Sophie. Besides the police would arrest me if I tried to fly out."

"You didn't hear this from me, but you could probably rent a boat."

Mark clenched the cell phone. "No, Homer. I need to get through this and clear myself. If I get arrested, Oana will find a way to get me killed in jail. My best chance is to stay here and resolve this."

"With Oana after you, you'll need to be prepared to defend yourself."

Mark paused. "I hate to admit this, but I borrowed your gun."

"What?"

"Look in your drawer."

Mark heard a sound of wood scraping and some paper being shuffled.

"I'll be damned. It's gone."

"If you're only noticing now, you haven't had any violent clients to deal with. I needed some protection. I'll get it back to you when this is over."

"That's all I need. One of my clients committing a crime using my gun."

"I'm not planning to use it. But as you've said, I need some protection against Oana."

"I'll have to report it missing."

Mark sighed. "Do what you need to."

"Just don't get caught with it. Stealing a weapon and possession of a stolen gun will add five more years to your jail time."

"Thanks for the encouraging news. I thought you were going to keep me out of jail."

"I don't know if even I can help with all the charges piling up against you. Yours is the most difficult case I've ever handled."

"That's reassuring, but one more in my list of crimes will hardly matter at this point. By the way, if you get any calls mentioning seeing strange people or cars near Muriel Tanabe's house take good notes."

"What's that about?"

"Puna hasn't located anyone who can help determine who killed Muriel. Alert Andrea as well so she can be prepared if someone calls with useful information."

"Are you using my office as a clearing house for clues?"

"Something like that. I don't have any other reliable place to have them call. Thanks for your help." Mark clicked off.

Next, he looked in the phonebook for a print shop. He found a listing for one in the Pilani Village Shopping Center and drove over. He left his order and went shopping for clothes.

He returned two hours later as the owner was preparing

to close the print shop. Paying, he noticed he had nearly run through Sophie's mad money.

The good news, he had the business cards he needed. They read: Pat Bartlett, Private Investigator, with an address in Kahului and Homer's phone number.

After changing into his new clothes, Mark drove to Muriel Tanabe's neighborhood and parked the pickup truck several blocks away and around the corner from her house. Then he walked to Muriel's street.

He knocked on a door.

A middle-aged woman opened it a crack. "Yes?"

"I'm Pat Bartlett, a private investigator. He handed a card to the woman. I'm checking with neighbors of Muriel Tanabe's to see if anyone saw any car stop near her house this morning. This may be very important in an ongoing investigation."

"No. What a horrible thing to happen to such a nice young woman."

"If you happen to remember anything, please call the number on the card and leave a message."

Mark continued down the street. At one house an elderly man said, "I was looking out my window and saw a beat up, brown pickup truck. A man got in it who was approximately your build but a lot scruffier."

"Any other cars or visitors after that?"

"Not that I noticed. But I didn't look out the window again until much later."

After working both sides of the street, Mark had nothing specific that helped. He tried the next block with an equal lack of results.

It was starting to get dark when he decided to work a few more houses on the block the other side of Muriel's house.

He knocked on one door, and a man's voice shouted, "Go 'way."

"Sir, I'm part of an investigation into one of your neighbor's death."

"I no talk to no one after dark. Beat it."

Mark wrote a note on his card and slipped it under the door.

At the next house, he spoke to an older woman who informed him, "No. Didn't see anything."

A voice from behind her in the living room shouted, "I saw something."

Mark's head jerked up.

An old man lifted himself off a couch and shuffled over, scratching his arm as if he had a flea bite. "I was walking our dog this morning. Kapu likes to stop and sniff everything. Saw a pickup truck parked down the next street."

"Oh," Mark said, disappointed that someone else had seen his truck.

"Yeah. Blue pickup."

Mark looked at the man more carefully. Keone's pickup was a rusty brown.

"You're sure it was blue?"

"I know all the cars and trucks in this neighborhood. Definitely not a regular."

"See anyone get in or out?"

"No. But after I got back to my house, Kapu stopped at the mailbox for one last sniff. I happened to look up the street. I saw a big guy with a scar on his cheek who was turning the corner. Don't think he noticed me."

It all fell into place. Oana's thugs had abducted him in a blue pickup. Malo had been here.

On his way back to the hotel, he saw a flashing light in his rear view mirror. His head felt light and his grip tightened on the wheel. He kept driving at the speed limit, trying to decide if he should make a run for it.

The light came up close behind. Mark slowed and pulled over to the right before the vehicle shot around him. Was he going to be forced off the road?

The police car sped ahead with its light flashing. Mark let out a sigh of relief. It was dark enough to hide the easy identity of his vehicle, given the number of beat up pickup trucks on the island. The police officer obviously had some other target in mind.

★ ★ ★ ★ ★

The next morning, Mark called Homer and asked, "Any messages from Muriel Tanabe's neighbors?"

"No. But I received another angry call from Puna. It seems one of the neighbors called the police to check on the business card that was left. The description of the man handing it out met yours, and the police found your fingerprints on the card."

"I guess that backfired."

"I'll say. And with my phone number on it. Puna is trying to find some charge of impersonating a private investigator or fraud to add to your long list of crimes. He also threatened me again. You've brought more police harassment on me than I've had in all my years in practice."

Mark gulped. "I'm sorry."

Homer chuckled. "Just joshing you. I know how to handle Puna. He has to take his shots, and I can deal with them. Not a problem."

"That's a relief. I'd hate to cause anyone more trouble than I'm causing myself. I did find out that one of Oana's men had been in Muriel's neighborhood yesterday. He probably killed her."

"Give me the details and I'll pass it on to our favorite detective."

Mark recounted what the neighbor had said and which house it was.

"And the man was certain he had seen the color of the truck?"

"Absolutely. And he gave an accurate description of Oana's henchman, Malo."

"I'll let Puna know, but I doubt he'll pay much attention to it. He's very stubborn and not one to change his mind. Everything you do reinforces his opinion that you're evil personified."

Mark clasped his cell phone in frustration. "And I used to be viewed as such an upstanding citizen."

"Not in Puna's mind. I've even been served with papers. I'll be hard pressed to claim attorney-client privacy privileges with Puna putting pressure on me as well, but I'll work that out."

"I'm sorry again to put you in this position. Problems seem to be compounding rather than getting solved."

"I did report my gun missing. Puna immediately leapt to the conclusion that you stole it. Now that charge has been added to your other many offenses. You're the most wanted man in Maui's history. The police have you listed for every crime except counterfeiting."

"What about Oana? Why isn't Puna trying to do something to capture him?"

"Oana's a Maui institution like death and taxes. Puna co-exists with him. You, on the other hand, are viewed as a new threat to both Puna and Oana. They both want your skin."

"It's nice to be thought of so highly."

"I'm concerned that when the police catch you, you're apt to be 'accidently' hurt or killed. I've never heard Puna so angry as when he talks about you."

"You said, 'when the police catch me.' Don't you mean 'if?'"

There was an audible sigh on the line. "Mark, it's only a matter of time. This is a small island, and everyone is looking for you."

"Too bad that Puna's emotions can't be directed at Oana. Then something might really be fixed on this island."

"Don't count on it."

"I'm going to keep trying. There's nothing else I can do at this point."

"As we've discussed, there's hardly anything else the police can charge you with. I think you've nearly covered all the possibilities already."

"If my parents were alive, they would be so proud of me."

★ ★ ★ ★ ★

Later he called Sophie to check in.

"I had another heart-to-heart talk with Arlene last night," she said.

"Any progress?"

"No, but here's a new twist. She and Ted have made up."

"How can that be? She acted like she wanted to kill both of us."

"She's still mad at you but not Ted. He sweet-talked her into forgiving him, and she dismissed the charges against him."

Mark looked down at the floor and saw a cockroach scurry by. He tried to squash it with his shoe, but it escaped under the bed. "And what about me?"

"You're the enemy. She's now convinced you're the one who led Ted astray. Her words were, 'Ted wouldn't try to take advantage of me on his own. I hate to say it, Sophie, but that husband of yours is no good.' I bit my tongue and listened, but I was ready to haul off and smack her."

Mark smiled in spite of the situation. "Thanks for the vote of confidence. I can't believe she blames me."

"Ted either overly or by omission left the impression that you're the culprit—this sleazy wheeler-dealer from the mainland. To keep on her good side, I didn't try to change her impression."

Mark squeezed the cell phone. "I have to speak with her."

"I don't think she'll see you."

Mark thought for a moment. "I need to plead my case with her and have an opportunity for her to discuss Ted's dealings. What about this? Why don't you arrange to have dinner with her? Set up a time, and I'll show up instead. That way she'll have to listen to me."

"I'll be happy to do it, but I don't think you'll get her to change her mind. She's a very stubborn woman. And you'll have to be cautious. Remember, she's armed."

"But she did reconsider her opinion of Ted, even though he's the guilty party."

"You're not as young and cute as Ted."

"But hopefully I'm older and wiser."

Chapter 24

Two hours later Sophie called back. "It's all set. I've arranged to meet Arlene at the Café Kau Kau for dinner here at the hotel at eight tonight. She arrives exactly five minutes late so plan to be here at 8:10."

"Thanks. I'll see what I can do."

"Don't expect much. She raved over the new emerald earrings Ted gave her. She's going to wear them tonight to show me; you can admire them instead."

Emerald earrings. He'd have to check them out. He remembered the emerald necklace he had found in George Tanabe's shoe at Muriel's house. Unique white gold fleur-de-lis imbedded in the chain between the emeralds. This had possibilities.

Mark needed to find some lead on Oana. Who could he turn to? He snapped his fingers. Of course. He looked up the number and called Dexter Kwan.

"Good of you to contact me, Mark, but I've heard some disturbing reports about you."

"Yeah, I can imagine. I'm in a lot of trouble because of illegal activity linked to a crime boss named Oana and his cronies."

"That's one bad man. Everyone on the island fears him, and the police have been powerless at containing him or even charging him with anything."

"That's why I'm calling. I'm trying to learn more about Oana, and since you've been on the island a long time, I thought you might have some information."

"No one I know has ever seen him. Very illusive man and dangerous. Stay away from him."

180

"Here's the thing. I've actually met him."

"Really! What did he look like?"

"That I can't say. I had a burlap bag over my head, but I heard his voice. Very surprising. A cultured voice that reminded me of an intellectual at a university."

There was a pause on the line.

"Dexter, are you there?"

"Your description reminded me of someone. Twenty years ago I met a man who moved here from the mainland. Spoke like an Ivy League professor. Knew a great deal about art and jewelry."

Mark gave a start. "Jewelry?"

"Yes. He had an excellent knowledge of different types of gems and gold settings. We got together for coffee several times. He was also very interested in island real estate, but we never finalized a deal together. I called him several times with no answer and finally received a message that the number had been disconnected. He didn't follow up, and I've never heard from him again. I assumed he went back to the mainland."

"And his name?"

There was a loud sigh over the line. "Henry something. I can't recall his last name. I bet Harriet will remember. She met him as well and has a better memory than I do. She's out running an errand, but when she returns I can give you a call."

Mark left his cell number and signed off. An interesting possibility, this Henry whoever. Two steps forward, one step back. He hoped Harriet remembered the name.

* * * * *

An hour later, Mark remained in the room, awaiting a return call from Dexter Kwan. He didn't want to drive around and risk being caught by the local constabulary. Too bad he couldn't take in some of those sights Dexter had mentioned to Sophie on the plane. He'd prefer to be relaxing at Fleming Beach or even joining Sophie on a dreaded shopping expedition in Kaanapali. How his perspective had changed now that he was a fugitive.

The jangling of his cell phone interrupted his ruminations. He answered to hear Dexter panting for breath as if he had been running up the stairs.

"Harriet just got home, and she remembered. She said she felt at the time that the guy was too smooth and was hiding something. His name is Henry Caldwell."

Mark locked that name into his memory bank. "Do either of you remember if he had a tattoo of a shark on the back of his right hand?"

"Doesn't ring a bell with me. Let me check with Harriet."

There was muffled discussion in the background, and then Dexter announced, "Good question. Harriet, as I said, has a much better memory than I do. She does recall a shark tattoo on Henry Caldwell's hand. Another thing she thought was out of character for the way he spoke. How about that?"

"Very interesting." The image of the man with a spear gun off Molokini raced through Mark's brain. What to do next? "Could you do me a big favor?"

"Depends."

"Call Detective Puna Pa'a. Give him the name of Henry Caldwell as the possible identity of Oana."

"But I don't know that for sure." There was obvious stress in Dexter's voice.

"I don't either, but it's a possible lead for the police to follow up on. It's something they should be aware of."

"Why don't you call the detective yourself?" Dexter asked.

"I'm not the most popular person in the world with him right now. He'd only accuse me of trying to distract the police. It will sound much more credible coming from an independent source such as you."

★ ★ ★ ★ ★

Mark remained in his room until after dark. He decided he would head over to the Maui Queen early, park well to the back of the parking lot and check things out before his dinner appointment with Arlene Henrick. He had to do everything to stay out of the sight of the police until he had put together the pieces to prove his innocence to Puna. *Right*. As if that was going to happen.

After fidgeting for half an hour, he peered out the curtain to verify that no police cars were in sight, left his room and walked the two blocks to where he had parked Keone's truck. Scanning the street, he determined that no one was watching him, quickly got in the truck and drove off.

As he entered the Pi'ilani Highway going south, a few cars traveled in both directions. Maybe this would be a calm evening. He thought of turning on the radio but decided not to become distracted. He had to be paying attention at all times. Besides, he didn't even know if the radio worked in this old clunker.

He checked his rearview mirror and spotted a flashing light. *Uh-oh*. He squinted and peered ahead. The traffic had dispersed. He was the only car in sight. The police car had to be after him. Had a patrol officer spotted the wanted truck or seen the license plate?

A drop of sweat rolled down his side. *What to do?*

He sped up, but the light remained right behind him. He spotted a dirt road heading to the left up the hillside. Waiting until the last minute, he jammed the steering wheel to the left, and skidded onto the dirt road. Correcting his steering, he put his foot on the gas and sped up the road kicking the dry dirt into the air. He could see a plume of dust behind him but then made out the flashing light following him. *Damn*. The cop car was definitely after him. He couldn't get caught. He'd end up in jail, and Puna would keep him incarcerated for the next century with all the charges against him. He had to get out of this predicament.

Risking a peek in the rearview mirror, he saw a faint flashing light through the dust. He had gained a small amount of separation from the following police car. Maybe the police officer was having trouble keeping up while driving through the dust.

He rounded a bend and a wave of dust splashed into his windshield. *Uh-oh*. Something was in front of him. He kept his foot on the gas until he spotted taillights right ahead of him.

He'd have to slow down or risk passing, but the road was so narrow he didn't know if he could make it past another vehicle, particularly with all the dust and darkness.

An idea occurred to him. He followed the vehicle ahead around a bend and once momentarily out of sight of the trailing police car turned off the truck's lights. In the dim visibility off to his left he noticed a break in the undergrowth. An old Jeep trail. He spun the steering wheel and shot onto the Jeep trail. It was overgrown enough not to kick up dirt. It headed uphill. He took his foot off the gas, and the truck jounced to a stop without putting on the brake lights. In his rearview mirror he could see billowing dust illuminated by headlights. Then a flashing light shot past.

The cop was still on the dust trail, now following the other vehicle and not his. He slowly backed up. When he reached the dirt road, the dust had settled. He went right. Once sure he wasn't being followed, he turned his lights back on and retraced his route back to the Pi'ilani Highway.

Resuming the route to the Maui Queen Hotel, he wiped his forehead with the back of his hand and flicked the perspiration onto the passenger side seat. His hand shook. That had been too close a call.

★ ★ ★ ★ ★

At ten minutes to eight, Mark arrived at the hotel. He parked near the back of the lot between two SUVs so Keone's truck wouldn't be easily visible. Taking a minute to compose himself, he wiped his forehead again and took several deep breaths to control his breathing and to allow his heart rate to drop to a safe level. He wondered what the police car had done when it caught up with the other vehicle on the dirt road. Some unsuspecting person had probably been questioned by a very pissed off police officer. Not his worry. He had to confront Arlene Henrick. A new challenge.

He walked to the edge of the driveway and checked the portcochere. No police cars, or for that matter, any cars parked along the sidewalk.

The bushes rustled, and Mark flinched at the sight of a shape coming toward him. Then he noticed the person was short. "You surprised me, Kea."

Kea put his fingers to his lips and whispered, "We need to speak quietly. I heard the police are after you."

"Yes, but I didn't do anything wrong."

"I know. You my good customer. I'm not going to rat you out. Besides I have to be careful since they don't want me here selling stuff."

"I won't tell, if you don't tell."

Kea held out his hand. "Deal."

They shook.

"I'll let you know if the assistant manager is snooping around, and you let me know if anyone is following me."

Kea gave him a thumbs up. "I got your back. Say, you have the comments on my business plan?"

Mark shook his head. "Sorry, it's in the trunk of my rental car, which I can't use for the time being. Once I clear up everything, I'll get it for you."

"No problem. Catch you later." Kea dashed off into the bushes.

Mark strolled across the circular driveway and headed into the hotel. With a twist of his wrist, he checked his watch and entered the restaurant at exactly 8:10.

He spotted Arlene at a table in the corner, dabbing at her mouth while looking in her compact mirror. Taking a deep breath to steel his nerves, he sauntered over and sat down.

Arlene gasped. "What are you doing here?"

He held up his hand. "Calm down. Sophie couldn't make it. I'm here to make peace with you."

She crossed her arms. "I don't know."

Mark gave his best salesman smile. "Beautiful earrings."

Arlene unfolded her arms and patted her right ear with her right hand. "Yes, Ted gave them to me."

"May I take a closer look?"

Arlene leaned forward, and Mark inspected the emeralds with white gold fleur-de-lis. He sat back in his chair. "I know you were upset, Arlene. Let's see if we can be friends."

"Friends? After you tried to swindle me with that absurd land deal? And taking advantage of poor Ted as well."

Mark clenched his fists along his side and nudged the gun inside his light jacket. "I'm not involved in any land deals. I apologize for whatever you thought happened, but that's between you and Ted."

"Ted explained it all. It was a misunderstanding on my part that he was involved, but that doesn't mean I'll forgive you." She shook her right index finger at him. "You talked Ted into an unscrupulous deal and tried to scam me."

Mark could only take so much of this. "So you've made up with Ted because he's given you stolen earrings, but you're blaming me even though I wasn't even involved."

"Stolen earrings! Now you've gone too far."

She reached in her purse and pulled out her derringer. "I'm calling the police... maitre d'!"

Mark looked at the small barrel pointed at him. When the maitre d' appeared, Arlene turned her head.

Mark leaped up from the chair and ran toward the restaurant exit.

Arlene fired.

Chapter 25

Mark felt a searing pain in his left arm. He continued running, almost knocking over a waiter.

When he got to the lobby, he checked his arm. There were two holes in his jacket, and he was bleeding. He could move his arm so he didn't think a bone had been hit. It must have gone in and out of flesh. He pressed his hand against his arm to stem the flow of blood and dashed through the lobby.

Outside, Kea appeared from the bushes. "Hey, Bruddah, a cop is checking your truck." He scampered back into hiding.

Mark skirted the side of the parking lot and saw Puna's sidekick, Akahi, peering through the truck's driver side window. Removing the gun from inside his jacket, he tiptoed up behind Akahi.

"Raise your hands. I'm armed." Mark pressed the barrel of his gun into Akahi's back.

Akahi carefully stood up with his hands in the air. "Don't do anything stupid."

"I want to talk to you without the threat of your gun being used against me." Mark kept his pistol against Akahi's back, removed the officer's gun and threw it into the bushes.

"Hey, Puna's going to be pissed if I don't have my gun."

"You can pick it up later. Into the truck. You drive."

Mark kept his gun on Akahi while he circled the hood and entered the passenger-side door. He handed the keys to Akahi, covering him with the gun.

"Where we going?" Akahi asked.

"Just up the road where we can talk. Puna around?"

"Nah. I'm here on my own."

"Good."

They exited the parking lot, Akahi driving carefully and staring straight ahead. "This isn't a good idea, Mr. Yeager."

"As I said, I only need to speak with you in a private place where we won't be interrupted. Turn left on the main road."

They drove in silence for ten minutes.

"Pull in there." Mark pointed to a dirt parking area along the side of the road.

They came to a stop.

"You aren't going to shoot me, are you?" Akahi asked.

"No. We're on the same side."

"Then why are you kidnapping me?"

Mark's arm was hurting, but the bleeding had stopped. "I'm not kidnapping you. Your boss has charged me with every crime on this island. I happen to be innocent, and I need to talk to someone on the police force who will listen before arresting me."

Akahi shrugged. "I'm listening."

"Let's start at the beginning. I met you right after I discovered George Tanabe's body by the pickleball court. As I said before, I happened upon the body by accident. I had nothing to do with his death."

"That's what you claim."

"It's also true. If I killed him I certainly wouldn't be the one reporting finding the body. Besides, I can deliver the real murderer to you."

Akahi's eyes widened. "Who's that?"

"I don't quite have enough evidence to prove it yet, but if you'll work with me rather than against me, I can get you enough proof to arrest the real murderer."

"Why should I believe you?"

"Hear me out on the whole situation. Then you can decide."

Akahi shrugged again, but he was watching Mark intently.

"When I started looking into the murder, the next thing that happened was I ran afoul of Oana's organization. I followed Lefty Kalama and came upon a drug transaction. Surely you and your boss know Lefty had connections with Oana."

"Could be." Akahi gave his signature shrug.

"They set me up. If you were to go after Oana and give Lefty witness protection, I'm sure he'd testify and support my claim."

"Look, Mr. Yeager. That kind of thing doesn't work here. You can't relocate someone within the islands. It's too small a place, and people find out. Even if Lefty wants to move to the mainland, a local boy like him would stick out. Oana would track him down."

"Only a thought."

"Okay, I'm listening."

"Then Oana's thugs kidnapped me and tried to kill me. They have a place Hana-side of Kahului. Cliff where they like to shoot people and push them into the ocean."

"Shark Cove."

Mark winced. That was the name he had heard from Abe of the photograph taken along the Hana Coast. "You know about it!"

"There have been several bodies recovered in that area."

"When you say bodies do you mean people swept off the rugged shore or other types of accidents?"

Akahi shrugged once again. "No one has ever found out what happened, but for some of them, there were bullets in the remains."

"Remains. I guess that says it all."

"Yeah and the sharks didn't leave the bullets in the bodies. You have any useful information for me?"

"Oana had his main enforcer take me to the Shark Cove to kill me. The guy has a big scar on his cheek and is named Malo. Do you know him?"

"I know who he is. We've suspected him of multiple killings but have never been able to prove anything."

"And he had a companion named Kimo."

"Don't know anything about him," Akahi said.

"Between Lefty and me, you should be able to nail both Malo and Kimo."

"What makes you think Lefty will cooperate?"

"I don't know for sure, but he's getting in over his head. I think we could convince him to start a new life. I bet he wants out of the trouble he's in with Oana's gang."

"Maybe."

Mark waved the gun. "None of this is certain, but it might work."

"What about the other charges against you?"

"All explainable. Keone kidnapped my wife. Puna must have understood that from talking to her and investigating Keone's cabin. Keone ran away and fell off a cliff. That's how he died."

"Pretty convenient for you. How can you prove it?"

"Why would I want him dead? I needed to have him admit the kidnapping."

"Revenge."

Mark looked at Akahi. "I have a gun. I could have shot him, but I didn't."

"Maybe you wanted to make it look like an accident."

"I think from my wife's testimony you can piece together what really happened."

"And the gun?"

"I admit taking it from Homer Nagano. I needed it to get Keone to take me to find my wife."

"We're also sitting in a stolen pickup truck."

"Look. This was Keone's. He doesn't have any use for it anymore. I need transportation while I'm trying to clear my name. I'll reimburse whoever is responsible for Keone's estate by providing the equivalent of a rental fee. Unfortunately, Oana's thugs slashed the tires of my rental car so I couldn't drive it."

Akahi gave a half smile. "I have to admit taking the truck's no big deal. But there is the matter of a complaint filed by Arlene Henrick."

"That's another one I had nothing to do with. If I can convince her to drop the charge, that should take care of it."

"As long as she's not found dead. You're forgetting the most serious charge. The murder of Muriel Tanabe."

Mark took a deep breath. "I met with Muriel twice at her

home. The second time we discovered stolen jewelry in the sole of one of George's shoes. I told her to report it to the police and left."

"We got a call from her. I even went to investigate. But I found that someone had killed her. No jewelry."

"Then again why would I have told her to contact the police if I planned to kill her? Doesn't make any sense."

Akahi shrugged. "Maybe she called on her own."

"Did she mention the stolen jewelry when she called?"

"Described it and gave a full report."

"Good. I need to find that missing jewelry. Another point you might not be aware of. A man matching Malo's description was seen by one of the neighbors around the time of Muriel's murder. He was driving a blue pickup truck."

Akahi's eyes narrowed. "No shit?"

"You can check it out yourself. It's the man who lives in the white house with flowers on the mailbox, one block toward the mountains and on the opposite side of the street from Muriel's house."

"There's one other thing Puna thinks you're involved with."

Mark tapped his non-gun wielding fingers on the dashboard. "What now?"

"He got a search warrant for your rental car. He found a marked up business plan for souvenir shops in the trunk. He thinks you plan to set up a money laundering operation in the islands with this as a front under the assumed name of Kea Puahi."

A spike of anger shot through Mark's chest. "You've got to be kidding. Do you know who Kea Puahi is?"

"I figured it was you."

"This is something you can easily check on. He's a twelve-year-old kid who sells necklaces and shells. He hangs around the Maui Queen all the time. Bright kid who wants to start his own business. He gave me his business plan, and I marked it up with some suggestions."

"That explains why the comments were in your handwriting."

"Why in the world would Puna think I was involved in money laundering?"

Akahi actually gave a faint grin. "He thinks it goes along with the other illegal activities you've been involved in."

"I'm trying my damnest to clear my name and help solve this series of murders. It's difficult with you and Puna after me as well. And my lawyer, Homer Nagano, mentioned there might be one more charge. Impersonating an investigator. I'm also guilty of that. That's how I found out that someone matching Malo's description had been in Muriel Tanabe's neighborhood. When this is all over, I'll be happy to face that charge."

"Don't need to. Puna checked, but couldn't find any law you violated." Akahi laughed. "That pissed him off as much as the illegal things he thinks you did."

Mark noted the word, "thinks." Maybe Akahi was starting to believe him. "If you will work with me rather than arresting me, I feel I'm getting really close to proving who murdered George and Muriel Tanabe. Let me gather the final evidence. Then I'll turn myself in to you."

"You could skip the island."

"I could have by now if that was what I was trying to do. I'm sticking around to prove my innocence. All I need is someone on the police force supporting my efforts."

"Let's be realistic, Mr. Yeager. Even if I buy everything you've said, which is a stretch given the dead bodies and broken laws, Puna isn't going to believe you."

Mark looked Akahi in the eyes. "Puna has his own agenda. I've asked you to listen and you have. I know it's hard to accept all of this. I have trouble believing everything that has happened to me as well. Give me a day or two. I'm convinced that I'm getting close. Work with me."

"You don't have to worry that I'll arrest you. You have the gun."

Mark glared at him. "The key will be what happened around the pickleball court the night George was killed. I'm going to figure that out."

"What happened to your arm?" Akahi asked.

"Arlene Henrick shot me. But I won't press charges."
Akahi grinned. "You one unlucky guy."

★ ★ ★ ★ ★

Mark directed Akahi to drive back to the tennis courts near the hotel.

"How do I get hold of you?" Mark asked.

Akahi reached into his shirt pocket and pulled out a card. "Here's my direct phone number."

Mark looked at the card. It read, "Alexander 'Akahi' Mendez, assistant detective."

"You're real name is Alexander?"

"Sure. My mom named me after Alexander the Great."

"I'll stick with Akahi the Great. I'll be calling you. Maybe as soon as tomorrow. It's a five minute walk back to your car from here."

Akahi got out, and Mark scooted over to the driver's side.

"You're letting me go like this?" Akahi asked.

"Sure. We're a team now."

"But I'll be in deep guano if Puna finds out what you did to me."

Mark winked. "Puna doesn't have to find out, does he? As you told me earlier, just don't do anything stupid."

Mark started the engine and drove away.

★ ★ ★ ★ ★

On the drive toward Kihei, Mark realized he had forgotten to tell Akahi one thing—that Oana's real name was Henry Caldwell. He'd correct that when they next met.

Back at his hotel, Mark removed his jacket and shirt. The gash in his left triceps was raw and surrounded by coagulated blood. He held up his jacket to see the two small holes. He now had an air-conditioned jacket. Good thing for both him and his jacket that it was only a small caliber bullet.

He washed the wound and tore strips from a pillowcase to wrap his arm. He'd later leave some money to compensate the hotel.

Bending his elbow, he had mobility in spite of the pain. At least it wasn't his pickleball arm. The only difficulty would be when serving, but with the underhand serve of pickleball, he shouldn't be hampered too much. Other than that, he could get by fine as long as he didn't get arrested or taken away by Oana's gang.

★   ★   ★   ★   ★

The next morning, he called Homer. "I'm checking in to find out any breaking news."

"Two things. First, in spite of the fact that you already have more charges than a battery factory, you've succeeded in collecting another."

Mark's chest slumped. "What now?"

"Kidnapping a police officer. Puna has charged you with threatening and abducting his assistant. What'd you do this time, Mark?"

"I had a little talk with Akahi." He couldn't believe Akahi mentioned the whole incident to Puna. He thought they had bonded. So much for his male intuition about police officers. "What's the other piece of news?"

"I got a call from one of Muriel Tanabe's neighbors. Your amateur sleuthing paid off. He reported seeing a young *haole* guy approximately six-foot-two wearing a blue UCLA baseball cap on Muriel's street at the time of the murder."

Mark snapped his fingers. "It might not be Malo after all."

"What are you talking about?"

"It's all making sense. Ted Franklin, the tennis pro I play pickleball with, wears a blue UCLA cap. Do me a favor. Call this number I'm going to give you and pass that information on to Akahi Mendez."

"The guy you kidnapped?"

"I didn't kidnap him. We merely had a man-to-man discussion. You might also ask him why he ratted me out."

194

Chapter 26

After Mark finished talking to Homer, he sat on the bed in his hotel room, deep in thought. The pieces were coming together, but he needed to make the final connection. He realized there was only one way to do this. It would require Akahi's cooperation, and he wasn't sure he could count on that. First, he had a call to make.

Ted answered on the third ring. "I wasn't expecting to hear from you. Arlene says you threatened her."

"What? She shot me in the arm. I think she has her story a little confused."

"She warned me not to have anything to do with you."

Mark felt like crushing the cell phone. Also wanting to blast Ted for his duplicity, Mark counted to three and continued in a calm, controlled voice, "You're a big boy. You can do what you want. As you know she gets very emotional. Only a little misunderstanding between her and me."

"Seems like a big deal. She's really pissed."

"I have a number of people really pissed at me. Remember. She was pretty angry with you as well. She's forgiven you. With me it will just take more time."

"You got that right, but I don't think she'll ever forgive you."

Yeah, because of what Ted told her. Mark sucked it up. "The reason for calling— I've lined up a pickleball partner. We want to take on you and Lefty tonight."

"I don't know. With Arlene the way she is, maybe I shouldn't be seen with you."

"She doesn't have to know. Besides, I'm going to bet one hundred dollars per game for three games."

"You're ready to lose three hundred dollars to me?" Ted sounded interested. "You must have a ringer."

"No. I'm ready to play and thought a little extra incentive would make the game more exciting."

Mark disliked the thought of losing three hundred dollars, as surely he would, but it seemed to be the hook needed to get Ted motivated.

"I'll call Lefty," Ted said. "We'll see you and your fellow victim at eight. Come prepared to be whooped."

Mark let out a sigh. Half the problem solved. How for the really difficult part. He dialed the number Akahi had given him.

"Detective Mendez's office," an official sounding female voice answered.

"I need to speak to Akahi."

"He's busy right now."

"Tell him it's important. I'll call back in half an hour."

"Who is this, please?"

"Inform him that if he wants to solve the George and Muriel Tanabe murders, to answer the phone in exactly thirty minutes."

Mark paced the room. He was getting tired of the off-white wall with an old black and white print of palm trees silhouetted against a beach. This was a hell of a way to spend a vacation. Couldn't see his wife, not able to walk around freely without looking over his shoulder for the police or a crime lord and stuck in a dingy room with a gun wound in his arm. So far he hadn't come down with dysentery from eating too many greasy hamburgers. Then he winced. That was the diet that had contributed to his prostate cancer. He needed to return to a regular lifestyle and better eating habits.

He peeked out the opening in the curtains and watched a family load suitcases and boxes into a dented white station wagon. Man, wife and two kids just like his family when he and Sophie were younger. He thought of the fun vacations they had taken as a family. No time for reminiscing. Letting the curtain fall closed again, he continued to pace, periodically checking his watch.

When it was time, he called again.

"This is Akahi."

"Mark Yeager here. I've found a way for us to solve the George and Muriel Tanabe murders."

"Which is?"

"You and I are going to participate in a pickleball challenge match tonight."

There was a pause on the phone. "How will that help?"

"Work with me here, Akahi. By the way, what's this charge that I kidnapped a police officer?"

"Sorry 'bout that. I had to report what happened to Puna. He noticed that I didn't have my gun."

"You knew where to find it in the bush where I threw it. I assumed you retrieved it after I dropped you off."

Akahi cleared his throat. "That's the problem. I went back to look, and it wasn't there. I searched through the bushes. No gun. When I went back to the police department, Puna asked me where my gun was. I thought of making something up, but he knows when I lie. Just before you surprised me, I had called in to say I spotted your truck. Puna asked me what happened to the truck. I had to tell him everything."

"That didn't help me."

"Didn't help me either. I told the truth, but now I'm on Puna's guano list as well. You have so many charges against you anyway, what's one more? For me, Puna thinks I need more training. You know, so I will never be surprised by a suspect and disarmed."

"I have an idea how you can redeem yourself—by solving the murder cases. I've figured out who the murderer is, and I'll help you prove it tonight if you work with me." Mark paused and crossed his fingers.

Akahi whispered into the phone. "Puna won't give me permission to work with you."

"This time you can't tell him."

The line went silent, and Mark hoped Akahi was still there. "Can you hear me?"

"Yeah, I'm thinking." He let out a burst of air. "I'm in enough *pilikia* as it is. I suppose I could do something to try to catch the murderer."

Mark let out a sigh of relief. "You show up at seven thirty tonight. Park in the lot at the Kamaina Tavern and wait by the curb. I'll be watching to make sure you're alone. If you are, I'll pick you up."

"And if I'm not alone?"

"You will blow the opportunity to solve two murders. We're in this together. You need me to break this case, and I need you to make my plan work. Come prepared to play pickleball."

"Do I need a paddle and balls?"

"No. The equipment will be provided. Also wear a baseball cap or something to cover your head. Will you meet me?"

There was another long pause on the line. "You're one cra-a-azy *haole*."

"Yes or no."

"I don't know. You might be setting me up to shoot me or kidnap me again."

"Look, Akahi. I let you go before. I have no intention of shooting you, and I didn't kidnap you before. We had a friendly chat. I want to team with you to solve the murders. Work with me here."

"I suppose you won't kidnap me again… Okay… I guess I'll meet you."

"That's the positive attitude I'm looking for. Keep Puna out of this for now. You can bring him in when it's wrapped up and you deliver the murderer."

"Only one murderer?"

"That's right. The same person killed both George and Muriel Tanabe. And it wasn't me."

* * * * *

Mark sat in the room reviewing plans for the evening. He now had Akahi's agreement, which gave him a shot at this plan. Next, would Akahi actually show up alone without informing Puna?

His cell phone rang, and he answered.

A voice said, "Your days on this island are numbered."

A shudder ran through his body. It was the voice he heard when he had the burlap bag over his head. Mark struggled to gain control, then said calmly, "What can I do for you, Oana?"

There was a laugh. "Very good. Get this through your head. I've had enough of your games. You and I are going to settle this once and for all."

"How did you get my cell phone number," Mark asked stalling for time. "It's unlisted."

"I have my ways. The problem is I'm tired of you being on my island."

"So, you're going to the mainland?"

"No more smart-ass comments."

Mark winced. "Okay. What do you have in mind?"

"You and I are going to meet alone. Mano a mano. One walks away."

Mark couldn't believe what he was hearing. "Is this some kind of macho island thing? Guns, knives, sling shots or spear guns?"

"Funny man. I'm going to enjoy killing you with my bare hands. This is you and me alone. No weapons."

"How do I know you won't show up with a gun and shoot me?"

There was a derisive laugh. "I give you my word on that. I don't need a weapon to kill you."

"And how good is your word?"

"On this island my word is golden. And my word is that I will hunt you down and kill you. I'm giving you a chance to pick your place to die."

Mark considered what he knew regarding Oana. Homer had said he was shorter than Mark and about the same age. Mark was physically fit, now that he had recovered from prostate cancer. He had wrestled in high school. This could be the one way to get Oana off his back. If he could neutralize him. His left arm was still sore, but he could move it fine. Mark calculated what time he needed that night. "Okay. I'll meet you at Maluaka Beach tonight at ten thirty. Just you and me. No Malo and no other enforcers."

"I'll be looking forward to it."

"So will I, Henry Caldwell." Mark ended the call. That would give the crime boss something to think over.

After all this brave posturing, the realization struck him. What had he got himself into? He had succeeded as an entrepreneur by having a strong will and not giving up, even when his company almost went belly up. He had gritted his teeth, persevered and won. That same attitude served him well when playing pickleball. Now he faced a homicidal psychopath with no conscience who intended to kill him. He'd have to use his wits to survive.

He noticed his "lucky" kukui nut where he had left it on the top of the dresser. Wouldn't hurt to have any extra help for this evening. He dropped it into the pocket of the swim trunks he'd play pickleball in.

He'd be at the court from eight until nine thirty. That would give him an hour to settle things, let Akahi arrest the murderer and then he'd meet Oana at the beach near the hotel where Sophie was staying. One way or the other, things would get resolved tonight.

*   *   *   *   *

At seven fifteen Mark parked behind a dry cleaners. He found a bush to stand behind, giving him a clear view of the Kamaina Tavern.

At seven twenty-five a car pulled into the parking lot. Akahi got out dressed in white shorts, T-shirt, tennis shoes and a baseball cap. He held a zipped closed sports bag and turned around as if looking for his ride.

Mark inspected him carefully. No place that he could be carrying a gun. Possibly the sports bag, but as long as he didn't open that, it should be safe.

Waiting five minutes to make sure no one else appeared, Mark climbed back in the truck, started the engine and pulled up beside Akahi.

"Jump in."

Akahi climbed into the passenger's side seat of the cab and dropped his sports bag on the floor.

Mark looked in the rear view mirror and took off. No headlights visible.

"Okay," Akahi said. "I'm here."

"First, here's a tidbit for you. Your island crime lord, Oana, may be a man named Henry Caldwell. An acquaintance, Dexter Kwan, may have already phoned Puna with this information. I thought you should know as well."

"No kidding. That's news to me. Puna didn't mention that name."

"When you next talk to Puna, you can check to see if he received the call."

"What's happening tonight?"

"You and I are going to play a pickleball match and make an arrest."

"And our opponents?"

"First is the tennis pro, Ted Franklin. I had you wear a baseball cap just in case Ted caught a glimpse of you the morning I found George's body. I don't want him to know who my mystery partner is."

"Other than possibly at that crime scene, he's never seen me. Even then, I didn't get close to him. And our other opponent?"

"Lefty Kalama. You said before you'd never met him."

"That's right."

"Good. I'll introduce you as Alexander because Ted might have heard Puna shouting 'Akahi' at the crime scene. Here's the plan. We're playing a three game match against Ted and Lefty. You said you've played before so I need you to be your best."

Akahi graced the cab with a huge smile. "No problem."

"We have a hundred dollars bet on each set."

"You going to split the winnings with me?"

"That's the spirit. We need to put up a good fight. After the match while Ted and Lefty are talking, you and I are going to search Ted's bungalow. I'm sure we'll find some stolen jewelry."

"And if we don't?"

Mark shaded his eyes from a car with bright beams on approaching them. "Let's assume success just like with the match."

"Even if we find evidence, I'm not going to be able to use it without a search warrant."

"All I want is for you to know where it is for a legal search. Then you're going to act like you're leaving, but stay on the grounds, hidden. I'll provoke Ted. If he reacts like I expect he will, you'll have what you need to arrest him and get a search warrant."

"Sounds like a great plan... if it works."

"It'll work. All we have to do is not get killed in the pickleball match."

Chapter 27

When they arrived, Lefty's car was already parked along the side of the road. Mark peered through the window and saw a tennis racquet and a racquetball. Nothing like an eclectic racquet sports player. But then again, if he ran a shop, it was necessary to represent a number of sporting interests.

"I'm going in first," Mark told Akahi. "You wait five minutes and then pretend that you've come separately."

"Jeez. I'm the police and you're bossing me around."

"Only a suggestion to make it less likely that they'll suspect something." Mark headed in through the open gate.

Ted and Lefty were warming up on the court, blasting balls at each other as hard as they could from behind the non-volley line.

Mark gulped, then remembered that he'd been able to handle their speed. But would Akahi?

"Here's part of the raw meat," Ted shouted. "Where's your ringer? I hope he's current on his medical, dental and life insurance."

Lefty chuckled. "Yeah, did you tell him to come with a bull's-eye on his chest and to wear a bulletproof vest underneath?"

"He'll be here soon." Mark stepped over to grab a paddle and joined them to practice his strokes.

A few minutes later, Akahi sauntered up, his baseball cap pulled well down over his forehead. He slouched as if much older than his real age. Mark figured Ted and Lefty wouldn't consider him a threat. He only hoped there was real ability behind the façade.

After introductions, they split up in their teams to continue warming up.

Mark kept an eye on Akahi, who hit solid ground strokes, volleys and dink shots and wasn't intimidated when Ted slammed the ball at him. *Not bad. Not bad at all.*

In the first game, Akahi miss-hit a couple of shots but settled down after that. He had great reflexes at net and poached regularly to win points. When Ted or Lefty drilled the ball at him, he handled it as if swatting a fly. They lost the first game eleven to seven.

"We can get these guys," Akahi said to Mark after they exchanged ends of the court with their opponents.

"That's the spirit." Mark gave him a wink. "We'll get them now and later."

By playing steady while Lefty went through a wild streak, they miraculously pulled out an eleven to nine victory.

In the third game, Akahi served, and during the rally Lefty hit a lob that missed the baseline by three inches.

Ted slammed his paddle onto the net cord. "Get with it, Lefty. We've got to beat these yahoos. I don't want you to cost me a hundred bucks." He turned to Akahi and Mark. "You two are dead meat in the third game."

Akahi smiled and shrugged. "Just like we were dead meat in the second game?"

Ted slammed his paddle onto the top of the net again.

"Hey, don't destroy the net," Akahi said. "We need it so we can beat you in the third game."

As they returned to the baseline, Mark whispered to Akahi, "Good job, you have him riled up. He'll make mistakes."

* * * * *

Early in the third game, Mark was positioned behind the non-volley zone, when Lefty drilled the ball at him. Mark had his paddle ready in front of him, but the shot clipped the net and continued with most of its force into Mark's leg. It hit right where he had the kukui nut in his pocket. Pain shot through his leg. Mark rubbed the spot convinced that he'd have a black and blue memento of being hit. *Damn "lucky" kukui nut.* It had caused nothing but trouble. He was tempted to throw it away, but he decided to give it one more chance. Maybe it would pull them through for the rest of the third game.

★ ★ ★ ★ ★

At four-all Mark made a successful lob over Lefty's head. Ted raced back to retrieve it but was forced to lob back.

Akahi retrieved the lob and hit a soft deep overhead to Lefty's backhand. Lefty lifted a weak return right to Mark.

Mark chopped a dink shot inside the line on Ted's side of the court.

Ted charged toward the net and hit the ball just clearing the net.

Akahi lunged and popped the ball up.

Ted, already up to the non-volley zone, slammed the ball, catching Mark in the stomach.

With a loud "oof" Mark sank to the court, gasping.

Akahi bent over him. "Take a deep breath."

Mark gulped in air, regaining a regular rhythm of breathing.

Ted didn't apologize but turned his back and returned to the baseline. Lefty gave him a high five and shouted, "Way to go, partner!"

Mark picked himself up and prepared for the next serve.

Akahi and Mark somehow held on win eight points, but Ted and Lefty easily reached ten points.

At match point, Ted hit a deep serve, which Mark returned equally deep back to Ted's side of the court. Mark raced to the non-volley zone, but Ted hid a perfect drop shot that landed within the non-volley zone to Mark's backhand. Mark lunged but was only able to hit a high dink—too high and too deep. Ted cleanly slammed the ball down the middle between Mark and Akahi.

In spite of the intensity of the match, Ted graciously shook hands with both of them at the net and gave them both an "aw shucks" smile.

Mark bent over feeling a twinge in his gut. "Ted, you're a much better winner than loser."

"Sure. I don't lose very often. Time for a beer." He opened a cooler sitting on the patio table next to the court.

Mark sipped his Primo and sat quietly while Ted and Lefty congratulated each other on the victory.

"We showed these guys," Ted said. "But, Alexander, you played a good game. You've obviously played before."

Akahi shrugged. "Picked up the game on a trip to the mainland."

"You'll have to join us again."

"We'll see."

Lefty drained his beer and smacked his lips. "That'll do it for me. I need to hit the road."

"Hot date?" Ted asked.

Lefty shook his head. "Nah. My girlfriend's on Oahu. I have an early meeting with a guy who may buy my shop."

Ted took a sip of beer and wiped his mouth. "You really thinking of selling out?"

"Could be. I need the money."

"That sucks. Where are we going to get pickleballs?"

"The new guy will carry pickleballs and paddles. Nothing will change."

"What about the discount you gave your good buddies?"

"You'll have to negotiate that with the new owner."

Ted waved his beer bottle at Mark. "By the way, you owe us a hundred dollars."

Mark held his stomach. "I'm still groggy from the hit in the stomach. I'll give you the money in a little while. Mind if I go into your bungalow and lie down for a few minutes first?"

"Go ahead. Your beer will keep."

"I need to use your bathroom," Akahi added.

"In the back next to the bedroom."

"I'll show you where it is," Mark said.

They walked into the cottage, and once the door was closed, Mark pointed toward the bedroom. "Let's start looking there. I know he's hiding jewelry somewhere."

Mark opened drawers and sorted through clothes. Akahi checked under the bed and the mattress.

Mark proceeded to the next drawer. "We have ten minutes before he gets suspicious."

Neither found anything. Mark went through the closet with equal lack of success. He checked his watch. It had been eight minutes.

Then he noticed the bookshelf. He grabbed books and looked behind them. On the second shelf he found a small wooden box tucked away behind a dictionary. He opened it and lifted out an emerald necklace with fleur-de-lis gold between the jewels.

Mark showed it to Akahi. "You'll find a matching set of earrings that Ted gave to Arlene Henrick who's staying at the Maui Queen. This also matches the description of the jewelry that Muriel Tanabe reported finding and was murdered for."

"Couldn't use the evidence without a search warrant," Akahi said.

"Well, get a search warrant. You know where to find the stolen jewelry." Mark held the necklace up to the light to examine it more carefully. He was so intent on his discovery that he didn't notice Ted standing in the doorway pointing a gun at him.

"So. Two intruders trying to steal from me."

Mark winced and put the necklace down. "No. We found what you've stolen."

Ted laughed. "Too bad no one will ever find out."

Mark kept his eyes on Ted. "You killed George and Muriel Tanabe for stolen jewelry. It was pretty stupid to give the matching earrings to Arlene."

Ted's eyes blazed. "I'd say it was pretty stupid to come in here. I'll also kill both of you."

"Why'd you kill the Tanabes, Ted?" Mark asked.

"A necessity. Like getting rid of the two of you."

"That would be pretty incriminating, finding us shot in your cottage with your gun. I'd say you'd spend the rest of your life in prison."

"This isn't my gun. It belonged to George."

"But I bet it's the same gun you used to kill George with."

"What of it. He deserved to die. He was trying to cheat me out of my cut. He and that wife of his."

"But you hit her over the head."

Ted waved the gun at Akahi and then back to Mark. "I tried to get the jewelry back, but she found me going through George's shoes. Couldn't have a witness."

Ted moved farther into the room.

Akahi had been standing motionless, not saying a word.

"I think you two are going to have a very serious accident," Ted said.

"That wouldn't be a good idea," Akahi said, leveling his gaze at Ted.

"You don't think I'd let you go, do you? Not on your life." Ted laughed. "That's a good one. Not on your life."

Mark never saw the move. There was a blur and Ted fell backward, clutching his throat. The gun clattered to the floor.

Akahi picked up the gun. "Mark, go get my sports bag. I'll watch him."

Mark trotted back to the courts and retrieved the bag. Lefty had apparently gone. When he got back, Ted sat on the floor rubbing his throat.

Akahi took cuffs out of the equipment bag and snapped them on Ted. "Good thing you confessed of your own free will. Mark and I both heard it."

"I want a lawyer."

"Once we get to the jail, that can be arranged."

"I didn't see Lefty out there," Mark said.

"He left. Jeez, what was that you did to my throat?"

"An Aikido move," Akahi replied.

"Where did you learn that?" Mark asked.

"As a kid I took lessons and competed in tournaments. Although I liked tennis, Aikido was my number one sport. Got a black belt. I still spar two times a week."

A sudden realization struck Mark. "You could have taken me out when I had a gun on you."

Akahi winked at Mark. "Sure. But then we wouldn't have caught the real killer."

"You must have bought what I told you."

"It seemed pretty far out at first. Then I figured there's more to you than being a one-man crime spree. My cop intuition. I took a chance, and it worked out. Don't tell Puna. He thinks you took me from behind and handcuffed me."

Mark scowled. "That will cause him to think I did something illegal. Attacking you."

Akahi shrugged. "We'll get that cleared up. You shouldn't spend more than five years in jail."

"What?" Mark shouted.

"I'm testing your sense of humor."

Mark looked at his watch. Nine fifty-five. Another twinge went through his stomach, and it wasn't from being hit by a pickleball. He needed to keep his appointment with Oana. Too bad he didn't possess Aikido skills like Akahi.

Then a thought struck him. "If you were in a life or death situation, what one move would be most useful?"

"Throat thrust, like I used on Ted."

"Teach me how to do it."

"It's simple. Let me show you."

Akahi demonstrated the move.

"Now try it on me."

Mark lunged toward his throat, and Akahi parried his hand away.

"Do it again."

Mark kept trying until he got the move down.

"You're armed and dangerous." Akahi slapped Mark on the back.

While Akahi called headquarters, Mark slipped away. He jumped in the pickup truck and drove back toward the Maui Queen Hotel. His stomach tightened at what lay ahead. How could he survive this encounter with Oana? He had one Aikido move that he had practiced for all of five minutes. How could that save him from a cold-blooded, psychopathic killer?

With these thoughts swirling through his head, he parked and headed along a walkway toward the beach.

The moon peeked out from behind a bank of slow moving clouds, and the gentle breeze rustled through the grove of coconut trees.

I have to maintain my cool. He had faced many tough business situations that necessitated nerves of steel and audacious moves to keep his company going. Those seemed like life or death situations at the time, but now his physical life was on the line. He trudged out to the beach.

Up ahead he saw a single figure step out of the shadows.

The man was shorter than Mark and in the moonlight looked to be his age. He wore a Hawaiian shirt that failed to hide strong arms. Hiking shorts partially covered spindly legs. Nothing out of the ordinary. Closely cropped brown hair that reminded Mark of a retired Marine officer. An equal fight?

"Mr. Yeager. It's a pleasure to meet you again."

The moonlight reflected off the shark tattoo on his hand.

"Yeah. This is our third meeting."

"Third? I only remember one other encounter."

"I saw you out at Molokini. When you were illegally spear fishing."

Oana laughed. "I don't do illegal things. Must have been someone else."

"It was you. I saw the shark tattoo."

Oana snorted. "It *is* my fish preserve."

This guy had a huge ego. *How can I use that to my advantage?* "And I suppose this is your island and you want me off it, Henry Caldwell."

Oana flinched. "Why are you calling me that again?"

"Because that's who you are. And by the way, the police are going to nail you."

A steely glint reflected from Oana's eyes. "I don't think so. I would enjoy talking to you more, but, unfortunately, it's time for me to take care of you… permanently. It's too bad my associates didn't follow my order to kill you earlier at Shark Cove." He

210

gave a false sigh. "It's a shame when I have to do everything myself."

Mark didn't like that. If he admitted that he was responsible for the murder attempt by Malo at Shark Cove, it didn't look like Oana intended to let Mark leave this encounter alive. He assessed his opponent. Moonlight fell upon a face with good complexion, supported by a firm jaw. Confidence and arrogance. Obviously ruthless with no regard for human life. How to use this to his advantage?

Wouldn't want his face messed up. Would assume a swift and easy battle. Mark had to find a point of weakness and a way to neutralize him.

They circled each other. Mark's strength rested in wrestling holds, not boxing. He'd have to get close if he were to be effective. And then try the move Akahi had taught him.

Mark feinted in and moved back.

Oana held his ground and took a step toward Mark.

Knuckles struck Mark's jaw.

Mark reeled, shaking his head. He hadn't seen the punch coming. He put his hand to his face. It came away covered with blood.

"Not used to someone this fast, are you?" Oana's fist shot out.

Another blow, this time to Mark's chest.

He staggered back, gasping for air.

The third blow hit Mark in the arm where he had been shot by Arlene, knocking him to the sand. He rested on all fours, pain shooting through his arm.

Oana unleashed a kick to Mark's ribs, sending him sprawling.

Mark rolled out of reach, blood and sand sticking to his face. He scrambled to his feet.

Oana took a casual stance and blew on his fingers. "You look like crap. I have all the time in the world." Then he flicked his fingers toward his palms. "Come and get me."

Mark tried to clear his head. This wasn't working at all. He hadn't even touched Oana yet. He looked around. No one in sight—the beach empty at this hour. *Think*. There had to be a strategy. *Arrogance. Over confidence.* Like being behind nine to five in a pickleball game and battling back to win eleven to nine. But this was more like being down ten to zero. He hadn't scored a point yet.

Blood covered his shirt. Taking a deep breath, he charged at Oana, who deftly sidestepped as Mark shot past, receiving a chop in the back, knocking him onto the sand again. His face struck a piece of driftwood, causing pain from a new laceration. He must have looked like a bloody sand monster from hell by this point.

Mark pulled himself up again, dusted the sand off his face and spat out a mouthful of sand and blood. Assessing the situation, he saw that they still had the beach to themselves. There was no assistance in sight. *No good charging wildly. It's got to be calm, not rushed. Have to take a hit, but find a way to engage him close in.*

Oana stared at him as if viewing a cockroach ready to be squished. The crime boss slowly moved toward him.

Mark stepped backward and went into a wrestling stance with his hands in front of him and slowly moved toward Oana.

Another punch to the jaw rocked him, sending sand flying off his face.

Mark raised his left arm to deflect Oana's next blow. His arm stung. Again the wound from Arlene.

Get in close. Somehow.

He deflected another punch with his right arm. Both arms hurt.

Mark gasped for breath. His whole body ached, the combination of three hard fought pickleball games, getting hit in the stomach and leg by a ball and being Oana's punching bag.

He only partially blocked the next jab, feeling his opponent's knuckles graze his cheek. He recovered enough to return an ineffective thrust toward Oana that only brushed his arm.

"Not much of a fighter, are you?" Oana jeered. "Come take a shot at me." He pointed to his jaw.

Arrogance. Over confidence. This was it. At that moment the moon went behind a cloud. Mark had one chance. He reached in his pocket and pulled out the kukui nut. Taking aim at a nearby kiawe tree, Mark hurled it with all his might. It connected with a satisfyingly loud, "Thwack."

Oana jerked his head toward the sound.

In that brief moment, Mark put his head down and charged, butting Oana in the stomach.

The move caught the crime boss by surprise.

Mark followed through, tackling and knocking him over.

Oana hit the sand, making an "Oof."

Mark dropped on top of him.

With the throat thrust he had learned from Akahi, he jabbed with full strength.

Oana's hands flew to his throat.

Mark saw the piece of driftwood his face had hit earlier. He picked it up and bashed it against Oana's head.

The crime lord lay on the sand, motionless.

Mark raised himself from the sand, staring down at the unconscious body. Placing his hands on his knees, he gasped for breath.

After a moment, Mark straightened, catching sight of a dark shape emerged from the trees along the beach. The moonlight broke through the clouds again revealing the scarred cheek of Malo, Oana's henchman, brandishing a pistol.

Chapter 28

"Looks like you're a dead man anyway," Malo said.

Mark's throat tightened. Would this nightmare never end? Oana remained out cold but now this additional predicament. *Think.* How to stall this thug.

"Your boss will be mad if you don't let him finish what he started."

Oana leveled the gun at Mark. "He'll be madder if I let you get away."

"So I have a fair fight with Oana, beat him, and he has to rely on you to finish his dirty work? What are you his nursemaid?"

"Shut up."

Out of the corner of his eye, Mark saw another shape materialize. At first he thought it might be another of Oana's enforcers, but then he realized it was someone short. The figure came closer. Kea.

"So you're going to get rid of me like you tried before," Mark said loudly.

Malo waved the gun at Mark. "That's right. Oana's orders are to kill you, one way or the other."

"I don't think so," Kea said from behind Malo.

"Run, Kea," Mark shouted. "He has a gun."

"So do I," Kea said.

Malo turned at the voice, and a shot rang out. Malo dropped his gun and fell to the sand.

Mark raced over and viewed the limp body. Still breathing. He kicked Malo's gun out of reach. "Where'd you get a gun, Kea?"

"I saw you throw it in the bushes yesterday. I kept it in my backpack. Tonight when I saw you sneak out to the beach, I followed you. I thought the gun might come in handy, and it did."

"And you know how to handle guns?"

"Sure. My mom has lots of guns—a 22, a 9 mm, a 45, a Winchester rifle and a shotgun. We go off in the woods lots of times and shoot at rocks and trees."

A loud sound came from someone crashing out of the bushes. Puna raced across the sand. Akahi had been right. Puna could really move.

"This is the first time I've been glad to see you." Mark leaned over, trying to catch his breath.

Puna bent over the wounded enforcer and felt for a pulse. "Out cold but still alive."

"How did you find me?" Mark asked.

"I followed Akahi. I was going to arrest you when you first picked him up but decided to wait and see what you did. Then I followed you here after you left the pickleball court."

"I'm glad you did. I didn't even notice."

"I'm good at what I do." Puna pointed at the wounded man. "Interesting conversation I overheard you have with Oana and this guy."

"His name's Malo. Oana's enforcer. He tried to kill me on an earlier occasion. He wanted to shoot me and throw my body into shark-infested waters. Fortunately, I escaped."

"You're like a cat with nine lives, Mr. Yeager."

"Just lucky."

Akahi came trotting down the path to the beach with another police officer, both with guns drawn.

"All under control," Puna announced. "Get cuffs on Oana and Malo and call an ambulance."

Mark put his arm around Kea. "And this young man saved my bacon."

Puna held out his hand.

Kea gave him the gun and smiled. "I don't need it anymore."

"What's your name?" Puna asked.

Kea whipped out a business card. "Kea Puahi. Any time you

need anything you call me. In addition to my other businesses, I'm always willing to help the police." He gave Puna his best smile.

Akahi stepped forward. "That's the kid I mentioned to you, boss. He's the one with the business plan you found in the trunk of Mr. Yeager's rental car."

Mark looked toward Akahi. "What happened with Ted?"

"He's off to jail."

"Oana's ready to join Ted," Puna said. "Wake him up."

"Right boss," Akahi said.

Akahi lifted Oana to his feet. The crime lord came too. "What's going on?"

"That's my question for you," Puna said.

Oana scanned the group of police officers and pointed a shaky finger at Mark. "That man attacked me. I demand that you arrest him."

Puna grabbed Oana, spun him around and in a flash had him cuffed. "I heard everything that went on. Very interesting what you admitted. You're the one under arrest."

"I demand a lawyer."

"You'll have your chance after you're booked. Take him to the squad car, Akahi."

Akahi and the other police officer dragged a struggling Oana up the path while Puna pulled out his notepad and wrote on it. Then he put it back in his pocket. "Pretty good fighting, Mr. Yeager."

"You can give the credit to Akahi. He taught me an Aikido move that came in handy."

"I thought I was going to have to butt in sooner," Puna said. "Good thing I didn't. Malo probably would have shot me."

"What about when Malo pointed his gun at me?"

"I waited to hear what he said, but you blocked my line of fire. Good thing the kid came along, although it's too bad he had to be involved in a shooting."

"You're not going to do anything to Kea, are you?"

"No way. The kid's a hero." Puna winked. "Even if he saved

the guy who has the most charges against him in the history of the island."

"I hope everything is cleared up now." Mark glanced at his watch and saw how late it was. "Am I free to go?"

"No. We have a lot to discuss at headquarters."

"I'll be happy to go over everything with you."

★ ★ ★ ★ ★

As Puna and Mark sat at police headquarters, sipping paper cups full of steaming coffee, Puna leaned toward him over the table. "You have many crimes to discuss with me. Where would you like to start?"

Mark leaned back in the uncomfortable chair. "Where to begin? I guess with George Tanabe. He and Ted were involved in jewelry thefts. They had a falling out, and Ted killed him. Ted also killed George's wife, Muriel. Akahi and I heard Ted's confession."

Puna nodded. "I'll check that with Akahi."

"Ted was also scamming widows and divorcées as well as stealing jewelry. Arlene Henrick overheard Ted and me discussing something else and assumed I was in cahoots with him. That's why she was mad and took a shot at me."

"I spoke with her earlier this evening. She's sorry for shooting you. She isn't going to press charges on anything."

"And neither will I."

Puna stared at Mark. "There's the matter of Keone's death."

"As I told Akahi, that was an accident. He went running off into the woods and fell over a cliff."

A small smile appeared on Puna's large lips. "Our crime scene investigator checked the top of the cliff. There was no sign of any struggle, only marks where Keone slipped in mud and went over the side. You're clear."

Mark let out a whoosh of air. "That's good."

"Care to comment more on the business plan that was in the trunk of your rental car?"

"I explained it to Akahi. Kea, the young man who saved me,

217

wrote that, and I added some comments. He wants to start his own souvenir stores. Quite a kid."

Puna put his hands on the table. "But you threatened Akahi, took his gun and kidnapped him."

Mark sucked on his lip for a moment. "No one would listen to my side of the story. If I gave myself up, you would have jailed me, and I couldn't have proven that Ted was the murderer. I didn't harm Akahi, and Kea with Akahi's gun actually saved me from Malo."

"Let me see what Akahi thinks." Puna left the room and returned with Akahi. "Mr. Yeager makes a case that he didn't kidnap you. What do you think?"

Akahi gave his usual shrug. "Not a problem. We went and had a little chat. Two pickleball buddies, nothing unusual."

"And your gun?"

"I must have lost it in the bushes."

"Okay. Take better care of your gun in the future. Get out of here."

"You got it, boss." Akahi scampered out of the room.

"Seems you're clear on that, Mr. Yeager. Keep going."

"Oana's goons put my rental car out of commission so I borrowed Keone's truck. I will be happy to reimburse anyone for the wear and tear I put on it."

"Keone has no relatives, so no one cares. Next."

"I had business cards made indicating I was a private investigator. That's not true, of course, but it served the purpose of finding a clue to Muriel Tanabe's death. Akahi said that wasn't a crime anyway."

"Yeah. That's right."

"I think that's about it. I was only doing these things to clear my name and to find the real murderer. Along the way I got crosswise with Oana and his gang. You have Oana and Malo in custody. And don't be too hard on Kea. He saved my life."

"Don't worry. I guess you and I don't have any more business together tonight. I want you to come back here tomorrow, and we'll take a complete statement for you to sign. Then you'll need to return to the Islands for several murder and attempted murder trials. Akahi will give you a ride back to the hotel. Other than that, have a good rest of your vacation and stay out of trouble."

* * * * *

Stay out of trouble. That would be his catch phrase for the remainder of the vacation. Outside, Mark took one last look at the police station. He'd be welcome there as a witness and not as a suspect.

It was two in the morning when Akahi dropped Mark off at the Maui Queen Hotel.

"We make a pretty good team," Mark said.

"Yeah. Both on the court and off. I'm going to have to convince some of my old tennis buddies to take up pickleball now that I know where there's a court. If I can round up one more player, you, Lefty and I can play another match." He snapped his fingers. "How about this? I'll draft Puna to come play. He's a good athlete and nobody's going to get a ball past him when he's at the non-volley zone. His intimidation factor would be worth a few points a game. What do you think?"

Mark tried to imagine Puna playing pickleball, which might be a sight to behold. But partnering with him would be like teaming with a steamroller. After only a few seconds of consideration, he held up a hand. "I think I'm done with pickleball on this trip. For the rest of our vacation, I'm going to dedicate myself to spending time with my wife and not getting in trouble."

"Sounds like a good decision."

Mark stepped out of Akahi's car. "The Reinholts will have to find a new house sitter. Maybe one of your tennis friends can apply."

"Good idea. By the way, when I put Ted in the squad car, he reminded me that you owe him a hundred dollars for winning two out of three games."

"Tell him to put it on my tab."

★ ★ ★ ★ ★

A sleepy Sophie opened the door for Mark. "I wasn't expecting to see you here." Her eyes focused more clearly. "What happened to you?" She held her nose. "You look like a piece of raw meat and smell as ripe as week-old fish."

"What do you expect after three sweaty games of pickleball and a tussle on the beach with a crime lord. I need to take a shower, and then I'll tell you everything. The good news—it's all over. I'm cleared, and the right people are locked up."

"Go!" She pointed toward the bathroom.

Mark threw his bloody clothes down on the bathroom floor and regarded himself in the mirror. What a sight. Blood, raw skin, scrapes, and purple bruises. He looked like the victim of a car wreck.

He turned the shower on full blast and soaked his tender skin, careful to rid himself of the sand without grinding it into his various wounds. Leaning his head back, he let the hot water soothe his face. What a day. All the tension, the arrest of Ted, the fight with Oana, the encounter with Malo and being saved by Kea. And it came very close to having a completely different outcome. In spite of his pain, he chuckled. And his lucky kukui nut. It had certainly been that… finally. He'd have to go out and look for it the next day. Maybe in the afternoon when he woke up. No early morning rising after this night. And he'd search for a few more seashells for Sophie. He didn't need to buy everything from Kea.

He toweled off, put on a robe and returned to find Sophie pacing the room.

"You look much more presentable, although a little worse for wear." She gave him a fierce hug. "So I don't have to be a moll for a fugitive anymore?"

"No. We can resume our vacation."

"It's about time. I was going to give you a few more days. That cabana boy was starting to look pretty good. Tell me everything that happened."

They went out on the balcony and pulled the two chairs together.

He spoke for an hour, while Sophie, wide-eyed, periodically nodded her head. When she heard what Kea had done, she clapped her hands together. "I'm going to buy everything he has in his backpack tomorrow."

"Better than that, I intend to invest in his business. Since that kid will probably become the Rockefeller of Maui souvenirs, we'll get in on the ground floor."

"Is this your new career? Being an investor?"

Mark yawned and stretched his arms. "Could be. I have to find something more to do than pickleball, since it seems to get me into trouble."

"You're not going to give it up, are you?"

"No, but I do need to reassess my retirement. Investing is a possibility. In any case, Kea's quite a kid."

"Now that everything is resolved are you going to try windsurfing again with Homer?"

Mark put his arm around Sophie. "No, I've decided no more sports on this trip."

"And dealing with the police?"

"I'll have to go back to the police station to make a complete signed statement. And we'll have to come back to Hawaii again in the future."

"Oh?"

"Yes. There will be trials for Ted, Oana and Malo. I'll need to testify."

"Won't that be dangerous?"

"With the mob boss in jail, Puna is going to put Oana's organization out of business. The serpent's head has been cut off. And I won't be the only witness. Credible police officers have also heard the confessions. But the important part is for the rest of our vacation it will be you and me with no further distractions."

"Good. I have a whole list of things for us to do including a trip to Hana so I can shop at the Hasegawa General Store. Then on to the 'Ohe'o Gulch with all the pools. We have to see how it matches the photograph we bought in Abe's shop."

Mark didn't even make a comment that on the way to Hana they'd be driving past Shark Cove. He had no intention of visiting that spot again. "What else do you want to do before we head home?"

"I want to see more of the west end of the island. We have lots of beaches to visit that are waiting for us. And every evening at sunset for the rest of our vacation, rather than you rushing off to play pickleball, we'll have to sit on our balcony and watch for the green flash."

"And we can take a helicopter tour or go on a whale watching expedition."

Sophie stuck out her tongue. "I've had my boat trip to Molokini, and I'm not sure my stomach would do any better in a helicopter."

"Any other requests?"

Sophie snuggled against him. "I want to look for shells, lounge around the pool and beach and one last activity. We need to go shopping in Kaanapali. I have to buy a least one new muumuu in Kea's cousin, Nora's, shop. And I'll get a bright new Hawaiian shirt for you as well."

Mark leaned over and gave Sophie a kiss. "Even shopping sounds good after what I've been through. I'm definitely ready for a few uneventful days."

"I'm not letting you off that easily." With that she took his hand and led him off to bed.

About the Author

Mike Befeler is author of six novels in the Paul Jacobson Geezer-lit Mystery Series (*Retirement Homes Are Murder, Living with Your Kids Is Murder, Senior Moments Are Murder, Cruising in Your Eighties Is Murder, Care Homes Are Murder, Nursing Homes Are Murder*), two of which were finalist for The Lefty Award for best humorous mystery. He has seven other published mystery novels: *Unstuff Your Stuff, Death of a Scam Artist, The V V Agency, The Back Wing, The Mystery of the Dinner Playhouse, Murder on the Switzerland Trail* and *Court Trouble;* an international thriller, *The Tesla Legacy;* and a non-fiction book, *The Best Chicken Thief in All of Europe.* Mike is past-president of the Rocky Mountain Chapter of Mystery Writers of America. He grew up in Honolulu, Hawaii, and now lives in Lakewood, California, with his wife, Wendy.

If you are interested in having the author speak to your book club, contact Mike Befeler at mikebef@aol.com. His web site is http://www.mikebefeler.com.

CPSIA information can be obtained
at www.ICGtesting.com
Printed in the USA
BVHW041700160523
664273BV00004B/82